Praise for the work of SYRIE JAMES

Dracula, My Love

"This tale about a fierce, forbidden romance will appeal to even the most jaded romance fan." —*Library Journal*

"A truly remarkable love story that keeps the reader glued to every page." —*Feathered Quill*

"Very romantic . . . powerfully sensuous . . . masterfully told." —*Single Title Reviews*

"I loved it! A gripping story, infused with passion, excitement, and emotional turmoil." —*American Book Center*

The Lost Memoirs of Jane Austen

"A thoughtful, immensely touching romance . . . well-researched, well-written, and beautifully plotted." —*Jane Austen's Regency World Magazine*

"Jane comes alive . . . the reader blindly pulls for the heroine and her dreams of love . . . offers a deeper understanding of what Austen's life might have been like." —*The Los Angeles Times*

"Deserves front-runner status in the field of Austen fan-fiction and film." —*Kirkus Reviews*

The Secret Diaries of Charlotte Brontë

"James takes the biography of Brontë and sketches it into a work of art. A can't-miss novel for Brontë fans and historical fiction buffs alike." —*Sacramento Book Review*

"A captivating and entertaining read. James is so winning in her narrative style that by the end of the tale the reader will be convinced that she, in fact, has discovered Charlotte's secret diary." —*Feathered Quill*

"Brings the beloved author to life as never before . . . This fascinating novel is a delight to read." —*Wichita Falls Times Record Review*

ALSO BY SYRIE JAMES:

Dracula, My Love:
The Secret Journals of Mina Harker

The Secret Diaries of Charlotte Brontë

The Lost Memoirs of Jane Austen

NOCTURNE

SYRIE JAMES

Vanguard Press
A Member of the Perseus Books Group

Copyright © 2011 by Syrie James

Published by Vanguard Press
A Member of the Perseus Books Group

All rights reserved. No part of this publication may be reproduced, stored in a
retrieval system, or transmitted, in any form or by any means, electronic, mechanical, photocopying, recording, or otherwise, without the prior written permission
of the publisher. Printed in the United States of America. For information and
inquiries, address Vanguard Press, 387 Park Avenue South, 12th Floor, New York,
NY 10016, or call (800) 343-4499.

Designed by Pauline Brown
Set in 11.75 point Centaur MT

Library of Congress Cataloging-in-Publication Data

James, Syrie.
  Nocturne / Syrie James.
    p. cm.
    ISBN 978-1-59315-628-2 (hardcover : alk. paper) I. Recluses—Fiction.
  2. Vampires—Fiction. I. Title.
  PS3610.A457N63 2011
  813'.6—dc22

                                                                2010030418

Vanguard Press books are available at special discounts for bulk purchases in the
U.S. by corporations, institutions, and other organizations. For more information,
please contact the Special Markets Department at the Perseus Books Group, 2300
Chestnut Street, Suite 200, Philadelphia, PA 19103, or call (800) 810-4145, ext.
5000, or e-mail special.markets@perseusbooks.com.

10 9 8 7 6 5 4 3 2 1

I dedicate this book to
all my readers—every single one of you.
Thank you for your support,
the blogs and reviews you write,
and the wonderful messages you send me,
sharing all the ways in which my novels
have touched you.
It means the world to me,
and inspires me more than I can say.

CHAPTER *1*

*I*T BEGAN SNOWING AT NINE. Delicate flakes were still sifting down two hours later as Nicole Whitcomb reluctantly loaded her carry-on suitcase and small backpack into her rental car and slammed the trunk. She took one last second to appreciate the hushed descent of the gentle white flakes against the iron gray sky and to drink in the picturesque view of the snow-capped hotel against the backdrop of the ski slopes and surrounding forest.

I wish I could live here, Nicole thought for the hundredth time, as she inhaled deeply the crisp, pine-scented mountain air. She hated to leave all this beauty to go back to the city, and to the stress and tedium of her job. After brushing off the accumulation of snow from her front and back windshields, she unlocked the car, slipped behind the wheel, knocked the snow off her fur-lined boots, and started the engine.

Nicole knew she had to hurry. The weather report had said a big storm was coming in to the Steamboat Springs area. When she'd called the Denver airport, however, they said it was sunny and clear, and assured her that her flight to San Jose was departing as scheduled. She figured it shouldn't take more than forty-five minutes up the mountain road to reach Rabbit Ears Pass, the first of several summits en route. All the roads were open, so after that it should be an easy three-hour drive to Denver.

It was cold inside the car and Nicole shivered as she turned on the windshield wipers, heater, and defroster. Leaving on her fuzzy light blue scarf and hat, she strapped on her seat belt, exited the parking lot, and drove through the quaint Steamboat Springs ski village. There was a good two feet of snow on the ground in the uncleared areas, but so far only a light dusting on the road. Even so, as she turned onto Highway 40 and headed south, she carefully moderated her speed. It had been awhile since she'd driven in these conditions.

It was her first time in Colorado, a place she'd always longed to visit—and it was as beautiful as she'd imagined it would be. She'd always loved the snow. During the years she'd lived in Seattle, it had been a hop, skip, and jump to the nearest ski area, and she couldn't count how many delightful hours she'd spent on the slopes with her friends. Since she moved back to California three years ago, however, she'd given up all that.

At the thought of that move and the reason behind it, Nicole's stomach knotted with anxiety. The memory of that awful day and all that happened afterward still filled her with self-recrimination and doubt. Would she ever be able to forget?

Nicole frowned, shoving the thought away, determined not to let it spoil her mood. She'd just spent a wonderful long weekend with dear friends she hadn't seen in years. When her best friend, Chloe, had announced her intention to have a ski resort wedding, Nicole had laughed at first—the idea had seemed ludicrous and impractical—but in the end it had been fabulous.

The wedding had taken place high atop a ski slope at Steamboat Springs, with the bridal party in formal wear and everyone on skis. After the ceremony, most of the people had ridden the chairlift back down, but Nicole—on a dare from one of the groomsmen—had blithely skied down the mountain. It had involved tucking her long bridesmaid's dress into her thermal leggings, which Chloe had laughingly insisted was scandalous and beneath the dignity of a twenty-nine-year-old woman. But Nicole hadn't cared; she couldn't resist the challenge.

The newlyweds and most of the other guests had left after two days, but Nicole stayed one more day to go skiing on her own—and what a blast it had been! Sailing down a white mountain with the crisp air in her face always felt like heaven. She couldn't wait to show the pictures to her coworkers and to the kids at the museum and the library that weekend.

The car had warmed up now. Nicole removed her hat and gloves, glancing briefly in the rearview mirror to smooth back her long, wavy, reddish-gold hair. She'd left the town of Steamboat Springs far behind. The snow was falling faster. Nicole increased the speed of the windshield wipers, focusing her attention on the road. For the first time, she began to wonder if she'd made a mistake in staying the extra day. The drive back to Denver would have been so much easier yesterday, when the weather had been clear.

The road began to climb through a wooded area now. Nicole had read that the highway gained an incredible 2,500 feet in about seven miles during this stretch, as it made its way up the side of the Gore Range through Routt National Forest toward the pass. The view here should be expansive, but instead it was obscured by low, dark clouds.

Nicole felt another stab of worry as she crept along. She'd been lucky to rent a car with four-wheel drive, but it wouldn't help if she encountered black ice. Worse yet, it was becoming more and more difficult to see. The storm had come in way faster than she'd expected. The wind howled. There had been a couple of cars behind her at the beginning, but they'd long since disappeared from view, and she'd only passed a few cars coming the other way.

Should I turn back? Nicole wondered. She didn't want to get stuck on this road in the middle of a blizzard—but she couldn't miss her flight. She'd already been gone five days, and she'd left a ton of work on her desk. She had to relieve the neighbor taking care of her cat. She didn't want to pay for another night's lodging or go through the hassle of changing her airline ticket. No, she decided; she'd press on. The hotel desk clerk had been confident that she'd be over the pass and out of this weather system before she knew it.

On the drive up, Nicole had made a point of looking for the sign marking the summit of Rabbit Ears Pass at 9,426 feet, announcing the precise location of the Continental Divide—the line that ran from northwestern Canada along the crest of the Rocky Mountains all the way to Mexico, and divided the flow of water between the Pacific and Atlantic oceans. Nicole remembered smiling when she'd caught sight of the gray rock formation on a forested peak to the north, for which the pass was named. When viewed from a certain angle, the formation did sort of resemble the ears of a rabbit. But she knew that the summit was still more than a dozen miles ahead. At the rate she was crawling, it could take almost an hour to reach it.

Nicole used the snowbank at the right side of the highway as her guide, staying just a few feet inside it. At a sharp crook in the road she reduced her speed even further, carefully navigating around the bend. Through the swirling flakes in the air, the steep, snow-covered slope on the north side of the road was partially visible.

Suddenly a loud crack erupted from above, followed by a low hissing sound. *What on earth was that?* Nicole wondered, alarmed, instinctively pressing on the accelerator and speeding forward. The hissing behind her grew louder, turning into an ominous, growing rumble. Glancing into the rearview mirror, Nicole was shocked to see an enormous slab of snow slide off the mountainside in a great, rushing torrent and cover the entire road behind her.

An avalanche! she thought in terror. If she'd been driving any more slowly, it would have buried her.

There was no turning back now, Nicole realized, even if she'd wanted to. With her heart in her throat, she continued up the road, crawling on for what seemed like a century. The highway soon leveled off. The harsh wind stirred up snow from the drifts below that mingled in a frenzy with the flakes falling from the sky. Snow was smacking against the windshield at such a furious rate that the wiper blades couldn't keep up. Nicole struggled to see through a gathering veil of white.

The highway was covered by at least six inches of snow now, and it was growing deeper by the minute. She had to get over the pass—and soon—before this turned into a total whiteout. She pressed harder on the gas and forged on, holding tight to the wheel.

The accident happened so quickly. One minute, Nicole was driving along under perfect control; the next instant, the road was slipping out from under her and the car was spinning into a terrifying right-hand slide. In a panic, she jammed on the brakes and jerked the wheel to the left, even as her brain shouted, *No, stupid, that's the wrong thing to do* and to her horror, it only made things worse.

The car skidded and then hurled itself off the road into the embankment. A scream tore from Nicole's throat as the entire world turned upside down. A shattering pain spiraled through her head as it slammed against something hard. There was a jarring crunch, an explosion of glass, another crunch, and then the rolling stopped and the world righted itself again.

Nicole sat unmoving, dazed and confused, her head pounding. She struggled to get her bearings. She was still seat-belted and sitting upright. A bitterly cold wind blew in through her shattered side windows. Her lap and the interior of the car were strewn with small, scattered fragments of glass. The windshield was still intact but heavily damaged with a spider web of cracks, and the view was obscured by snow and pine branches. From what she could make out, the car had landed beneath a tree.

Okay, she told herself. It's not as bad as it looks. You ran off the road, but you're still alive.

There were no cuts on her hands, but she felt an oozing from the left side of her throbbing temple and touched it. Her fingers came away smeared with blood. *Blood.* Panic spiraled through her and she gasped aloud, extending her hand as far as humanly possible from her face. *Blood.* She couldn't look at it. The sight made her stomach churn. The pounding in her skull increased, as the horror came flooding back. *Blood. Blood everywhere. Blood pouring onto the bed and covering the floor . . . She was bleeding. From the head. Stop the blood. Stop it. Now!*

Glancing around frantically for her purse and a tissue, she gave up and grabbed her neck scarf instead, pressing it firmly against her forehead. *What should I do?* she wondered, fighting down the panic, struggling to think despite the throbbing in her head. *Call 911?* Woozily, she retrieved her cell phone one-handed from her coat pocket and cursed. No signal.

The faint hum of a car engine made her tense with anticipation: was someone coming? No, she decided, disappointed; it was just her own motor idling. She snapped on her flashers but couldn't see any evidence that they were working. She tried to open her car door, but it wouldn't budge. Peering out through her broken side window, she realized that the car had sunk so deeply into the snowbank that it was half buried. The only way to get out was through the window. But—did she *want* to get out? Her head was bleeding. There was no way she could dig the car out and get it back on the road.

And where would she go on foot? She was in the middle of nowhere, surrounded by a national forest. As far as she knew, no one lived here; it was all government-owned land. The road behind her was blocked by an avalanche. Who knew how many miles it was to the pass up ahead, much less to the next town? She couldn't recall seeing any call boxes on the road, and even if she could find one, how long would she last out in the blizzard? Visibility was poor and getting worse. She wasn't sure she could properly judge distance or direction; she might walk off the road and become hopelessly lost.

Better to stay in the car, she decided, and pray that someone would come along—however unlikely that might be. She gave the horn a few sharp blasts, and then leaned on it long and hard, but the sound was muffled by the roar of the wind. With a sigh, she gave up. What was the point? Who was going to hear a horn out here?

Nicole shivered. She considered leaving the engine running to keep the heater on, but realized it could never keep the car warm with snow blowing in through the open windows. She turned off the ignition, leaving the key in place, knowing that it was going to get very cold, very fast. Why did she feel so light-headed?

Still pressing the scarf against her forehead, Nicole leaned back against the seat and closed her eyes against the excruciating pain. Her thoughts drifted. She was dizzy. So dizzy. Disconnected images flitted through her mind: the blue-green gleam of her tabby cat's eyes; the potted red Anthurium on her apartment windowsill; her friends' laughing faces over nachos and frosty margaritas; building a sand castle on a sunny beach with her darling nieces; the giddy, gap-toothed grin of a little Native Alaskan girl.

No, Nicole thought desperately, *stay awake. Stay conscious.* Her last thought, as she felt her hand drop uselessly to her side, was: *Is this it? Am I going to die?*

CHAPTER 2

*H*E WAS ABOUT A QUARTER MILE above the main highway, plowing his private road to keep ahead of the storm, when he heard the approaching vehicle. Through the methodical *whap whap whap* of the truck's windshield wipers, he stared down through the snowy gloom, waiting for the car to appear below. Who the hell was idiotic enough to drive in these conditions?

With a squeal of brakes, a small white sport utility vehicle sped around the curve of the highway and into view. It looked brand-new—perhaps a rental—an out of towner from the ski resort, no doubt. To his dismay, the car suddenly fishtailed into a perilous slide, skidded off the white ribbon of highway, then rolled over and crunched faceup against a tree in the snowy embankment.

Bollocks, he thought, staring down through the swirling storm at the half-buried car. The distance and heavy snowfall made it impossible for even his keen eyes to ascertain who was behind the wheel or how many people were in the vehicle, but he could see that the impact had damaged the roof and windshield and had blown out the driver's side window.

He forged ahead with his plow, shoving snow off to the side of his road as he drove down the hill toward the highway. The snow was so deep around the stranded SUV that there was no way its occupants could open the doors. He watched to see if anyone would try to get out through the windows, but there was no sign of movement. Was the driver unconscious? Or dead?

The car's horn beeped a few times, followed by a long retort.

Okay. Not dead. Trapped? Injured? Staying inside to keep warm?

As he urged his truck down the hill, irritation prickled within him. It certainly wasn't the first time there'd been an accident on this stretch of road in winter, but in the past, emergency services had come along and saved the day. That wasn't going to happen this time. From the look of things, this storm was going to be a nightmare. He'd just heard about an avalanche on the road to the west on the police scanner. The car must have just gotten through. They were closing the pass in the other direction due to heavy snowfall. It could be days before the storm ended and the county got around to clearing the roads. That car would be stuck there the entire time.

He told himself that it wasn't his problem. If he went down there, he'd have to invite up whoever was in that car—and *he'd* be stuck with them for days. It was the last thing he wanted. He'd never had a visitor in his home, if you didn't count Jhania—but he always made himself scarce on the days she came by. He'd worked hard to maintain his anonymity and his distance. He'd never met the people he did business with, and had no desire to. He was alone, as alone as it was possible to be—if you didn't count the two souls in the barn—and he liked it that way.

He had absolutely no wish to open his house to strangers. It might well be like opening Pandora's box. His sense of privacy and tranquility would be shattered, possibly forever. He wasn't equipped to host, much less feed, anyone. And more to the point, he thought bitterly, their safety would be in question every minute.

Could he exist with a person or persons in the house for days on end? Did he dare take that chance?

On the other hand, did he have any choice? It was only noon, but the temperature was already well below freezing and dropping fast. The entire car would be buried in snow in no time. Whoever was inside it would freeze to death.

With a disgusted sigh, he jammed down on the gas pedal, moving forward at a faster clip. At the end of his road he drove across the highway, clearing away the snow in front of him in an arc and pulling to a halt not far from the stranded vehicle.

Donning his hat and gloves, he yanked open the cab door to the howling wind and snow. He planted one booted foot down onto the black ice, then stepped out carefully. Grabbing his snow shovel from the back of the truck, he made his way to the edge of the road.

The snow in the embankment was waist high at least. He plunged down into the deep accumulation and waded through it, an exercise which no doubt would exhaust a normal person but merely irked him. The roof and hood of the half-submerged car was already shrouded in a quarter inch of new snow. He bent down by the driver's shattered window and peered inside.

A young woman sat behind the wheel, held upright by her seat belt, her head slumped to one side. The left half of her face was drenched in blood, which had left a crimson trail across her light blue scarf and was dripping onto her parka. The sight made him tense with alarm. He knocked sharply on the roof of the car and called out, but she didn't budge. She had just pressed the horn a few minutes before. Had she passed out? Or was she. . . ?

Working very rapidly with the shovel, he cleared away the snow from around the driver's door, yanked it open, and leaned inside, steeling himself against the heady scent of fresh blood which invaded his nostrils. A quick survey of the vehicle's interior confirmed that the woman was alone. The air bags had not deployed, no doubt because the car had rolled sideways in the accident instead of hitting something head-on.

He laid a hand on the woman's shoulder. "Miss? Miss?" he said urgently. "I'm . . . here to help you."

She didn't respond. He instinctively took her wrist and felt for a pulse—something he hadn't done on a human, he realized, in a very long time. He was surprised by the relief he felt when he found a steady beat. She wasn't wearing a wedding ring, he noticed. He heard and saw her regular and even respiration, and visually assessed her status. She probably had a concussion. Did she have a bleed inside her head? The only other things obviously wrong were a contusion on her left cheek and the blood flowing from the temple above it.

At the sight of all that blood he frowned in annoyance, fighting back the dark feelings it stirred within him. Quickly he withdrew a handkerchief from his pocket. Pressing it firmly against the wound, he studied her face. Even with blood splattered across half of it, she was pretty; beautiful, in fact, with a pale complexion and long, reddish-gold hair. She was young, perhaps in her mid-twenties. Who was she? Where was she from? What was her name?

Gazing at her, he was suddenly aware of a very different kind of attraction and desire, a sensation that startled him. It had been so long since he'd spent any real time around a woman, so long since he'd allowed himself to even remotely care about anyone for that matter, that he'd almost forgotten what it felt like. *Forget it*, he told himself. *It isn't going to happen.*

He briefly removed his handkerchief from her forehead and studied the wound: a small gash just below her hairline. Head wounds, no matter how tiny, always bled profusely, more so than any others, and this one was no exception. He could heal her cut rapidly and permanently right now, without leaving a mark, but how would he explain that away when—if—she awakened? No, he decided, he'd have to stick to traditional doctoring methods.

He uncoiled the scarf from her neck and tied it around her forehead to hold the handkerchief in place over the wound. The wind continued to howl, blowing in snow through the open car door. He had to get her out of this weather. Spotting the key in the ignition, he removed and pocketed it. Unbuckling her seat belt, he brushed off the litter of safety glass from her lap, carefully lifted her out of the car, and carried her to his truck, blinking his eyes to keep out the wind-driven snow. Her weight was trivial. Despite her bulky parka, he could tell that she was slender and probably stood at about five feet eight.

He belted her into the passenger seat of the truck cab, then retrieved all the belongings he could find in her car. He'd only cleared half of his winding road so far, and he used that side to drive back up to the top of the hill.

Once inside the house, he removed her parka and laid her down on the sofa before the hearth in the great room, spreading a towel beneath her head and propping it with a pillow. Moving fast, he added more fuel to the fire, retrieved a clean T-shirt and a few other items he kept on hand, and returned to her side.

He unwrapped the blood-spattered scarf from her forehead. To his satisfaction the wound was staunched. After disinfecting the site, he placed a small butterfly bandage over it, then cut a long strip from the T-shirt and used it to tie a compress to her head. That should take care of it, he thought. Still, he was worried about possible internal bleeding.

He withdrew the penlight from his pocket, opened her eyes with his fingertips, and shone the light into them. Her eyes were a lovely shade of green. Her pupils were equal, round, and reactive. Good. No severe intracranial issues. He took her pulse again. Its strong beat and the color in her cheeks reassured him that there was no worry of internal bleeding anywhere else. She seemed stable. If all went well, she'd wake up soon with nothing more serious than a headache.

He went to fetch a bowl of warm water and a soft wash cloth. Crouching down beside her, he gently cleansed the blood from her face. He liked the subtle spray of freckles across her small, straight nose, the shape of her ears, and the gentle curve of her light red eyebrows. Her long, wavy hair spread out like a reddish-gold cape across the pillow beneath her, and invited his touch. She wasn't wearing any makeup and looked even prettier because of it.

As he worked—his body in such proximity to hers, his fingers grazing her warm flesh, the cloth soaking up her blood—the act felt very intimate. His eyes lingered on her mouth before moving to her throat. In the quiet of the room, the sound of her heartbeat thudded tantalizingly in his ears. Despite himself, his eyes traveled down her body. She was wearing a royal blue, V-neck sweater over a striped cotton shirt, tucked and belted into tight-fitting blue jeans that hugged her shapely figure. Her long legs, which disappeared into tall, insulated boots, were slender and perfectly proportioned.

Once again, a stirring welled within him, the pull of a physical attraction so powerful it made his nerve endings tingle. He silently cursed himself and stood up, exasperated, resisting the urge to slam the bloody bowl of water onto an end table. This was going to be even more difficult than he'd imagined. What happened to the sense of professional distance he'd once been so adept at? He was far too long out of practice.

Drawing a blanket up to her chin, he made a mental note to keep a careful distance between them while she was here, or the consequences might not be pretty.

CHAPTER 3

NICOLE'S HEAD THROBBED. She heard and smelled a crackling fire and could feel its warmth, but she couldn't see any flames. What had happened to her? It was dark, so dark that she couldn't see her hand in front of her face. Was she in a cave? A warm liquid oozed down her cheek. She was bleeding! No, she thought with equal horror, someone—or something—was bending over her, washing her face.

Nicole's heart began to pound in cadence with the violent drumming inside her skull. The dark figure moved away, but she could still hear it breathing, could sense its feral presence. It was a Thing. A beast. A monster. Terror snaked through her, setting her every nerve on edge. She wanted to move, but she was paralyzed. She wanted to scream, but she couldn't make a sound. She was a fly caught in a spider's web. The Thing was going to kill her. She had to get away!

Nicole awoke with a start, her heart and head still pounding. Opening her eyes, she saw to her great relief that she was not in a dark cave, but gazing up at a light-filled, open beam, vaulted ceiling lined with a pale-colored wood. Turning her head, she discovered that she was lying on a comfortable leather couch, covered by a soft blanket, in someone's very spacious living room. *What a strange, strange dream*, she thought in groggy confusion as she silently took in her surroundings. Where was she?

The room was decorated with a masculine flair. Assorted leather easy chairs were grouped around an oak coffee table with curved legs and an eclectic mix of hardwood tables that looked antique. An expensive-looking area rug stretched out atop a shining hardwood floor. On one side of the room stood a black grand piano, its shiny surface gleaming beneath a strategically placed lamp. On the other side was a gigantic flat screen TV. The rest of that wall was taken up by a massive stone fireplace. A fire burned brightly within, giving off a comforting heat. The entire place looked scrupulously clean and neat as a pin.

A man was bent over the fireplace, his back to her. He wore a dark green, long-sleeve shirt. Who was he?

Muted daylight shone in through a row of tall windows that reached the peaked, vaulted ceiling. A blizzard raged outside.

Then she remembered. The storm. The accident. *The blood.*

Nicole's hand went to her left temple. Her fingers encountered a strip of fabric wrapped and tied around her forehead. Some kind of bandage? She slowly sat up, an action that caused her head to throb even more painfully and the man to whip around in her direction.

"Don't touch that," he said abruptly.

His tone was so sharp that Nicole immediately dropped her hand to her lap. To her surprise he spoke with a refined British accent.

"My head hurts," Nicole said, staring at the man's scarred, brown leather boots, which peeked out from beneath his dark blue jeans.

"That's to be expected." Although his deep voice revealed concern, it seemed tempered by wariness and reserve. He stood a good eight feet away and made no move to come closer. "You received a rather nasty blow."

Nicole looked up at the man's face for the first time. An unexpected fluttering began in her stomach. He had lovely blue eyes and was extremely handsome—so good-looking, in fact, that Nicole couldn't help but stare. He appeared to be in his mid-thirties and was about five feet ten, a couple of inches taller than she was, with a lean, athletic build. His light brown hair was of medium length and combed back loosely from his fore-head. The silver buckle that adorned his leather belt looked like an antique or something a cowboy might wear. But cowboys didn't have British accents—did they? And they were always deeply tanned. This man's complexion was fair.

"How long was I out?" Nicole asked.

"A couple of hours."

"Oh my God, really?" She glanced at her watch and saw that it was after three. There was no way she'd make her flight now, unless she could teleport to Denver. "Is this your house?"

"Yes. What's your name?"

"Nicole Whitcomb."

"How old are you?"

"Twenty-nine."

"Do you know what day it is?"

An odd question, she thought. "Monday, March 4th." She touched her left cheek. It was tender but clean. *Had he washed her face and bandaged her?* The thought brought another flutter to her stomach. *If so, this gorgeous man was hardly a monster.* "Where are we, exactly? How did I get here?"

"Do you remember what happened to you?"

She recognized the intent of his questioning now, realized he was testing her to see if she was fully coherent. "Yes. One minute, I was in complete control of my car, and the next I was sliding off the road and flipping over. It was terrifying."

He nodded as if her answers satisfied him. "Four-wheel drive doesn't mean four-wheel stop. Black ice is a dangerous hazard, even if you have years of experience driving in these conditions. The accident happened on the highway just below my house. I saw it when I was out clearing my road."

There was a captivating elegance to his speech and mannerisms that felt a little old-fashioned for a man so young. At the same time he seemed tense and aloof, as if for some reason he was deliberately holding himself in check, forcing himself to be polite.

"Clearing your road?" she asked. "How far is it down to the highway?"

"About a half mile."

"Wow. That must take a pretty big shovel."

He darted a glance at her, as if trying to decide whether or not she was kidding. "I hang a blade on the front of my truck. Otherwise, I'd be snowed in all winter."

"I figured."

"Anyway, I found you. You'd passed out. I dug you out, brought you up here, and cleaned you up a little. Your scarf and parka are in the wash." He stepped away with unhurried grace and lowered himself into an easy chair across the room— as far off, she noticed, as it was humanly possible to sit, although there were plenty of closer chairs.

"Thank you." Nicole felt a jumble of contradictory emotions: a rush of gratitude to this total stranger who had saved her life; the light tingle of her attraction to him; and an overwhelming feeling of awkwardness. Although his words seemed to convey an interest in her well-being, his voice and body language implied otherwise. Whoever he was, despite all he'd done for her, she felt instinctively that he didn't want her here, that she was imposing on his privacy, that he'd rescued her against his will.

She wished she could leave immediately. But how? Her car was buried in a snowbank and it was blizzarding outside.

He studied her from where he sat. "Are you thirsty? Would you like a glass of water?"

"I'm okay, thanks."

"Do you feel dizzy? Nauseous? Any abdominal pain?"

"No. Just a headache."

"How bad is the headache? Moderate or severe?"

"Moderate. Are you a doctor?"

He hesitated. "No. But I've . . . studied first aid. Can you stand up? Touch your hand to your nose, like this?"

She stood and mimicked the requested movement.

"Good. You appear to be fine. The headache should go away in a couple of hours."

She sat down, still ill at ease. "Thank you again for rescuing me and everything you've done to take care of me. I'm really sorry to be in your way, but—" She paused, hoping he would contradict her, but he didn't. "I'm very grateful. What kind of injury do I have? As I recall, my head was a bloody mess."

Her statement brought a brief, dark glimmer to his eyes that sent an unexpected chill up Nicole's spine. *What's that about?* she wondered. She had no reason to be afraid of this man. Did she?

"A small cut on your temple—nothing severe," he answered, his features resuming their prior complacency as he glanced away.

Nicole's heart began to beat erratically. She'd heard scary things about mountain men who'd lived too long in isolated places. Who was this guy? He seemed cultured and spoke very formally, as if he belonged in the Queen's court or in a palace surrounded by servants. What was an Englishman doing in this remote corner of the Colorado mountains, unless he was hiding from something? But if he was a killer, surely he would have murdered her already, instead of carefully tending to her wounds. Wouldn't he?

"You haven't told me your name," she said, straining to keep her voice even.

"Haven't I? I beg your pardon. Michael Tyler."

"How is it that you live up here? I thought this was national forest land."

"It is. But there are pockets of private land scattered throughout. This property has been in my family since the 1860s, when my great-great-great grandfather homesteaded it, more than forty years before Theodore Roosevelt established the national forest."

"I see. But your accent. Aren't you from England?"

"I grew up in England."

"And you moved here. . . ?"

"About twenty years ago, when I inherited the property."

"Twenty years ago?" He looked no older than thirty-five at most. Which meant he must have inherited the place when he was fifteen. "To emigrate all the way from England to this remote spot at such a young age—that's very brave and unusual."

"I wasn't so young," he said testily. "I was nineteen and ready for a change."

Okay, so he was older than he looked. "Do you live here all year long?"

"I do."

"By yourself, or . . ."

"I live alone."

Her questions seemed to annoy him. He stood up and Nicole sensed that he was about to leave the room. In an effort to lighten the mood—or maybe just to put herself more at ease—she glanced at the grand piano and said with a forced smile, "So I take it it's either you who plays that piano, or the resident ghost?"

A surprised twinkle lit his blue eyes. He sat back down in his chair with the first hint of a smile. "Definitely the ghost. Watch out for her. She plays at the oddest hours and has been known to leave candles burning in the most unlikely places."

"She?"

"A raven-haired beauty. From her clothing and hairstyle, I deduce that she's from the previous century. Which is strange when you consider that I only built the house ten years ago."

Nicole laughed. His smile was charming and only enhanced his good looks. His accent was so lovely, she could listen to it all day long. Maybe there was nothing to be afraid of after all; maybe he just wasn't used to being around other people. "What do you do for a living out here, Michael?"

"Various things."

"Such as?"

"I write, I make things."

Clearly he didn't want to share any details. "Well, you must be very successful. This is a beautiful house."

"Thank you." He seemed to relax a bit as he studied her from his chair. "Where are you from?"

"San Jose, California. I was here for my best friend's ski wedding. She got married at Steamboat Springs."

"A ski wedding?" His eyebrows lifted in amusement.

"It was great—a perfect, beautiful day, the ceremony on a mountaintop. My best friends from college were there. I hadn't seen them in a while and it was fun to catch up. Just now, I was on my way to the Denver airport to fly home. I thought I could make it over the pass before the weather got too bad."

"You won't be flying anywhere today, I'm afraid. The pass is closed."

"Closed?"

"And according to the radio, an avalanche was reported in the other direction, to the west."

"I saw it! It happened a few seconds after I drove by. It covered the entire road."

"You're very lucky to be alive."

"I know. And I probably wouldn't be, if not for you. So again: thanks."

"You're welcome."

Nicole stood, crossed to the picture windows, and looked outside. From what she could see, the house was a modern chalet style with stained wood siding and a wide wraparound wooden deck, the front of which was sheltered by an extension of the high, peaked roof. They were nestled in a pine forest. The air was so alive with swirling snow that she couldn't see more than fifty feet or so in any direction.

"How long do you think this storm will last?"

"A good long while. The weather report said it won't blow itself out until tomorrow night at the earliest or perhaps the day after. And I'd guess it'll take a good two days after that before the county clears the roads."

Nicole stared at him, stunned. "Are you kidding? Is there any other way out? Do you have a snowmobile?"

"I'm afraid not."

"Could I walk out? I mean, two days from now, after the storm is over?"

"On an unplowed road? No." He stood, shoving his hands in his jeans pockets. "Steamboat Springs is more than twenty miles away and blocked by the avalanche. My closest neighbor is twenty miles in the other direction, and it's a good fifteen miles beyond that to Kremmling, the nearest town. Even with snowshoes, that'd be an impossible trek."

"What am I going to do?" Nicole said, distraught. "I have to get home and back to my job. And my cat—"

"I'm sorry. You seem to be stuck here." His tone and expression made it crystal clear that he wasn't any happier about the prospect than she was.

"But four days! I can't expect you to put me up all that time."

"It seems that we have no alternative, Miss Whitcomb."

Miss Whitcomb? Nicole couldn't remember anyone ever calling her that in her entire life. Before she could comment, he went on:

"It's awkward, I admit. You don't know me and I don't know you—and I'm not accustomed to having guests. But I'll do my best to stay out of your way. And don't worry," he added, with a dark glimmer in his eyes and a surprisingly playful smile, "I promise I won't bite."

CHAPTER 4

A SHIVER PASSED THROUGH NICOLE'S BODY. When he looked at her that way, she felt an inexplicable sense of apprehension again, despite her attraction to him. It was a very confusing, unsettling feeling, and she was glad he was halfway across the room.

"Do you have a phone?" Nicole asked. "I need to make a few calls, but I couldn't get a signal with my cell phone earlier."

"Cell phones don't work in this area. They don't run phone lines up here, so I use my satellite Internet connection to make calls. You're welcome to use it, but in this kind of weather it will operate for only a few minutes at a time, if I keep brushing snow off the dish."

"Oh—that sounds difficult. Is the dish on your roof?"

"I installed it on the deck. I didn't want to have to go up on the roof every time it snowed. Just let me know when you're ready to make your calls, and I'll take care of it."

"Thanks." Nicole's head began to pound with renewed vigor. "Do you have any aspirin or Tylenol?"

"Sorry, no."

"I have some in my suitcase, in the trunk of my car."

"Your bags are here. I brought up all your things for you."

"All my things? Thank you."

He rose, gesturing toward a set of closed double doors on the far side of the living room, where she now saw her bags neatly stacked beside her purse. "Would you like to get settled in?" he asked with calm politeness. "I can show you to your room."

"That'd be great."

At the door, they both bent to pick up her backpack at the same moment and his hand inadvertently closed over hers. His fingers were strong and slightly cool, and the contact between them caused a tingle to rush up Nicole's arm. His reaction was very different, however. To her confusion, he yanked his hand back as if her touch had burned him. Quickly he grabbed her other case, shoved the door open, and strode wordlessly into the room.

Nicole followed, bristling. Was he a wealthy hermit who despised people in general—or just her in particular? What was it about her that he found so offensive? She chided herself for her unwelcome feelings of attraction to him, vowing to wipe them entirely from her mind.

The bedroom was large and airy with the same open beam ceiling as the great room, picture windows with heavy curtains,

and a smaller stone hearth and fireplace. It was attractively decorated, with finely crafted oak furniture and a king-size bed
topped by a puffy dark blue comforter that looked like it was
filled with down.

"This is beautiful," Nicole said, suddenly uncertain,
"but—isn't this the master bedroom?"

"It's the only bedroom." He set her bags on top of the
dresser.

"You don't have a guest room?"

"No."

Only one bedroom, in a house this size? He wasn't kidding when
he said he wasn't accustomed to having guests. "I can't take
your room."

"I'd like you to take it. I'll sleep on the sofa in my study."

"No, really—" she began, but he cut her off.

"I insist. You'll want your privacy. The bathroom's through
there," he said, indicating an adjacent door. "I've already taken
my things out so I won't disturb you."

Nicole felt incredibly guilty kicking him out of his room,
even if he couldn't manage to hide his antipathy for her. At
the same time, he was being such a gentleman about it, she
didn't see how she could refuse. "Well, okay . . . thank you,
Michael . . . but I feel really bad about this."

"It's fine, really. I tend to work late and have caught forty
winks in the study on many occasions." He gestured toward
a phone by the bed. "There's a phone if you'd like to use it.
Just give me a minute to clear off the dish." He turned to go.

"What's your number in case someone needs to reach me?"

He paused, frowning; then he found a pen and notepad in
the nightstand, jotted down a number, and handed it to her.

"Just warn them that I doubt any incoming calls will get through until the storm ends."

He left the room. Nicole heaved a sigh. This was all so uncomfortable and strange. She reminded herself how lucky she was that this man had rescued her. If not for him, she surely would have died out on that road today—but he was a hard man to figure out. Maybe he was an English lord or duke who'd left his title behind to rough it in the Colorado mountains. Although this beautiful house could hardly be called roughing it.

Nicole retrieved her vanity bag from her suitcase and took it into the bathroom, which was large and luxurious, and outfitted with gold-plated fixtures and an oversize marble tub and shower. As she grabbed her travel vial of Tylenol she caught sight of her face in the mirror and nearly recoiled. In her preoccupation with her headache and her circumstances, she'd almost forgotten her injury. The left side of her face sported a small, purplish bruise, and a makeshift bandage cut from a strip of white fabric (one of his T-shirts?) was wrapped and tied around her throbbing forehead, holding a small compress in place. *I look hideous*, she mused. *No wonder he can't stand the sight of me.*

She glanced about for a glass so she could take the Tylenol, but couldn't find one anywhere. *Weird*, she thought. *Doesn't everyone keep a glass in their bathroom? He must have taken it when he removed his stuff.*

Her stomach growled, reminding her that she hadn't eaten since breakfast. She'd planned to stop for lunch on the way to the airport. It wasn't a good idea to take Tylenol on an empty stomach. Better to wait, Nicole decided, until she finished her phone calls, and then ask Michael for something to eat.

Returning to the bedroom, Nicole mentally reviewed the people she needed to call: her boss, her neighbor, her mother, and the car rental company. She sat down on the edge of the bed and was about to make the first call, when she noticed a beautiful wooden box on the nightstand. It was about the size of a hardcover book but a couple of inches taller, and made from a polished hardwood. The lid was inlaid with an intricate design fashioned from different colors of wood. Nicole couldn't resist picking it up and examining it more closely. The lid was hinged at the back and there was a small windup key on the bottom. When she lifted the lid, it began to play a snippet from Mozart's *Eine Kleine Nachtmusik*, a song she was very familiar with.

Nicole smiled. A music box! It was truly lovely. The cylinder and all its workings were visible in a compartment beneath a glass window. It seemed like a whimsical thing for a man like Michael to own. And yet—was it? What did she know about him, really?

MICHAEL COULD HEAR EVERY WORD she was saying on the phone, even though she was halfway across the house behind a closed door. It was an ability he had always found more aggravating than useful. Not that he didn't like the sound of her voice; it was quite pleasant, in fact. But he didn't like invading other people's privacy anymore than he liked them invading his.

It sounded like she was talking to her employer, and yet it could quite possibly be her boyfriend. A woman like that—attractive, charming, good sense of humor—was bound to have a boyfriend. He could envision the chap in his mind: a self-involved young upstart who took everything in his life for granted and was oblivious to its value. Why else had he let her attend her best friend's wedding alone? On the other hand, maybe she wasn't involved with anyone.

Michael caught himself with a laugh and shook his head. What was he doing? Where were these thoughts coming from? She seemed like a nice enough young woman, but why did he care whether or not she was involved with anyone? Admittedly, he was physically attracted to her—*very* physically attracted to her—and he'd enjoyed their short conversation. But it had been so long since he'd been alone with a woman, he no doubt would have started salivating over any female who was alive and breathing and was dropped on his doorstep. The less he knew about her—and the less contact he had with her while she was here—the better.

Michael strode into the kitchen. When he built this house, he'd thought it a waste of money to put in a kitchen at all, but he had to appease the architect, the contractor, and the building commission; he didn't want to do anything that would call attention to himself. He kept the shelves stocked these days for the same reason—to keep up appearances for Jhania, his cleaning lady—buying a little bit of this or that whenever he went into town, even going so far as to leave empty cans in the trash and dirty dishes in the sink. Up to now, he'd always found the charade to be a nuisance. Now he was grateful for it. It meant there was enough food to keep his guest alive.

And that was the whole trick, wasn't it? To keep her alive?

Michael quickly surveyed the contents of the refrigerator and cabinets. Thank God he'd had time, before she'd regained consciousness, to supplement the meager offerings with a few edible items he usually kept elsewhere. The pickings were slim, but she ought to be able to make do.

The sound of her voice continued to infiltrate his brain. She was talking to someone about an animal now. That's right; she'd mentioned something about a cat.

Returning to the great room, Michael sat down at the grand piano and began to play. Hopefully, Rachmaninoff would tune her out.

As he poured his frustration into the instrument, he reminded himself that his reaction to her was just an innate physical response to her humanness and femininity; there was no more to it than that. He just had to put up with her for a few days and then she'd be gone and life would be back to normal.

NICOLE'S SPIRITS LIFTED at the first sound of the bold, thrilling piano music coming from the other room. Smiling, she finished making her calls, the last one ending just as the connection dropped out.

Not wishing to disrupt Michael's playing, Nicole quietly entered the great room and stopped by a chair a few yards away to watch and listen. A highly accomplished pianist, he was playing the piece by heart, concentrating with a rapt expression as his fingers flew over the keys. The room resounded with the vibrant melody.

Nicole had loved the piano ever since she was six years old, when she'd attended a friend's recital and had begged her mother to let her take lessons. Her mom had immediately bought an old upright piano. When she was a few years older, Nicole had helped pay for lessons and sheet music by mowing lawns and doing odd jobs for neighbors. She'd practiced every single day, all the way through high school, had kept it up whenever she could throughout college, and she'd moved that same old piano up to Seattle into the house she used to share with her friends.

She'd only heard a grand piano in concerts and recordings. She'd only played one once, years ago, at a recital held inside a gymnasium, and the music had become lost in the immense space. Here and now—listening to Michael play this magnificent piece on this huge instrument within the confines of his living room—Nicole felt swept away. Holding on to the back of the easy chair before her, she closed her eyes, letting the music feed her soul. Her fears and anxieties receded. Anyone who could play this well, she decided, was a man to admire, not to fear.

Michael finished the song with a flourish, the final chords reverberating through the room. Nicole applauded.

"You're amazing," Nicole said, joining him at the piano. "Rachmaninoff, isn't it? Moment Musical in E Minor?"

He seemed both surprised and pleased that she recognized the song. "You know Rachmaninoff?"

"I do. Half the music on my iPod is classical. I love listening to it while I walk or exercise, and when I work in my garden plot."

"Your what?"

"My garden plot. It's just a ten foot square in my community garden—but I live in an apartment so it's the only patch of dirt I've got."

Michael looked at her, intrigued. "What do you grow in this patch of dirt?"

"Herbs and vegetables and a whole bunch of flowers. I love spending a couple of hours there every Saturday. I find it therapeutic to dig in the earth."

His eyebrows lifted and a hint of a smile tugged at his lips, but he didn't comment. Changing the subject, he asked, "Were you able to get through on the phone?"

"Yes. Thank you. The car rental company said to call them when the roads are clear, and they'll send out a tow truck."

"Good." Gazing out the window, where the snow was now drifting down gently against a background of white mist, he said, "Speaking of which, it looks like the wind's died down for a moment, and it'll be dark soon. I'd best finish clearing my road while I have the chance."

"You're going out in this weather? It's so foggy, I can hardly see."

"I know every curve of that road. I could probably plow it with my eyes closed."

"But why clear it now if, as you say, the storm's going to last a few days?"

"If I wait, there could be so much buildup I wouldn't get out until the end of spring. And I have to keep the back road open to the barn." He stood up. "It occurred to me that while I'm gone, you might be hungry."

"Actually, I am."

"Let me show you to the kitchen, then." He led the way across the room.

"By the way, is it okay if I do some laundry? I only brought enough clothes for a few days, and I'm down to my last pair of clean socks."

"Certainly. The laundry room is on the lower level. Feel free to make use of it."

"Thanks."

They passed a curio cabinet Nicole hadn't noticed before. She paused, glancing in at the contents. A dozen or more small wooden boxes were arranged on the glass shelves, all slightly different in size and shape, and all crafted with the same veneered marquetry technique as the box she'd seen in the bedroom, with a uniquely designed lid of inlaid wood. Some looked relatively new, while others appeared to be antiques.

"What a wonderful collection. Are they all music boxes?"

"Yes."

"They're beautiful and all so different. I think that one's my favorite." She pointed to an antique-looking box of burl wood with an inlaid design depicting a stunning red rose lying on a parchment scroll of music, surrounded by an intricate border. "Where is it from? Switzerland? Italy?"

He hesitated, an odd expression crossing his face. "I . . . don't know. I've had it a long time. It was . . . my father's."

He turned and walked off. Nicole followed him into the kitchen, which was surprisingly small but modern and immaculate, featuring gleaming oak cabinets, stainless steel appliances, and black granite countertops. An oak table and four matching chairs with elaborately carved legs stood in an alcove by a back window.

"You're welcome to fix yourself something to eat any time you like," he said in the aloof, polite manner that seemed to be his forte. He opened a few cabinets, revealing a very scanty stock of canned and dry foods. "I'm sorry I don't have many provisions on hand. It's been awhile since I went to the store.

My cleaning lady's always complaining that I don't eat right and leaving me homemade meals. She left a casserole in the fridge the other day that I haven't tried yet. Please help yourself."

"Thank you. I'll have a snack now if you don't mind, but I'd just as soon wait until you get back for dinner."

"*No,*" he said emphatically. "Don't wait for me. I'll be gone awhile, and in any case, I prefer to dine *alone.*"

Nicole was so taken aback by this statement and his unfriendly tone that she could formulate no reply.

He turned for the door, pausing halfway there to fling back at her, "Watch a film if you like, or you can borrow a book when I get back. Let me know if your headache gets worse or if you feel unwell for any other reason. And stay out of my study."

With that, he was out the door.

CHAPTER 5

NICOLE STOOD FROZEN FOR A MOMENT, staring after him in dismay. *I prefer to dine alone. Stay out of my study.* How rude could you get? What did he think she was going to do, steal a book and run off with it into the snow? She understood that he needed to clear his road. But would it kill him, when he got back, to sit down and eat a meal with her?

The man was a confusing set of contradictions. On the one hand, he was curt and ill-mannered, made no disguise of his reluctance to have her here, and flinched at her very touch. On the other hand, she'd glimpsed signs of genuine charm and wit beneath that cool exterior. He'd saved her life, doctored her, had graciously given up his bedroom for her, and had given her the run of his kitchen. He seemed to be genuinely concerned for her welfare, even if he didn't have much of a bedside manner.

Nicole sighed. It wasn't as though she was an invited guest. She'd been dumped on him out of the blue, against his will. Why should he trust her, a total stranger? He was doing his best in his own way to accommodate her. She had to give him credit for that. And anyone who played the piano with such passion couldn't be completely dead inside.

Maybe, she mused, her heart softening, *that's what happens when you're rich and live all by yourself in a megachalet out in the sticks. You lose touch with people and the way they ought to be treated.*

Nicole eyed the contents of the refrigerator, her stomach rumbling. Wow. He really *hadn't* been to the store in a long time. The fridge was practically empty. There was a six-pack of soda and the casserole he had mentioned. The vegetable drawer was stuffed with carrots and the fruit drawer was full to the brim with apples. That was it. Not a leaf of lettuce, an egg, a loaf of bread, or any other fresh food.

Is this all there is to live on for the next four days? she wondered, alarmed. *What a weird guy. He must really like carrots and apples.* Well, it looked like she was eating the casserole—whatever it was. Nicole took out the container, set it on the counter, and lifted the lid. It was enchiladas, topped with red sauce, cheese, and sliced olives—and it looked really good. Finding a plate and a serving spoon, Nicole dished herself up a nice-size portion, then put the plate in the microwave.

As the food heated, it filled the air with an appetizing aroma. To familiarize herself with the kitchen, Nicole glanced through all the drawers and cabinets. She found only the barest minimum of pots, dishes, and cooking and eating utensils, which all looked shiny and new, as if they'd never been used. There were wine glasses but no bottles of wine. The whole kitchen was outfitted so sparsely, in fact, it reminded her more of a vacation rental than someone's home, and like the rest of the house, it was as neat as a pin. The kitchen towels, hanging neatly from the oven door handle, looked as if they'd come straight from the store shelf.

Typical bachelor, Nicole thought. *He never cooks for himself and probably lives on frozen dinners.* When she checked the freezer, however, it was completely bare—not a frozen dinner in sight. She was still puzzling over that as she checked out the stove and dishwasher. They were in pristine condition—the dishwasher was empty—and she couldn't find a dish rack anywhere. *What does he do?* she wondered. Wash his dishes by hand, dry them immediately, and put them away after every meal? How anal retentive could you get?

That one casserole wasn't going to last very long between two people, Nicole realized. She was going to have to get creative over the next few days to figure out something to eat.

When the microwave dinged, she brought her plate and a glass of water to the kitchen table and sat down. She took a forkful. It was delicious. For the next few minutes, Nicole ignored the oddness of her situation and surroundings and devoured the enchiladas, enjoying every bite. For dessert, she ate an apple. When she'd finished, she took two Tylenol, then found a sponge and dishwashing liquid under the sink and washed her dishes by hand. Feeling obligated to follow his strict routine, she dried everything and put it back where it belonged, carefully replacing the dish towel on the oven door handle so that the kitchen looked as pristine as it had when she entered.

Nicole checked her watch and glanced out the kitchen window. It was 5:30 PM and pitch-dark outside. The wind whooshed through the trees and she could hear the distant hum of a truck engine. Michael must still be clearing his road.

She decided to take a few minutes to get the lay of the land and to do her laundry. On the opposite side of the main living area from the master bedroom was a closed door. She didn't explore it, presuming it to be his study. Following the polished oak staircase downstairs, she found the laundry room, where her stained scarf was soaking in a tub of blood-tinged, soapy water. Her parka lay on the counter beside it. There were spots of blood on it that appeared to have been treated with a spray-on stain remover.

That was nice of him, she thought.

While her clothes were in the washing machine, Nicole hand-washed her scarf and a few other items. A diligent scrubbing of her jacket removed almost all traces of blood. After hanging it up to dry and putting her clothes in the dryer, she moved on to investigate the next two rooms—a bathroom and a gym filled with top of the line exercise equipment. Framed movie posters decorated the walls, and she couldn't help but smile. Two of the posters were from movies adapted from novels by Patrick Spencer, one of her favorite authors. It looked as though she and her host shared the same taste in film.

At the back of the house was a mud room. Coats and parkas hung on pegs, alongside a pair of snowshoes. Knee-high leather boots, cowboy boots, thick-soled insulated rubber boots, sneakers, and sheepskin-lined slippers stood in a neat row beneath a bench next to a door leading outside. Another door led to a chilly, three-car garage that was lined with cabinets and housed a Range Rover. The remainder of the cavernous space was empty and damp from melted snow—where he parked his truck, no doubt.

Leaving the garage and mud room, Nicole returned to the hall where she found another door. It was locked. She wondered if he always kept it locked, or only did it because she was here. *What's the room for?* she mused. *His private wine reserve? His weapons collection? His store of gold bullion?*

A row of old framed photos hung on the wall in the corridor. One of them—a sepia tone print of a bearded old man standing in front of a rustic cabin—looked like it dated back to the 1800s. Was this Michael's ancestor? Nicole wondered. The one he said had homesteaded this property? If so—except for the heavy beard and mustache—he looked just like him. The other photos were mostly black-and-whites of various horses or people standing proudly with horses, and looked like they dated from the 1930s through the 1970s. It was an unusual and curious collection.

Heading back upstairs, Nicole tried to decide what to do with herself. Thankfully, her headache was gone. She wasn't tired and she didn't feel like watching a movie. If her cell phone was working, she'd happily spend a couple of hours catching up on her email—but that option was out. She briefly wondered if Michael owned a computer—but he'd made it clear that his study was off-limits—and in any case, his Internet connection relied on a satellite dish that was covered with snow.

It felt weird to be so out of touch with the rest of the world. But, Nicole realized, it was the perfect time to read. Reading had been one of Nicole's most treasured pastimes ever since she was four years old. Her parents had made reading a treat by "allowing" her to read for pleasure whenever she'd finished her chores and her homework. Clever, Nicole thought, looking back. She'd brought one book with her, the newest historical fiction by Patrick Spencer. She only had a few chapters left and was dying to finish it.

The house was a bit chillier than she liked, so after Nicole retrieved her book she grabbed a couple of logs from the wood bin in the living room and added them to the fire. Sitting down in a comfortable chair facing the hearth, she wrapped herself up in a soft blanket, turned on a nearby lamp, and began to read.

Her attention was so riveted to the novel that the next hour passed in the blink of an eye. The book—the story of a British doctor in Victorian England and the woman he loved—was so good that she didn't want it to be over. The ending, although bittersweet, was real, heartfelt, and satisfying, and left her in tears. She lay back and closed her eyes, her head filled with vivid images from the novel, the warmth of the fire so relaxing that she drifted off.

When Nicole next opened her eyes, to her surprise, it was after nine o'clock. She stood up, stretching, wondering where Michael was. The muted sound of classical music emanated from behind the door that she guessed to be Michael's study. Book in hand, she started in that direction, then stopped. He'd been so aloof and unfriendly when they last spoke, she hesitated at the thought of disturbing him—but she'd welcome another book to read, and he *had* offered to lend her one.

She rapped on the door. "Michael?"

Half a minute passed. The door opened halfway and Michael looked out, his hand on the knob, his lean frame filling the gap. "Yes?"

He was so very attractive, and standing so close, that Nicole's thoughts scattered like leaves in the wind, and she almost forgot what she was going to say. "I'm sorry to bother you, but—"

"How's the headache?" he interrupted.

"Better, thanks."

His glance fell on the novel in her hand and his eyes widened, but he didn't comment. "I saw you napping and didn't want to wake you. Did you find something to eat?"

"Yes. Your cleaning lady's an excellent cook."

"So she tells me." He spoke quickly, impassively. Whatever he was thinking, he was a master at hiding it.

"So she tells you?" Nicole repeated. "Haven't you ever tried any of the food she brings over?"

"Of course. I just meant . . . that she's proud of her culinary skills, and constantly reminds me of them."

"Oh." She waited for him to invite her into the room, but he clearly had no such aim in mind. "I thought I might read," she continued, mustering her resolve, "and you said I could borrow a book. So . . ."

"Oh. Yes. Of course." He hesitated as if this somehow presented a problem. "What kind of books do you like? I'll bring one out for you."

"Can I just see what you've got?"

He didn't reply, obviously reluctant.

"Oh for God's sake," Nicole said, losing patience. "I won't take up too much of your precious time. I'll just pick a book and be out of here." Without further ado, she gave the door a shove, pushed past Michael, and swept into the room.

Three steps inside the door she stopped, captivated. He had called it a study. Nicole had expected a cozy retreat with a desk and a bookcase. It was so much more than that, it almost took her breath away.

It was an expansive gentleman's retreat and a library. A fire blazed in another grand stone fireplace, and three walls were filled with floor-to-ceiling bookcases crammed with books. A comfortable-looking black leather couch and easy chair faced each other on one side of the room, opposite a mahogany coffee table and end tables that held small, elegant collectibles. On the other side stood a huge, L-shaped mahogany desk, on top of which rested stacks of papers and a state-of-the-art computer system.

"Oh. Wow. This is really . . . nice."

"Thank you," he said simply. He lowered the volume on the stereo with a remote.

Nicole saw what looked like a document open on his computer. Noting the direction of her gaze, Michael quickly crossed to his desk and put the computer to sleep. The screen went blank.

Nicole silently reminded herself not to be offended. He was a privacy freak; she already knew that. He dined alone, he worked alone, he didn't want her to see what he was working on. Whatever.

"I'll just grab a book." Nicole moved straight for one of the bookcases and studied the titles on the shelves. All the classics of British and American literature seemed to be represented: Daniel Defoe, Jane Austen, Charlotte and Emily Brontë, Edgar Allan Poe, Lewis Carroll, Charles Dickens, Mark Twain, Louisa May Alcott, Bram Stoker, Arthur Conan Doyle. Many of the books looked very old and were beautifully bound in leather.

"You have all my favorites," she said with delight. Taking out and examining a stately edition of *The Complete Adventures and Memoirs of Sherlock Holmes,* Nicole quoted in her best Holmes impression, "'When you have eliminated the impossible, whatever remains, however improbable, must be the truth.'" Smiling, Nicole replaced it on the shelf. "Some of these look like collector's items. Can I really borrow one?"

"Whatever you like, Miss Whitcomb."

She heard something different in his voice—a quieter, mellower tone than he'd yet exhibited—and she turned to look at him. He was leaning up against his desk, his arms crossed over his chest, his long legs stretched out before him. His guard was down, and he was studying her with an expression that resembled something like tentative delight. It was the first time he'd looked at her that way—as if she might prove to be an interesting human being after all and not just an inconvenience. It wasn't the most flattering look in the world, and yet the newfound warmth in his blue eyes made her heart skitter.

"This isn't *Pride and Prejudice.* You can call me Nicole."

"Nicole, then. Choose away."

"It's not going to be so easy to choose."

"That's all right. It's a big library. Take your time."

The ice wall he'd built around himself was visibly thawing. Nicole wasn't quite prepared for this new, relaxed attitude, but she was grateful for it. "Are you sure? I know you're busy."

"For a true literary enthusiast, I'm happy to take a break."

Nicole continued her study of the books on the shelves. "*David Copperfield!* May I?"

Michael nodded slowly. "Just be careful with it."

Nicole removed the book from the shelf, marveling at the dark green half leather binding with its gilt-embossed title and the marbled board covers and edges. It looked very old, but was in nearly perfect condition. Gently, she opened the book to the title page, which featured a black-and-white illustration beneath the flowery title and byline. It was inscribed by hand in an old-fashioned writing style that could only have come from an antique, steel-nibbed pen:

> *To Malcolm Taylor,*
> *With many thanks,*
> *Charles Dickens*

Nicole stared, hardly able to believe her eyes. "Is this really Charles Dickens' signature?"

"It is."

On the facing page, Nicole saw the imprint announcing the publication date:

> *London: Bradbury & Evans, 11, Bouverie Street. 1850.*

She knew enough about Dickens to guess what that meant. "This is a first edition, isn't it?"

He nodded.

Nicole gingerly shut the book and carefully returned it to its place. "You have a signed first edition of *David Copperfield*," she said in wonder, "and you just keep it sitting on a bookshelf? Why don't you keep it in a glass case?"

"I don't believe in putting the things I value behind glass. It belongs on a shelf where it can be read and enjoyed."

"Well, I wouldn't dare read something so valuable, rare, and precious. Do you have any other first editions in here that I might find accidentally?"

"A few. Most of them are in that book case."

"Would you show me?"

He strode over and let her examine another extraordinary book: *The Old Curiosity Shop*, signed by Charles Dickens to the same Malcolm Taylor. He even had an early, unsigned edition of *Ivanhoe* with the byline *Author of Waverley*, which he said was even more rare.

"Of course this one couldn't be signed," Michael said.

"Why not?"

"Because Sir Walter Scott was so mindful of his reputation as a poet, he published all his books anonymously. A facade he continued even when it became clear that there'd be no harm in coming out into the open."

"Interesting." Nicole studied the old book, enthralled. "What a beautiful edition. I read *Ivanhoe* the first time when I was twelve. I loved it so much, I wished it were true— especially the parts about Robin Hood."

"Even legend is founded in a kernel of truth. Robin Hood has been around since medieval times in ballads and such, so perhaps he did exist. Did you know that *Ivanhoe* is the precursor of the modern Robin Hood story?"

"In what way?"

"The character Scott gave to Robin Hood in *Ivanhoe* established everything we know and love today about that cheery, noble outlaw and his band of merry men. And it's the first time Robin was depicted as a contemporary of Richard I and given 'Locksley' as his title."

"I didn't realize that. What an impact Sir Walter Scott had on literature and film!" They exchanged a smile, warmed by this shared interest and connection. "Where did you get such rare books?"

"Auctions," he replied smoothly. "You can find anything if you're willing to pay for it."

And if you have the money, Nicole thought. Michael was standing barely a foot away from her now and his nearness caused her heart rate to quicken again. "Well, they're incredible. Thank you for showing them to me." She handed him back *Ivanhoe*, careful not to let her fingers come into contact with his, lest she experience a repeat of his earlier, adverse response. "I'll pick out something published a little more recently."

As Michael replaced the book on the shelf, she moved on to the next case. It was full of books and biographies that seemed to cover the gamut of world history, from ancient Greece up through the present day. There was an especially large concentration of works on Regency and Victorian England and the American Civil War. "So you're also a history buff. Do you have any . . . Oh! Here it is."

Two other bookcases were filled from top to bottom with historical fiction. To Nicole's surprise, five entire shelves were devoted to the works of Patrick Spencer, the world-famous writer who'd penned fifteen historical novels, every one a *New York Times* bestseller, and three of which had been made into films.

"I see you like Patrick Spencer. He's one of my favorite authors, too."

"Is he?" Michael returned with interest.

"Yes. I love his Dr. Barclay series. I just finished the latest one a few minutes ago." She indicated the book she'd brought with her, now lying on the coffee table, then turned back to run her fingers over the familiar spines of the books on the shelves. "And the Dr. Robinson series—it's fascinating and so well researched, don't you think?"

He didn't answer, instead asking quietly, "What do you like best about his work?"

"Well, I love the way he weaves actual historical events into his story lines. Like the books about the Civil War—I always learn something and it brings the period to life for me. And the ones that take place in that little country village in Victorian England—he writes with such exquisite period detail and evocative language, I always feel like I'm being transported back in time."

"Do you like the characters?"

"I love them. They're all so memorable and true to life. Even though they lived hundreds of years ago, their problems are still relatable—and he always includes such a haunting love story. Once I start reading one of his books I can never put it down, and at some point I always end up in tears."

Although Michael didn't respond, Nicole noticed a strange glint in his eyes and suddenly felt self-conscious. She sighed. "I'm babbling, aren't I? Sorry, I get like this when I talk about Spencer's books. I can't help myself. I've read every novel he's ever written, some of them three times." She glanced back at the shelves. "But you must feel the same way. I mean, look at this. You're even more of a die-hard fan than I am! You have every single one of his books, in hardcover *and* paperback! And multiple copies of some."

For some reason Michael looked peculiarly uncomfortable.

Studying the books in the case more carefully, Nicole realized that he didn't just have Patrick Spencer's entire collection in English; he had many dozens of foreign editions as well, which she'd never seen before. "You must have a copy of every foreign language title Spencer ever published. Where'd you get all these?"

Michael seemed to be struggling to hold back a smile. "I . . . collect them."

Nicole pulled out one volume, which—judging by the artwork on the cover—clearly was from the Dr. Robinson series, but the alphabet was foreign to her. "Is this Russian?"

"Bulgarian."

"Wow. You put my collection to shame."

The look on his face was such an odd mixture of guarded pleasure and unease that Nicole didn't know what to make of it. What was going on? Why couldn't he look her in the eye?

And then it hit her.

Everyone knew that Patrick Spencer was the pseudonym for an author who was not only rich and famous but famously reclusive. He so fiercely protected his privacy that he never revealed any personal information about himself, allowed no biographical details or photographs on his book jackets— ever—and he never did interviews. Some journalists thought he might be English, while others were certain he was American. No one had a clue where he lived, and no one knew his real name.

"It's you, isn't it?" Nicole said softly, staring at him. "You're Patrick Spencer."

CHAPTER 6

H E KNEW THERE WAS NO POINT in denying it. No
matter how many excuses he dreamed up, she'd
probably see through them. Well, he thought, maybe
this was a good thing. Maybe it would help divert her attention,
and explain away some of the other . . . oddities . . . so that she
wouldn't suspect his darker secret.

It was funny, though. Jhania had been cleaning this room
every week for ten years, and she'd never suspected a thing.
Nicole Whitcomb stepped in and figured it out inside of fifteen minutes. She wasn't just a beautiful woman—she was
smart, well-read, and very perceptive.

"You got me," he said finally, lifting his eyes to hers. "But
since you know my work so well, I assume you also know that
my personal life is something I prefer to keep confidential."

"Yes."

She was looking at him like a deer in headlights, stunned amazement wrapped up with a dose of awe. It was discomfiting, yet at the same time it was somehow . . . *gratifying*. In all the years he'd been writing and selling books, he'd only spoken to an actual fan a couple of times: once, in casual conversation when he'd dared to enter a bookstore where his novels were on sale; the other when he saw a nurse reading one of his books at the clinic. They hadn't known who he was, of course, but it had been interesting to hear their views on his work nevertheless.

He got his feedback solely through the Internet. There were various fan sites, and by now many thousands of reviews in the media and blogs across the globe. It was rewarding to know that people enjoyed what he wrote. It made all the effort worthwhile, made him feel like he was participating in the world again, making some sort of contribution. The comments about his historical accuracy always amused him. If anyone could write about the past with authentic detail, it was him. He had little need for history books, except as a refresher and to verify facts; most of it was there in his memory, ripe for the picking.

"I hope I can count on your discretion?" he said quietly.

"Of course," she said quickly. "I won't breathe a word. But . . . why?"

"Why?"

"Why don't you want anyone to know who you are? I thought most authors enjoyed their fame."

"I can't speak for most authors. I can only speak for myself. My personal life is my own. My readers enjoy the fictitious characters and stories I create, and I see no reason to mix the two. I'm not the first author to jealously guard my privacy. Many authors of yesteryear did the same."

Nicole nodded and flicked her eyes away, biting her lip as if still a little in awe of him. "I get it now. I feel terrible. No wonder you don't want me here."

He cringed at the bluntness of her statement. "I never said I didn't want you here," he said quickly.

She darted him a look that said: *please, don't insult my intelligence.* "I don't blame you," she added softly. "You must see me as a threat to the way of life you've built up for yourself."

Well, that was certainly true, for more reasons than one. Still, no matter how noble his intentions—he'd tried to keep her at arm's length for her own good—he didn't want to come off as a jerk. "I'm sorry if I've made you feel . . . unwelcome. As I said before, I'm just not accustomed to having visitors."

"I understand. It's a relief, actually, to learn the truth. I thought it was something about me. Look: I don't want to interrupt your work anymore than I already have. You were writing when I first walked in, weren't you?"

"No," he admitted. "I'm in between books at the moment. I was just working up some ideas of what to write next."

"Oh. Still, I should get out of your hair." She turned back to the bookcase and grabbed one of his Civil War novels, *The Wind of Dawn.* "I'll read this one again, if that's all right."

"That's fine, but there's no reason for you to rush off." The statement escaped his lips before he could stop it. But now that he'd said it, Michael realized that he really didn't want her to go.

"I don't want to disturb you," she insisted.

"You aren't disturbing me. I don't mind taking a break. And to be honest . . . I've enjoyed talking to you. And I promise it's not just because you appreciate my work."

She laughed. "Really?"

Really, he thought. It had been so long since he'd had a meaningful, face-to-face conversation with someone—and he liked her far more than he'd expected to. He also liked the sound of her laugh, the soft curve of her mouth, the way her green eyes sparkled when she smiled. If only he couldn't hear her pounding heart and pulsing blood . . .

But he'd managed to retain control thus far, hadn't he? Surely he could indulge himself a little while longer, without putting her in jeopardy?

"Please stay."

IT WAS INCREDIBLE TO THINK that she was actually in the same room as the mystery man who had all the literary world guessing. Nicole had tried to imagine who Patrick Spencer was, where he lived, and what he was like, hundreds of times. She had always revered his mind and talent. Now, as she sat down on the couch watching him stoke the fire in the hearth, she couldn't take her eyes off him.

The firelight threw long shadows against the walls and played against his handsome face, bathing his skin in a warm glow and revealing the red highlights in his light brown hair. His jeans hugged his long legs, and his shirt pulled tight across the muscles of his hard, lean back. He was truly a beautiful man, and he exuded an energy, sophistication, and intelligence that made him seem different from any man she'd ever met.

Of course he's different, Nicole reminded herself silently, her heart dancing an erratic rhythm. *For God's sake, he's Patrick Spencer. Get a grip!*

Nicole tore her gaze away, struggling to censor her thoughts and to rise above the sudden shyness that had pervaded her ever since she'd learned who he was. It was only a fluke that had brought her here. This famous and accomplished man would never be interested in someone like her—except, perhaps, as a diversion on a snowy evening—and he'd be only too glad to see her go.

"What should I call you?" Nicole asked. "Patrick or Michael?"

"Michael, please. Patrick is a pen name. I doubt I'd answer to it if you called."

"Okay." She glanced at him, willing her heart to return to its natural pace. "You're very different from what I expected."

He sat down in the easy chair opposite her. "In what way?"

"I don't know. Your writing . . . it's so brilliant and self-assured, I think . . . well, I imagined you'd be a much older man."

"Ah." For some reason a smile flitted across his face. He didn't say anything else, so she went on:

"Your first book is just as wonderful as your last one. The critics all think you must have written under a different name for years, long before becoming Patrick Spencer. But now I know that's impossible. Your first novel came out eighteen years ago, right?"

"Yes."

"If you moved here twenty years ago when you were nineteen—that means you would've been what—twenty-one when your first book was published?"

He gave her a silent, almost imperceptible nod.

"You couldn't possibly have written much before then."

He leaned forward in his chair, clasping his hands together, and seemed to be choosing his words carefully before he answered. "I guess I just got lucky with that first book. My publisher did a great job promoting it, and it found an audience."

"It wasn't only luck. I'm sure you worked very hard, and you have talent."

He shrugged modestly. "I leave that judgment to the readers and critics. Anyway, the publisher asked for another book after that, and . . ." He gestured toward the picture windows that overlooked the blustery night sky. "This is the ideal setting for a writer to work. So I just kept writing."

"It *is* beautiful up here. And I imagine it's very quiet, when the wind isn't howling."

They talked on for a while, with the storm raging outside and the wind whistling through the eaves. Nicole was interested in what inspired his novels, which he rather whimsically explained came from a love of history and a desire to travel through time.

Michael seemed fascinated to hear what Nicole thought about his books, what she liked and disliked, which books were her favorites and why, and which characters she liked best or least.

"I'll never forget that scene in *The Wind of Dawn*, when Dr. Robinson is single-handedly taking care of all those wounded soldiers in the Union field hospital," Nicole enthused. "The way he fought back against that Confederate raiding party, grabbing a gun and killing those Rebs—that scene haunted me for weeks. He was so consumed with guilt afterward, yet he was such a hero. "

Michael looked at her, his mouth fixed in a tight line. "*Was* he a hero?"

"Yes! He saved all those men."

"But he murdered half a dozen others."

"In wartime, killing isn't murder."

"Isn't it?"

The grim look on his face led Nicole to realize she'd unintentionally touched a nerve. "Not when it's done in self-defense or to hold off an enemy attack. But I empathize with your character's point of view. He was a doctor, dedicated to saving lives. To take any life at all was painful to him."

"I'm glad you understood that about him." He stood up and stoked the fire in the hearth again. "But enough about my books and about me. Let's talk about you. You said you're from San Jose, California?"

"Yes."

"And that's where you have your garden plot?"

She smiled. "Yes."

"Have you lived there all your life?"

"Not yet."

He laughed. It was the first time Nicole had heard him laugh. It was a deep, hearty sound, and the smile that accompanied it lit up his entire face.

"I grew up in San Jose. I went to college in Seattle and then . . ." Nicole caught herself. "I came home a couple of years ago."

"Home?" He sat down across from her again.

"My mother still lives there in the house where I grew up. I live on my own."

"Except for your cat."

Nicole was surprised and flattered that he'd remembered such a tiny detail she'd only mentioned once in passing. "Except for my cat. She's a mottled and striped black, gray, and golden tan tabby. She adopted me—strolled into my apartment one day when I was picking up the newspaper, and never left."

"What's her name?"

"Audrey Catburn."

That elicited a wide grin. "As in *Breakfast at Tiffany's*?"

"Exactly." Nicole couldn't help but smile in return. "She struck me as the feline equivalent of an elegant brunette. She's slightly Rubenesque and has the whole feminine/princess thing going. The underside of her paws and her arms all the way up to her elbows are black, like long evening gloves. She comes when I call her, is very chatty, loves people, is part dog I think, and hates cats. A few months ago, she brought me a gift—a live mouse that she proudly dropped on the living room floor at my feet. I spent the next three hours trying to flush it out the front door with a broom."

Michael laughed again, then rested his chin on his hand as he regarded her. "Why did you move back to San Jose? Is . . . that where your boyfriend lives?"

He seemed to be striving for a tone of offhand casualness, but Nicole sensed that he had a greater personal interest in her answer than he wished to convey. The idea threw her thoughts into temporary disarray. "No, I don't have a boyfriend."

"How is that possible? I would have thought you'd be involved with someone."

"I *was* involved with someone. I had a long relationship with a really great guy, but we broke up a few years ago."

"What happened?"

"Let's just say it got to the point where it didn't feel right anymore. What about you? You live alone. Has it always been that way?"

"Yes."

"Don't you ever get lonely?"

Something changed in his eyes. For the briefest of instants, an almost haunted look pervaded them; then he blinked and the look vanished. The look spoke of such profound pain that Nicole's heart went out to him, and she wished she hadn't asked the question.

"I do get lonely," he admitted softly, "but it's the price I pay for . . . anonymity."

What happened to him? Nicole wondered. Had he run away from something or someone in coming here? Was it a lost love? Is that why the tragic love stories he wrote were always so deeply felt?

His voice broke into her thoughts. "You haven't told me what you do."

"Me? Oh, let's not go there. My work isn't one-tenth as interesting as yours."

"Somehow I doubt that."

"Trust me, it's true." Since he was patiently waiting, Nicole felt obligated to continue. "Well, every Saturday I volunteer at the Tech Museum, demonstrating science experiments for children. And on Sundays I'm the Story Lady at the library."

"Story Lady? You mean you read to children?"

Nicole nodded. "I love children. I always have. They have so much energy and enthusiasm, and such a vivid sense of imagination. Don't you think? To them, the whole world is an exciting place full of wonders just waiting to be discovered. Growing up, I spent time with kids every chance I got. I baby-sat, I tutored elementary school kids after school, and I was a camp counselor more summers than I can count. I always knew that somehow, some way I'd work with children when I got older."

"That's wonderful—to know at such an early age what you wanted to do. But you've only described weekend volunteer occupations. You said you had to get back to your job, so I ascertain that you're not a lady of leisure. What do you do the rest of the week? Do you teach? Run a child care center? Do legal or social work?"

"No." Nicole hesitated. "I work for a medical insurance company, processing insurance claims."

He looked surprised. "Really? What does that involve?"

"Taking client phone calls, answering questions. Mostly it's a computer input job. Amount of claim column A, amount not covered column B, process, print, repeat."

"If you don't enjoy it, why do you do it?"

"I didn't say that I don't enjoy it."

"You didn't have to. It's clear enough."

"It's a good job," Nicole insisted.

"I'm sure it *is* a good job for a great many people—just apparently not for you."

"That's not true. I'm carrying out a service, helping people to cover their medical expenses—and that's rewarding. At the same time I try to protect the company. I'm good at it. There are a lot of fraudulent claims and I can smell them a mile away. The benefits are good and it's located close to where I live. I like the people I work with. It's a good environment."

"You said *good* four times but not once with conviction."

"Forgive me if my description of my work doesn't meet your required code of enthusiasm," Nicole bristled. "Not everyone gets paid to spend all day in a beautiful office on a mountaintop, spinning stories."

"I beg your pardon," Michael replied gently and with heartfelt apology. "I didn't mean to sound harsh or critical. I was only making an observation. It seemed an unusual choice for you, that's all, given your love for children. How long have you worked in medical claims?"

"Three years."

"What did you do before that?"

Nicole frowned. The familiar prickle of dread, guilt, and anxiety descended on her, just as it always did whenever anyone asked that question. How could she tell him? It would inevitably lead to questions about why she left—the one subject she wouldn't, couldn't discuss with anybody—particularly not with this man, whom she'd admired for so many years.

"I had various odd jobs," she said vaguely, feigning a yawn and looking at her watch as she stood. "I'm sorry. It's late, and suddenly I'm really tired. I think I need to go to bed."

"That's understandable. You had a concussion. It takes time and energy for the brain and body to recover. The best thing for you is a good night's sleep."

"Would you do me a favor?" Retrieving the copy of his novel she'd brought with her, she held it out to him. "Would you sign my book for me?"

"I'd be happy to."

He took the book, grabbed a pen, and paused. "Do you know, I've never done this before?"

"Never? In all these years, you've never signed a book for a fan? A friend? A relative?"

"Never."

She shook her head in wonder. "That is really . . ."

"Sad?" he finished for her, a self-effacing glint in his eyes.

"I was going to say *astonishing*."

He smiled, opened the book to the title page, inscribed something there, and returned it to her. She thanked him.

Standing up, he said, "If you don't mind, I'd like to take another look at that cut on your head before you retire, to make sure it's healing properly."

MICHAEL LED THE WAY BACK across the house to the master bathroom, where he instructed Nicole to hop up onto the counter and sit facing him. Her legs dangled between them.

"Now I understand why you know so much about first aid and medicine," she said suddenly. "You must have learned it while researching your books about Dr. Robinson and Dr. Barclay."

He nodded. As he began untying the bandage from her forehead, his hips came in contact with her knees. The contact caused him to draw a breath that was out of rhythm with the others. *You're playing with fire*, he reminded himself. *This is madness.* And yet he continued.

"The medical scenes in your novels are so detailed and explicit. How do you do your research?" she asked.

"I read a lot. I have shelves of medical texts and books about the period. There's a wealth of information online. And . . . I have a doctor friend I consult with from time to time, to make sure I get the facts right."

What a shame, he thought as he slowly unwound her bandage, *that I have to keep lying to her.* He'd been manufacturing identities with corresponding back stories for such a long time, it came as easy as breathing—but he'd grown weary of it. For once, he wished he could be open and honest with someone—*with her.* To his surprise, he realized he wouldn't mind talking with her all night long. It seemed they had a lot in common. He felt they'd never run out of interesting topics to explore.

What would she think, he wondered, if he told her the truth?

Don't be an idiot, he warned himself. The truth was something that simply couldn't be shared. And it wasn't as if she was being entirely up front with him. For some reason, she was being cagey about *her* past. The minute he'd asked about her former occupation, she'd cut him off and changed the subject. What was she hiding?

As he removed the dressing, he tilted her chin slightly with his hand and tried to examine the spot on her temple beneath the butterfly bandage—but he couldn't seem to focus on the wound. Her skin felt hot against his fingers. He could hear her heart pounding more quickly than usual, which made his mouth go dry, even as her nearness inspired a very different kind of desire. Her lips were just inches from his, and he resisted an unexpected impulse to kiss her.

"It's healing nicely," he said abruptly, taking a step back. "The bleeding's stopped and there's no sign of infection."

She turned and critically studied her injury in the mirror. "Oh, that's ugly."

Michael gazed at her mirror image in sympathy, grateful that the legend about his kind having no reflection was either a myth or for some reason did not apply to him. "It looks worse than it is. The head bleeds more than any other part of the body—"

"—due to the thin skin," she mused.

"More or less, but—"

"—it wasn't deep enough to require stitches?"

"No. It should heal quickly and cleanly and only leave a small scar, most of which will be covered by your hair."

"That's a relief."

She turned back to face him again, still seated on the counter. He put on a clean compress, opting to leave off the head bandage this time and simply secure it with a small piece of tape. "In the morning, if you don't see any blood seepage, you can remove the compress. But it's important that you keep the wound dry, so don't wash your hair."

"Got it. Thanks."

He put his hands around her waist and helped her down off the counter. Her hands touched his shoulders as she steadied herself. Her feet touched the floor and their eyes locked. His heart began to pound. It was everything he could do to keep from pulling her into his arms and pressing that wonderful feminine body against his.

"I hope you . . . have everything you need?" he said quietly.

"Yes," she answered. "Do you have . . . whatever you need? From your room, I mean?"

"Yes."

"Then I'll . . . see you in the morning."

Michael could feel her trembling slightly, could feel a heat rising within him and settling behind his eyes like twin flames. *Get out*, an inner voice shouted.

"Good night," he said, tearing himself away.

CHAPTER 7

A S HE STRODE OUT THE DOOR, Nicole's heart hammered in her chest. What had she just seen? In that moment before Michael turned to leave the room, she'd noticed something strange in his eyes. For an instant, they'd seemed to glow like red flames. *But that's impossible,* Nicole thought. Clearly that hit on the head was causing her to see things, or it was her own heated imagination gone amuck.

Her imagination wasn't the only thing that was heated up at the moment. The entire time that Michael had been undressing and redressing her forehead, Nicole had found herself wishing he'd been undressing a very different part of her body. *Stop thinking like that, Nicole,* she reprimanded herself, mortified. She'd barely known the man for half a day, and here she was having wanton thoughts about him. *Besides, he's totally out of your league.*

The irony of her situation, medically speaking, wasn't lost on her. With her education and training, she was far more suited than he was to examining and taking care of her own wound—but she wasn't about to bring that up.

Now that he was gone, Nicole took a moment to see how he'd signed her book. In a neat, elegant script, he'd written:

> For Nicole,
> With all best wishes,
> Patrick Spencer

Well, she thought. That was simple. Could it possibly be true that he'd never signed a book before? If so, that made this copy especially rare and valuable. She knew she'd treasure it always.

Nicole quickly brushed her teeth, put on her pajamas, climbed into the king-size bed, and shut off the light. The luxurious feather-top mattress was as soft as a cloud. The sumptuous down comforter quickly enveloped her in a cocoon of delicious warmth.

Nicole closed her eyes, trying to relax. But the wind wailed incessantly, repeating the same note over and over, as the events of the day kept playing over and over in her mind. The frightening drive across the snowy mountain. The accident. Waking up in this beautiful house. A shiver ran through her at the thought that she'd nearly died today. She didn't, thanks to one man. He'd been so aloof and prickly at the start. Now that she knew who he was, she understood why. It still seemed impossible to believe that she was lying in *Patrick Spencer's bed*.

For so many years he'd been her literary hero. She'd developed a crush on him from afar, even without knowing a thing about him. Tonight, after they'd talked awhile, she'd felt a thrilling, unspoken connection between them—something she hadn't experienced in years, not since the early days of her relationship with Steven—and she'd begun to relax. She'd sensed a change in Michael, too. He'd seemed pleased by her company, as if he'd enjoyed talking with her as much as Nichole had enjoyed talking with him.

Just because he was gorgeous, brilliant, charming, and famous, she reminded herself, there was no need to feel nervous around him. He was still just a person like everyone else.

As Nicole recalled the exquisite shudder of sexual desire that had run through her when Michael had touched her chin—and again when he'd lifted her down from the counter—adrenalin coursed through her in a white heat. Nicole was certain he'd felt the same desire; she'd seen it in his eyes, had sensed it in his touch.

But when she recalled the look she thought she'd witnessed in that last moment as they stood together, she started to shiver again. It was a hungry look, like a parched man staring at a glass of water. A parched man whose blue eyes danced with red flames.

The image of those red flames haunted Nicole, causing her to toss and turn for hours before she finally drifted off to sleep.

WHEN NICOLE DID SLEEP, she had a terrifying nightmare.

She was walking down the corridor of some strange, nameless hospital. The walls were brightly lit but endless, windowless, making it impossible to tell if it was day or night. People scurried past in both directions: doctors in white lab coats, surgeons and nurses in scrubs, visitors carrying armfuls of flowers.

A bald child in a wheelchair was being pushed in her direction beside his rolling IV pole. The boy gave her an odd, curious look, then held up a mirror he was carrying in his lap.

As the boy rolled past, Nicole glimpsed her reflection in the mirror. To her dismay, her nose was bleeding and a drop of blood was leaking from the corner of her eye. She glanced down and saw that both of her hands were covered with blood! She gasped but couldn't breathe. There was no oxygen in the building!

Nicole raced down the corridor, pushing past all the people, desperately seeking an exit, finally reaching double doors and barreling through them. Suddenly she was outside, taking deep, shuddering breaths of the cold night air as she ran. Inexplicably, she wasn't in a hospital parking lot. She seemed to be in a city, but it was a very old city she'd never seen before.

She couldn't stop running. Nicole had no idea where she was or where she was going. Her feet pounded against the cobblestones as she followed narrow, twisting streets, past dark stone buildings lit only by the moon. She heard lapping water and paused in an ancient doorway to catch her breath, her heart thudding in her ears, her hands still coated in blood. Just ahead she saw a river, moonlight gleaming on the murky, slow-moving water.

A young man was strolling idly along the riverbank, whistling to himself. Strangely, inexplicably, he was wearing a costume—knee breeches, a ruffled shirt, a powdered wig, and a silk frock coat—something Mozart might have worn. Another man, his face shrouded by the hood of his long, black cloak, was striding toward him.

The first man nodded with a smile, tipping his tricornered hat. Suddenly, the cloaked figure pounced, yanking the young man toward him with such uncanny speed that his victim barely had a chance to cry out. The young man struggled futilely against his attacker's superior strength. His cravat was ripped from his neck. The cloaked man opened his mouth wide, revealing sharp fangs. With a ferocious snarl, he instantly sank his teeth into the whiteness of the young man's throat.

Nicole gasped in terror. The cloaked figure continued feeding until his victim was limp and lifeless, then unceremoniously dropped the body into the river. He turned now, staring at Nicole from the dark folds of his hood with glowing red eyes. Who or what was he? Had he smelled the blood on her hands? Did he mean to kill her next? He began moving deliberately in her direction. Nicole screamed.

Nicole's eyes flew open and she sat up in bed, breathing hard, her pulse still racing.

THE WORLD WAS EERILY SILENT when Nicole next awoke. The bedside clock announced that it was 10:30 AM. Nicole slipped out of bed, still tired after her restless night. The memory of her vivid and frightening dream still lingered and made her shiver. Why on earth had she been dreaming about vampires? Was it because she had lost blood when she was injured?

The central heating was going full blast, keeping the house at a pleasant temperature, but the floor was cold on her bare feet. Padding to the front windows, she opened the curtains, diffusing the room with a grayish light.

It was still snowing, but the wind had died down. For the first time, Nicole was able to glimpse the property around them. The hillside below the house was densely forested. Stands of bare, wintry aspens alternated with snow-laden evergreens. The world was blanketed in a deep layer of fluffy white, all except for Michael's private roads—and from the look of it, he must have just cleared them again. There was a wide circular driveway at the side of the house. One road twisted and turned downhill from there, no doubt leading to the main highway, although Nicole couldn't see that far. Another road—short and straight—led directly away from the circular driveway into a nearby grove of trees.

Beyond the trees, Nicole thought she caught a glimpse of another building, although the distance and snow gloom made it impossible to make out what kind of building it was. Michael had said there were no neighbors for miles, so the building— whatever it was—must belong to him.

Nicole tied her hair up and took a quick shower, taking care not to get her hair or bandage wet. She then removed the dressing and inspected her forehead in the bathroom mirror. The gash was still red and angry, but the little butterfly bandage was doing its trick. Thankfully it didn't hurt as much as before. The bruise on her cheek wasn't pretty, but her headache was gone. After carefully brushing her hair, Nicole dressed in her jeans, a burgundy scoop neck pullover sweater, her navy blue zip-up fleece, and her fur-lined boots. Ah. Blessed warmth.

Starving, she made her way to the kitchen. *Where is Michael?* she wondered. Did he have breakfast yet? Although he'd made a point, earlier, of saying he preferred to eat alone, she hoped after the conversation they'd shared that he'd changed his mind. There wasn't much of anything in the fridge, but hopefully he had a plan and would find something for them to eat.

To her disappointment, the kitchen was empty and just as immaculate as she'd left it the evening before. The only evidence that Michael had been there was a bowl and spoon sitting in the sink, half-filled with water. The house felt very still, as if she were its only occupant.

Michael wasn't in his study or in the gym. She tried the mysterious door on the lower floor but it was still locked. Checking the garage, she discovered that his truck was gone. Hmm. He must have more roads to plow than were visible from the front windows. Nicole recalled him saying something about a barn. She felt bad that he had to keep going out in this storm.

With a sigh, Nicole returned to the kitchen. What she wouldn't give for scrambled eggs and toast, some crisp fried bacon, orange juice, and coffee—but *that* wasn't going to happen. The practically bare refrigerator stared back at her mockingly. The enchilada casserole was still missing only one portion—the serving she'd had the evening before. Hadn't Michael eaten dinner while she napped yesterday? What on earth did he eat?

Although it was almost noon, Nicole couldn't stomach the idea of enchiladas for the first meal of the day. Nor did a diet of carrots and apples sound appetizing. A search through the cabinets revealed assorted cans of soup and vegetables, and a large bowl filled with rolled oats, the same type of oats you'd find in a Quaker Oats box. That must be what Michael had for breakfast, she decided. But why did he empty them out of the commercial container into a bowl? The bowl wasn't even covered by plastic wrap—surprising for such a neat freak. *Just another one of his quirks*, Nicole thought with a shrug. She scooped a half cupful of oats into a cereal bowl, added water, and heated it in the microwave.

There was no coffeemaker. There was no tea in the cupboard—just an unopened jar of instant coffee and a half-empty box of sugar cubes. Nicole grimaced. Her mom used to drink instant coffee. Nicole had tried it a couple of times when she was little and could hardly stand the stuff—but it was better than nothing.

She ate alone at the table by the window. The coffee wasn't as bad as she'd expected, but would have been a whole lot tastier with milk or cream. When she finished, Nicole washed both her dishes and his and put everything away.

Michael still wasn't back yet. What could be keeping him so long? Nicole folded her laundry, then decided to occupy herself by reading—but remembered that she'd left the book she was going to borrow in his study. He wouldn't mind if she went in and got it, would he?

The study door was ajar and she slipped inside. The book wasn't on the sofa where she'd left it, so she decided to make another selection. Studying the vast array of titles on the shelves was both intriguing and entertaining. It was a wonderful collection, and it included more rare, old books than he'd led her to believe.

One bookcase housed two rows of tall, slender, notebook-size volumes with unmarked spines in a variety of colors. There were dozens of them. Curious, Nicole pulled out one of the volumes. It was an old journal, bound in cracked burgundy leather, its pages inscribed in ink in an elegant hand. Nicole read a bit of the first entry with fascination.

September 17, 1928

Sun again, third day in a row. Worked in the shop. Looking for rain tomorrow. 30 head of horses ready to fill the army contract. Training Midnight for Mrs. Andrews in New York; she's a beauty and I'm going to miss her.

Whose journal was this? Nicole wondered. Michael's great grandfather? The reference to "the shop" was vague and curious. How incredible to have inherited such a precious document—this record of the past. For some reason the handwriting looked familiar, but Nicole couldn't figure out why. Were the other volumes also journals? Would Michael consider this snooping?

Unable to resist, she took a similar book from the shelf above—this one bound in dark green leather—and opened it. The script inside was similar to the other one but more antiquated, as if written with a quill or nib pen instead of a fountain pen, and the ink was a faded brown.

When she noticed the date, Nicole stared in amazement. This must be the journal Michael's great-great-great grandfather kept when he first homesteaded this land!

June 12, 1867,
Fish Creek, Colorado

Still cloudy and overcast. Caught two wild horses yesterday, a stallion and a mare, which I hope to train and breed. Will keep them in the round pen until I build a barn. This valley is the ideal spot for them to

79

winter. Wildlife is abundant. Haven't seen another soul in months—
thank God. I am grateful for my books. Still plagued by memories—do
the painful ones ever fade? I—

Her reading was interrupted by the sound of a truck approaching and the automatic garage door opening. Nicole quickly replaced the journals on the shelves, heat rising to her face; she doubted Michael would approve of her reading these private documents. She hurried out of the room and down the stairs.

A door slammed on the lower level. Nicole found Michael in the mud room, hanging up his black parka by the back door. He was wearing a long-sleeve blue work shirt, his usual jeans, and a pair of square-toed, dirt-encrusted black leather boots with scarred heels and toes.

At the sight of him, Nicole felt all lit up inside— ridiculously happy—as if it had been days since she'd last seen him instead of just overnight. She hadn't forgotten how good-looking he was, or the effect he had on her.

Her intended bright greeting, however, died on her lips when she saw the look on his face. It was remote, withdrawn, impassive.

"How's the head?" He pronounced the greeting with such indifferent politeness, she sensed he didn't really care about the answer.

"Better. Thanks," she replied uncertainly.

"Good."

He didn't say another word, just sat down on the bench and removed his dirty boots, exchanging them for sneakers, without even glancing in her direction.

Nicole's heart lurched with disappointment. She felt as awkward again as she had when she first arrived. The man who'd talked with her so congenially for hours last night, and had later looked at her with such intensity in his eyes, had once again disappeared behind his stony, breathtakingly handsome exterior.

Why? she wondered. What had she done? Or did it have nothing to do with her at all? Could it be that this brilliant, highly successful author was just an eccentric and socially ungraceful hermit? She suddenly became determined to break through that icy shell. Somehow, she'd keep a conversation going, even if it killed her.

"So," she said, "were you out clearing your roads again?"

"That, and taking care of the horses."

"Horses?" She should have guessed that Michael would have horses. The main characters in his books often loved the horses they owned or cared for, and even great-great-great grandpa what's-his-name had apparently raised and trained them.

"I just keep two," he said matter-of-factly. "They live in the barn down in the valley at the back side of my hill. I have to feed them twice a day, snowstorm or no snowstorm."

Michael stood up and started past her toward the open doorway. Nicole cast about for a way to engage him further. "You must be freezing. Can I make you a cup of coffee? All I could find was instant, but with a couple of dozen sugar cubes, a sprinkle of verve, and a dash of imagination, it actually tasted pretty decent."

Michael paused and looked back at her, a smile tugging at his lips which he seemed to be struggling to contain. "No thank you. I don't drink coffee. I keep the instant for my cleaning lady."

"I could make tea, if you tell me where you hide it."

"I think I'm out of tea."

"An Englishman without tea. Now there's a contradiction in terms. How will you survive?"

"In difficult times, we all must learn to make do."

"Indeed. I had oatmeal for breakfast—not that you asked—and I've never much liked oatmeal. But that's all there was."

As if despite himself, his smile now broke out full force. "They say, never look a gift horse in the mouth."

She shook her head, grinning back at him. "What does that even mean?"

"It's a warning not to question the quality or use of a lucky chance or gift, but to appreciate the spirit behind it."

"But what does it have to do with a horse?"

"A horse's value is determined by its age, which can be roughly determined by examining its teeth. St. Jerome first said it in AD 400 in reply to his literary critics. I believe his exact words were, 'Never inspect the teeth of a gift horse.'"

"How on earth do you know that?"

Michael shrugged. "I have no idea. But let it be a lesson to you."

"Aye-aye, captain." Nicole gave him a mock salute, pleased that he was talking to her again. "I will eat oatmeal every morning and be grateful for it. But what else do *you* eat? There's no food in this house!"

"There's food—I expect we'll get by—I've just been preoccupied with writing lately, and didn't plan for the storm. Had I known you were coming to visit, I would have given the matter more serious thought, I assure you."

Nicole followed him into the hall, dying to ask about the journals in the study, but she decided not to mention them. Instead, she gestured toward one of the photographs on the wall—the one of the old bearded man beside a cabin. "I've been meaning to ask you: who's the man in this old photo? Is he the guy who homesteaded this property?"

"Yes. He was the first Tyler to set foot in America." Michael paused, then added, "Three generations of Tylers lived in that old cabin before I got here. I found those pictures in my grandfather's trunk."

"Who are the people and horses in the other pictures?"

"I'm not sure," he replied quickly. "Probably some of the animals my grandfather and great grandfather trained over the years, and the clients he sold them to. I thought they were interesting, so I kept them."

"They are interesting," Nicole agreed. She wanted to study the pictures more closely, but Michael moved on to the mysterious door she'd been unable to open, and withdrew a set of keys from his pocket.

"I hope you'll find some pleasant way to occupy yourself today," he said, glancing her way with another brief smile.

Nicole sensed that he expected some equally polite response and that she'd be on her way. Instead, she blurted abruptly, "Why do you keep that room locked?"

"To keep my cleaning lady out."

"Why? What do you keep in there? The skeletons of all your ex-wives?"

"Not all of them," he replied, without missing a beat. "Just the last six or seven."

"Six *or* seven?"

"I've lost count."

"I'd love to see them. I've always had a deep interest in osteology."

A smile took over his face. He jingled the keys in his hand, and she saw his mind working on the problem, the way he'd deliberated the night before when she'd brashly intruded into the private domain of his library. Finally, he inserted his key in the lock and opened the door. "I'm not deliberately trying to be rude. I've just never had anyone else in here before. You might find it boring, but you're welcome to come in."

CHAPTER 8

*M*ICHAEL ENTERED, flipped on a light switch, and stood aside, motioning for her to join him.

Nicole had no idea what to expect, nor any time to reflect on it. Entering the room, the first thing she became aware of was the pungent, fresh aroma of new wood, as if she'd entered a grove of trees. Looking about, she caught her breath in surprise.

It was a woodworking shop. Like the rest of the house, the spacious room was meticulously clean, and it was outfitted with a wealth of woodworking equipment—dozens of machines, saws, presses, and other things she didn't know the names or functions of—some that looked new, and some that looked quite ancient. An array of cabinets and drawers was built in along one wall, and beside it—somewhat incongruously—stood a full-size refrigerator. A large pegboard held a neat display of tools hanging on hooks. New wood of various sizes, lengths, and types was racked against the wall on the opposite side.

Scattered throughout the shop were several woodworking projects in different stages of completion. Among them were a small end table with scrolled legs, similar to the table and chairs in the kitchen, and an elegantly carved picture frame that appeared to be ready for painting or staining. Overwhelming all this was the delectable, balsam-flavored scent of cut wood, a fragrance that seemed almost visible, as if the trees were still alive and breathing around her.

"Michael, I had no idea," was all she could think to say, hoping that her tone and expression gave some indication of her delight.

Her gaze fell on an object that lay atop the large workbench in the center of the room, and she crossed to it with a little gasp. It was a music box—at least, it would be a music box when it was completed—she felt certain of that. The bottom of the box was fully formed of unstained hardwood with delicately curved sides and corners. The lid was as yet unfinished and lying in pieces. She recognized the style of the craftsmanship and looked up at Michael in astonishment.

"You made most of the music boxes in the cabinet upstairs, didn't you?"

He crossed the room and stopped at the edge of the workbench a few feet away. "Yes."

"And the furniture in the house?"

"I made a lot of that, too."

Nicole shook her head, awestruck. The man had so many talents. "When I admired them yesterday, why didn't you tell me?"

He shrugged unpretentiously. "I wanted to, but . . ."

"Where do you find the time? You write a new book almost every year."

"I can't write 24/7. Everyone needs a hobby. And," he added with a small smile, "I don't have much of a social life. This keeps me busy, and I enjoy it."

"Everything you make is so beautiful."

"Thank you." His blue eyes were humble but he seemed genuinely pleased.

A tray on the workbench held a variety of little templates and pieces of multicolored, precut wood. Nicole picked up a colored pencil sketch and studied it. "Is this the design for the lid?"

"Yes."

The design featured a quill pen and ink pot in the center, surrounded by a rectangular border of alternating geometric shapes enclosed between thin black-and-white stripes.

"It's so complex. I've never met anyone who did inlaid woodwork before. How do you do it?"

"It's really not all that complicated. Would you like a demonstration?"

"I'd love one."

Michael seemed delighted by her interest. "All right. We'll make the inset band for the border."

He explained what he was doing as he worked. First, he glued together three long, thin strips of wood in three different colors, melding them together like a sandwich.

"Now we cut this strip at a 45 degree angle into a few dozen small segments." Fitting a hand saw into a contraption he called a miter box, Michael cut through the wooden strip as if it were butter.

Nicole stood beside him, her eyes drawn to his hands. They were beautiful, his fingers long and slender and uniquely masculine. Each slow, precise movement was the practiced effort of a skilled artisan.

Michael picked up the first product of the saw in his fingers, took Nicole's left hand in his, and dropped something into her palm. The firm pressure of his hand on hers sent a shiver dancing up her arm, rearranging her heart rhythm, distracting her from the object she was supposed to be admiring.

She'd never felt such immediate, all-encompassing physical desire for a man before, and it was both startling and disconcerting. Yet she knew this desire was more than physical. She'd had a fierce crush on Patrick Spencer ever since she was a girl, based on the man she'd imagined him to be, inspired by his writing—and the man in the flesh was even more attractive and fascinating than she had envisioned.

"What do you think?" he asked, abruptly letting go of her hand.

Freed from his touch, she gave her attention to the tiny mosaic piece in her palm. It was no larger than her little fingernail, pyramid shaped, and made up of three ultrathin stripes of the different colors of wood.

"This is very cool," Nicole said, willing her heart to regain its natural pace.

"We have to make a few dozen more just like that." Michael flipped the wooden band over and sawed through it again and again, creating a succession of the tiny pieces.

"How do you know where to make the cut?"

"I just eyeball it. They're going to vary a bit no matter what you do."

"Where did you learn how to do this?"

"My father taught me. I've been working with wood ever since I was a child."

"So you learned in England?"

"I did."

Nicole watched him work, captivated—not so much by the activity but by his proximity, which was so intoxicating that she had to remind herself to keep breathing. Trying to distract herself through conversation, she asked, "You inherited this place from your grandfather, right?"

He nodded, his eyes on his work.

"If your grandparents lived here, how is it that you were raised in England?"

He hesitated before answering. "The Tyler who home-steaded this place—my great-great-great grandfather—emigrated from England. My own father was born here. One day, he decided to follow his roots. He went to England, where he met my mother. She disappeared soon after I was born. Dad raised me and taught me the woodworking skills he'd learned from my grandfather."

"I see. And what happened to your father?"

"He got sick and died." Impatiently, Michael went on: "My grandfather left this property to me, so I came to Colorado."

Nicole's heart went out to him. "So you never knew your mother or your grandfather?"

He frowned. "No."

"I'm so sorry."

"It's in the past. I don't think about it." Michael had sawed off more than two dozen little wooden pieces by now and paused, looking at her. "Would you like to try?"

"Sure."

Michael handed her the small saw, which felt sturdy in her grip. Nicole fit what was left of the wooden band into the miter box, guessed at the proper point to begin, and started sawing. It took more arm strength than she'd anticipated—he'd made it look so simple—but it was such a little piece that she cut right through it.

"Easy, right?" he said.

"And fun." She was delighted with her accomplishment. "Can I make a few more?"

"Be my guest."

Nicole flipped the band over and continued sawing. She felt his eyes on her, studying her in a steady way that made it difficult to focus on the task at hand. *Careful, or you'll saw your finger off,* she silently warned herself.

When she'd added several more pieces to the pile, Michael said, "I think we have enough. Now we sort them." Spreading out the tiny wooden pyramids on the workbench, he added, "We just want the ones with the white stripe at the bottom and the bit of brown walnut at the top."

As Nicole helped him sort through the pieces, their hands came close to touching several times. The mere anticipation of that contact caused a fluttering in Nicole's stomach that mimicked the rapid cadence of her heart.

When they'd set aside the pieces he wanted, Michael showed her how to clean off the fuzz on the edges that had been left by the saw blade. "They have to be nice and smooth so there aren't any gaps."

Following his lead, Nicole picked up a tiny triangle and rubbed off the little wood fibers with her fingernails. Michael worked immediately beside her, his body inches from hers. Did Michael feel the same riot of sexual tension that was threatening to destroy all rational thought in her head? If so, he gave no indication of it. She wanted to throw down the bits of wood, wrap her arms around his neck, and kiss him senseless.

Nicole blushed at the thought, which was most unlike her, and sought relief in conversation again. "So where did all these tools come from? Some of them look really old. Did they belong to your grandfather?"

"Some did. I bought the newer ones."

"What about this house?"

"The house that Jack built?"

He said it with a teasing smile—referring, Nicole realized, to the funds generated by the sale of his Dr. Jack Barclay novels.

"You mentioned yesterday that you built this place ten years ago. You didn't actually build the entire house *yourself*, did you?"

"No. That would require far more time and skill than I possess. I stick to furniture and music boxes. The box you were looking at yesterday, with the red rose design? That was one of the first boxes I ever made."

"Really?" she replied, puzzled. "But that one looked like an antique. And I thought you said it was your father's."

"Oh, that's right," he responded quickly. "I was thinking of another box I made. Okay, these pieces are ready to go. The next part—the final step—is the best part."

"What do we do?"

"We assemble all these bits into a nice geometric shape in between some strips of holly, and make a band."

Michael glued together two more thin strips of wood—one white, one black. At his instruction, Nicole interlocked the tiny striped, triangular pieces in a straight line atop one of these wooden bases, creating a lovely pattern of alternating shapes and colors. Michael stood just behind her as she worked, looking over her shoulder and reaching around with his right hand to dab drops of glue in between each tiny pyramid as she added it.

He moved even closer now. Her breath caught as she felt the hard length of his body press up against her back, the weight of his muscled arm against hers, and the cool caress of his breath on her cheek. Rattled, Nicole struggled to concentrate on the delicate process at hand. He drew a zigzag of thick white glue across the entire geometric band they'd created, then placed the other band of white and black wood on top of it.

"Push all the pieces together now and hold them," he murmured against her ear, his voice rough and deep, "until they're nice and tight and locked in position."

Still nestled against her, he reached around with his other arm, and both hands closed over hers. They sandwiched the fragments and strips of wood together, holding them in place for a long moment—a span that might have been a minute or two, but was so awash with erotic sensation, it felt to Nicole like a dizzying eternity. Her fingers were wet with glue. His fingers, pressed tightly against hers, were equally moist and slippery. She felt the warm roughness of his cheek pressed against hers. Against her back, she could feel each breath he took, each tightening of the muscles in his arms and chest, each thudding beat of his heart. Even the fluorescent lights above seemed to brighten, pulsate, and whirl, in rhythm with the pounding in her ears. She wanted to feel his lips on her neck. She wanted to turn and melt into his arms.

"Hold tight to that," Michael said softly. "We have to clamp it together."

Without changing his body position, he grabbed two small clamps from the workbench and expertly fitted them around their little creation, locking it in place with two supporting pieces of wood.

"You can let go now." His voice was low and husky against her ear. Nicole let go of the piece as instructed—but Michael didn't let *her* go. Still pressed against her from behind, his arms still wrapped around her, he picked up a soft, clean rag and, with gentle strokes, methodically wiped all the glue from her fingers.

Nicole swallowed, light-headed from his touch and the effort not to show it. Forcing herself to look down at the intricate wooden mosaic band inside the clamps, she said, "I can't believe we just made this." She'd only seen the like in exceptionally crafted pieces and fine antique furniture. "It's . . . a work of art."

"Was it as complicated as you thought?" he asked quietly, still pressed up against her, now cleaning off his own fingers.

"N—no."

Michael dropped the rag on the workbench, then brought his right hand up to caress her shoulder. "It has to sit for several hours." His hand massaged up and down the length of her arm, finally dropping to her waist and moving sensuously forward to graze across her midriff. "Or better yet overnight."

Even through the layers of her clothes, his touch on such an intimate part of her body made Nicole quiver in response, and the tips of her breasts began to tingle. She felt a heat rise within her and couldn't prevent a small, low sigh from escaping her lips.

His free hand played with the tendrils of hair at the side of her head. "Then," he went on softly, "we can cut it into strips to make a border."

"That's . . ." she began, but was incapable of further speech. His fingertip lightly traced the outline of her ear, across her cheekbone, to the curve of her chin. Then his broad hand lifted her long, wavy hair away from the side of her neck.

"Nicole," he said in a slow voice. "You are so lovely."

His lips were against her hair now. She felt their pressure, at first with the gentleness of a butterfly's wings, then more strongly as they moved lower until they came to rest against the tender flesh behind her ear.

Nicole began to sway under the powerful feelings he stirred in her, her head falling back slightly, her eyes closing. Her heart thundered violently in her chest. Her breath came in little gasps as she felt him plant kisses along the sensitive skin at the side of her throat. Heat suffused her. Perspiration broke out on her brow. She was just about to spin around and fold herself into his embrace when suddenly, to her dismay, she heard him curse under his breath.

Just as suddenly, he was pushing her away.

Disappointment cut through her like a blade. Why had he stopped? Nicole felt hot, flustered, bereft, abandoned. Her eyes flew open. He was already clear across the room, leaning one palm against a woodworking machine, the other hand covering his eyes. As he stood there, breathing heavily, between his spread fingers she saw that his cheeks and forehead were flushed and red.

Nicole struggled to regain control over her own breathing, equally flushed and perspiring.

"Forgive me," he said in a ragged voice.

"No, it's . . ." she began. She couldn't finish the thought. Why was he apologizing? His touch had made her dizzy with yearning and need. He'd felt the connection, too, she felt certain of it; she'd heard it in his voice, sensed it in his fingers. Maybe he was too much of a gentleman to continue—was afraid she'd think he was taking advantage of her, the helpless female guest with nowhere to run.

But she hadn't wanted to run. She'd wanted to turn into his arms and feel his lips against hers.

At length Michael dropped his hand. As he glanced at her, the thwarted longing she'd heard in his voice was visible on his face. He said, "I promised myself I wouldn't do that."

Unable to think of an appropriate reply, Nicole took a few steps back, trying to collect herself. She was hot. So hot. She'd give anything for a cold drink. She looked around desperately, searching for some way to cool down, some words to alleviate the tension in the air.

Her glance fell on the nearby refrigerator. In a few quick steps she was there, grabbing the door handle, striving for a light tone as she said, "I hope you keep soda in here."

Nicole yanked open the refrigerator door and froze in consternation.

The sight before her was the last thing she'd expected.

The refrigerator contained only one thing—or rather, nine things—and they were all identical in size and nature. They lay side by side in three neat rows on the shelves: the same clear plastic drip bags with IV catheter ports that she'd worked with at the hospital.

Nine bags, all filled with a deep, ruby red liquid.

They were all labeled HUMAN BLOOD.

CHAPTER 9

COLD SWEAT STREAMED IN silver pellets from Nicole's pores. A chill ran up her spine. She couldn't look at the bags of blood. She couldn't look at them! Yet neither could she tear her gaze away. The memory of that horrible night three years ago came rushing back. Her stomach constricted and she backed off, light-headed and nauseous, one hand anxiously seeking the table behind her to steady herself as she pushed the terrible images away.

At the same time, her mind echoed with one bewildered thought:

What was Michael doing with all that blood?

Before Nicole could find a reassuring anchor, the refrigerator door was violently slammed shut and Michael was standing in front of her, fury in his eyes. "Stay the hell out of there!" he roared.

Trembling, head spinning, Nicole stammered, "I'm sorry, I was just looking for—" But he interjected angrily:

"Don't look so terrified. It's just blood. I have a clotting deficiency. I could bleed out in minutes if I were to be injured. Because I live so far from any clinic, I'm allowed to keep a few units of blood on hand in the event of an emergency. Okay?"

"Okay," she replied, her throat too constricted to say more.

"We're done here," he added heatedly, whirling for the door. "Let's go."

In a daze Nicole followed Michael into the hall. He quickly locked the workshop door. As he turned away, his shoulder caught the edge of a picture on the wall, sending it crashing to the floor in a splintering of wood and glass. Heedless, he stormed off and up the stairs.

Nicole leaned against the wall for support, staring at the empty space left in Michael's wake. *What the hell is going on?* she wondered, stunned. This man blew so hot and cold, she couldn't keep up. For the last hour or two as they'd worked together, Michael had held her and touched her with such tenderness and sensitivity, she'd felt as though she were under an erotic spell. Then suddenly, just because she'd seen blood in his refrigerator, he'd stalked off like a madman. Why was he so upset? Did her fearful reaction put him off? If so, she was sorry for it, but it had been an involuntary response.

His explanation confused her. Nicole had a certain amount of experience with blood. It was true that hemophiliacs required a specific blood factor after injury or prior to surgery, but as far as she knew, individuals were not allowed to obtain or keep human blood of any kind for personal use. Where and how did he get it?

Maybe rules were different in Colorado, Nicole thought, and this was one of the perks of the ultrarich. Maybe he'd gotten special permission to store blood, and was trained in the techniques of venous access and hanging an IV. But even so, blood had a useful life after donation of only six to eight weeks. She could conceive of a hemophiliac keeping a single bag on hand—but nine? Why did he need nine bags of blood?

Nicole wracked her brain but couldn't come up with an answer. All she could figure was that Michael really *did* have a clotting deficiency—a very serious, life-threatening problem, as she knew only too well—and was more prone to injury and blood loss than most people.

Knowing that Michael could, God forbid, potentially bleed out and die from a wound—while they were snowbound here and far from help—did nothing to ease her tension. Any other medical problem Nicole could have faced without a second thought, but not that.

Something else occurred to her. Maybe Michael's fury was due to embarrassment—the fear that the world would find out the celebrated author, Patrick Spencer, was only human. As if she would tell anyone!

With a sigh, Nicole crouched down to clean up the mess left by the broken picture frame. After she gathered up the shattered pieces of wood and glass, she studied the photo that had become detached from the frame. It was an old 8 by 10 black-and-white of two men standing proudly on either side of a horse. Nicole turned over the picture and saw that it had been inscribed on the back:

To William with many thanks,
Leonard Small, 1925

Who was "William"? Nicole wondered. Studying the picture more closely, she noticed that one of the men in the picture—a very handsome man wearing chaps and a cowboy hat—looked remarkably like Michael. His face wasn't perfectly in focus, but even so the resemblance was uncanny. It must be Michael's great grandfather, she decided, when the man was in his thirties—the same man who'd no doubt written the first journal she'd seen in Michael's study.

Carefully balancing the photo atop the fragments of broken frame, Nicole moved on to another picture on the wall, the sepia tone print of Michael's great-great-great grandfather, the bearded old man standing in front of a cabin. On closer examination, Nicole realized that the man wasn't old after all; his heavy, dark beard and mustache just made him appear that way. Again, she could see the family resemblance in his eyes.

She had a fleeting thought: if this was the patriarch of the Tyler family, why were there no wife and children in the picture? Maybe, Nicole mused, the picture was taken before he got married and had a family.

Nicole returned to the main floor of the house, where she threw away the pieces of glass and set the broken frame and picture on the coffee table. The door to Michael's study was closed, and she heard music blaring within. Remembering the way it had felt just now when he'd pressed his body to hers and touched her with his lips and hands caused a heat to rise in her cheeks. Michael was just as attracted to her as she was to him— there was no longer any doubt about that.

Nicole considered knocking on his door, to reassure him with a friendly word or two that she meant no threat to his carefully built private life—hopefully he'd sense that she wel- comed his advances and yearned for more—but she thought better of it. Clearly he wanted to be alone at the moment.

It was late afternoon and she was hungry again. All she'd had to eat since she woke up was cereal and coffee. Nicole wondered if Michael had any plans for lunch. He'd risen much earlier than she had, and by now he must be starving. What if she made lunch for the two of them? Would that bring a smile to his face again? Although there wasn't much food to work with, Nicole was determined to find something.

The enchilada casserole had been delicious; surely he'd enjoy that. Nicole was dying for a green salad, but there were just the ubiquitous bags of carrots and apples in the fridge. An idea came to her for a kind of salad of grated carrots and ap- ples. You had to work with whatever was on hand when you were snowed in—and it would satisfy her desire for something fresh and light.

In the cupboard, Nicole found cans of black beans, corn, and chopped tomatoes. Combined, they'd make a nice side dish. She spent the next three-quarters of an hour happily peel- ing and grating carrots and apples, then she mixed them to- gether and added a little juice from the canned tomatoes to prevent the apples from turning brown. When the other dish was ready she exited the kitchen and went to set the table, thinking they might sit together in the dining room.

She stopped in her tracks, glancing around in surprise, suddenly aware that Michael didn't *have* a dining room. The space in the expansive great room that might have been devoted to a dining table was taken up by a grand piano. The only place in the house to eat was the small table and chairs in the kitchen alcove. That seemed strange at first; but then Nicole realized it made sense. Michael lived here by himself and never entertained visitors. Why would he bother with a formal dining room area that would never be used?

Nicole set the kitchen table, making it look as nice as possible. For napkins she folded paper towels in half. She popped the ceramic container of enchiladas into the microwave and turned it on, then arranged the side dishes she'd made on the table. There were only two choices of beverage: tap water and a six-pack of soda in the fridge. Not knowing what he'd prefer, Nicole put both soda cans and filled water glasses at each place setting.

The appetizing aroma of the heating casserole filled the kitchen. She wondered if Michael would smell it and come out of the study on his own.

As Nicole listened to the hum of the microwave, she stood at the kitchen's rear-facing window looking out at the tree-shrouded, white landscape. Incredibly, it was still snowing with no sign of stopping. There was a kind of beauty to the wild, wintry tempest, but Nicole was grateful to be inside, warm, and dry. It had only been twenty-four hours since she'd awakened to find herself in this house under Michael's care, yet it seemed like weeks—and even longer since she'd seen a blue sky and sun, sent an email, or watched TV. It felt odd to be so cut off from the world—yet at the same time, without that constant barrage of information and entertainment, Nicole felt freer than she had in ages. It was almost like stepping back to a simpler time.

The microwave dinged and the room fell silent again. The only times Nicole could remember being surrounded by such deep quiet were the hours she'd spent on ski slopes. It was a wonderful, calming environment, and for the first time since she arrived, she felt herself truly begin to relax.

Using kitchen towels as hot pads, Nicole retrieved the piping hot casserole and set it on the table, then surveyed the display. It looked both colorful and inviting. With a smile, she strode to Michael's study door and rapped lightly. There was no answer. She tried again, louder, calling out, "Michael?"

His quiet footsteps approached and then the door was thrown open. Michael's mouth was set in a deep scowl and his blue eyes flashed dangerously.

"What do you want?"

"I—" Nicole faltered. "I thought you might be hungry. It's way past lunchtime, so I made us something to eat."

"I'm working," he said irritably. "And I told you: I prefer to dine alone."

"I know, but I thought . . . surely you can take a break. Come see what I made. It's on the table. It's—"

"I'm not hungry," he snapped, "so don't bother me about food or anything else. Just stay in your corner of the house, and I'll stay in mine." He slammed the door in her face.

For the second time that day, Nicole stood frozen in dumbfounded silence. This time, anger rose within her. *What a prick*, she thought. *What a rude, insensitive asshole.* After all the trouble she'd gone to, he couldn't even be bothered to take a look or a bite? Or at the very least, to thank her for thinking of him?

Nicole marched back into the kitchen, fuming, the knots in her stomach tangling with her ravenous appetite. Heatedly, she spooned heaping portions of the three dishes onto her plate. Who did he think he was? Being rich and successful didn't give him the right to treat her like some insignificant, nagging nuisance. She was only trying to be nice!

Nicole stood at the counter and shoveled the food into her mouth, hardly tasting it. What was his problem? Was he bipolar and off his meds? Or was there something he wasn't telling her? A reason he couldn't or wouldn't be intimate? The way he barked at her reminded her of an ex-boyfriend from college. Anytime he felt his masculinity or personal space being threatened, he went nuts and treated her like garbage. Was that what was going on, an introvert's neuroses entwined with male bravado? Had she completely misinterpreted his feelings in the workshop? But how could she have?

Well, whatever. He'd made it clear, once again, that he didn't want her here. Thank God it would only be for a couple more days.

Nicole couldn't find any plastic wrap or storage containers for the leftovers, which only added to her cantankerous mood. She slammed the salads into the refrigerator uncovered. She dumped her dirty dish and silverware in the sink unwashed. Then, to spite him, she grabbed the dish towels from the oven door handle and dropped them in a heap on the floor.

Still seething, she returned to the great room, where she found the fire in the hearth had burned down to nothing but embers. *Nice*, she thought sarcastically. *He can't even be bothered to keep the fire going for me.* With wood and kindling from the bin she built a new fire, watching as the flames slowly spread, until they leaped like a golden crown around the logs and gave off a comforting heat. Rubbing her hands together before the fire, Nicole glanced about, her entire body tight with tension and frustration.

So, Michael wanted her to keep to herself, did he? *You stay in your corner of the house, and I'll stay in mine.* Fine. It was a big house. She could find things to do on her own. He could stay in his study all day and night and starve to death for all she cared.

Her gaze fell on the grand piano at the front of the room, by the picture windows overlooking the forest beyond. Nicole couldn't resist crossing to it and running a hand along its polished black surface. It was a beautiful instrument. She'd sold her own piano when she left Seattle three years ago, and had only played a handful of times since.

Music had always offered her a wonderful escape from the outside world, a means of releasing her anxiety and emotions. She hadn't realized until that moment how much she'd missed it. What better method was there to release her pent-up frustration than to play the piano?

Nicole hesitated. Given Michael's foul mood and his proclivity for being alone, he might not appreciate someone else touching his piano. He was a far superior musician, and she felt a little intimidated at the thought of playing when he could hear. The music might disturb him.

Screw him, she told herself, mentally squashing all thoughts of awkwardness or consideration. *If he doesn't like it, he can come out and tell me to stop.*

The late afternoon light was dim and gray. Nicole switched on the brass lamp atop the piano and opened the bench. It was stuffed with piano music, some of which looked very old. She shuffled through it until she came to something familiar—Chopin's Prelude no. 24—a thrilling piece she'd once known by heart, and had played often with great enjoyment. Setting the sheet music on the stand, she sat down on the bench, lifted the lid over the keyboard, arranged her hands in position, and began to play.

Nicole warmed up with a few scales, then plunged into the piece itself. It was complex and required great concentration. From the first bold stanza, an unanticipated surge of pleasure raced through her. As she followed the score, it was as if her brain was siphoning off all her excess energy into the task of getting her fingers into the right place at the right time.

The longer strings of the grand piano produced a larger, richer sound than the instrument she was used to, with truer overtones and lower inharmonicity. With every vibration of the instrument, she could feel the music as well as hear it. The song was glorious and beautiful. A smile built deep down within her soul, and all her tension and frustration began melting away.

Nicole was halfway through the piece when, from the corner of her eye, she caught sight of movement as she played. She glanced up, startled, to find Michael standing by the hearth, arms casually folded across his chest, watching her intently.

Ignoring him, Nicole played on, the room filling with the extraordinary beauty of the music.

"You didn't say that you played," he said quietly.

"You never asked," she retorted bluntly.

She gave her full attention to the music, feeling a little self-conscious now because he was still staring at her. She made a few mistakes, which had more to do with being out of practice than it did with him watching. When she came to the end of the piece, Michael applauded with enthusiasm. She sat back, wondering what was going through his mind. Considering the antagonistic remarks he'd made earlier, she couldn't begin to guess what he expected of her—so she said nothing and waited. Finally, he spoke.

"I'm sorry."

She glanced at him sharply. His expression was equal parts surprise, admiration, and contrition.

"I behaved like the most vulgar, offensive, and ill-mannered Neanderthal," he continued. "You went to great effort—I imagine—to prepare a nice meal for me, and I was entirely un-appreciative. I said things I didn't mean. Please forgive me."

Okay, as apologies went, it was satisfactory. Nicole sensed that it was genuine and came from the heart. Still, she was in no mood to forgive him.

"I appreciate the apology," she said coolly, "but it doesn't excuse or explain the behavior. What were you so angry about? That I found out you have a blood disorder? It's not such a big deal."

"You're right. What can I say? Except, again: I'm sorry. Can we chalk it up to cabin fever?"

The look in his eyes was so hopeful, repentant, and filled with teasing good humor that—despite herself—Nicole felt her anger scattering to the wind, like the billowy parachutes of a dandelion seed head. *Damn him*, she thought, straining to hold back the beginning of a smile. *I can't even stay mad at him when he deserves it.*

"If I seemed frightened, it had nothing to do with you," she said. "It was the sight of all that blood."

"The sight of blood makes you squeamish?" He stared at her, shaking his head slightly, as if for some reason he found that ironic.

"Yes. It didn't used to. But . . . anyway. If you're worried that I'm going to tell the press you're a hemophiliac, don't be. You're a private person. I get that. And I would never tell anyone who you are."

"Thank you."

"I hope you don't mind that I played your piano."

"Not at all." In a few graceful strides, he crossed the room and joined her. "I haven't heard anyone else play in a long time. I can't begin to tell you how wonderful it was—how wonderful *you* were. That's a very difficult piece, and you're very good."

"Not as good as you."

To his credit, he didn't try to refute that. "Perhaps I've just had more practice. You have a lot of talent. How long have you been playing?"

"Twenty-three years. You?"

"A bit longer."

He stood beside the bench, a foot from where she sat, one hand resting on top of the piano as he gazed down at her. The look on his face was tender. Nicole wanted to bang her head against the keyboard. A few minutes ago she'd been so furious with him that she was ready to cut his head off. All it had taken was a few sweet, well-chosen words and a certain look in his eyes to wash all that away. Once again, her heart was beating fast and butterflies were starting to flit in her lower regions.

"The piano has long been my solace," he said, "a source of pleasure when things go right, and a place to escape when things go wrong."

"The same for me," she admitted.

"It's like opening a door to the subconscious."

She nodded. "To allow the mind to wander."

"When I play Chopin's Nocturne no. 2 in E-flat Major, I sometimes feel as though I'm in a kind of trance."

"Have you played his Nocturne no. 5 in F-sharp Major?" she asked.

"I have."

"It always carries me away."

"Me, too. I've gone through entire pieces of music without being able to actually remember playing them." The excitement in his voice was infectious.

"When I get really angry, I play scales and arpeggios."

"If that doesn't work, I launch into massive chords."

"It's like magic," she enthused. "I love hearing the music, knowing that I can create this big, beautiful sound all by myself."

"And the best part is how your own emotions change the meaning of the music."

"Yes! The same tune played by three different people can express three entirely different things."

Their eyes were locked now and they were both smiling broadly, bound by mutual interest and excitement. "Would you like to play a duet?" he asked.

"I don't know any."

"I used to have some old music for a piano duet that you could sight-read in your sleep. Let's see if it's still in the bench."

Nicole stood. He rifled through the contents of the bench, finally coming up with the music sheet he was looking for. He handed it to her. "Are you game?"

It was Mozart's Sonata for Piano Duet in D. She'd never played it before. "Why not?"

Setting the music on the stand, Nicole resumed her seat. Michael sat down beside her. The bench was just big enough for the two of them. Nicole felt the now familiar quiver deep inside her as Michael's thigh and upper arm touched hers. They both moved their hands into position. Michael inhaled an anticipatory beat, they exchanged a glance and a nod, and began to play.

The music sprang forth from the instrument at the touch of their fingertips, resounding throughout the room. Michael's skill was masterful. Nicole worked hard to keep up with him, matching his precise cadence. As their fingers moved along the keys, Nicole was hyper aware of his taut body pressed against her own. Each unsteady pop of her heartbeat seemed a sharp point and counterpoint to the rhythm they played.

It was wonderful. Delirious. Breathtaking. Exhilarating. Together, they were creating something beautiful, just as they had earlier in his woodshop downstairs. The memory of what had followed after that event made Nicole's heart thud in her ears, and it became increasingly difficult to concentrate on the score. When they finished the piece, she sat with lowered eyes, fingers still at the keyboard, struggling to control her rapid breathing, knowing that if she looked at him, he'd see the longing on her face that she could not hide.

Suddenly, Michael's fingers were at her chin, gently lifting and turning it. His eyes smoldered, wordlessly communicating an attraction that matched her own. His other hand sifted through her long, wavy hair, then tucked a stray lock behind one ear. Lowering his head now, he touched his lips to hers.

His kiss was gentle, soft, and deeply arousing. Nicole turned to face him on the bench, her arms weaving up instantly around his neck and tangling in his hair. His hands smoothed their way around her back, drawing her more closely to him. As Nicole's breasts pressed softly against the hard expanse of his chest, a melting heat rose within her.

The kiss became more insistent now, Michael's tongue probing the soft openness of her mouth. As his hands roamed her back, the tingle of desire rushed through her. Their lips parted as each took a sharp breath, then clung together again.

"Nicole," he whispered tenderly, his lips at her ear, "you bring out feelings in me that I didn't know existed."

Michael's mouth brushed hers again, then traveled down to her throat. Nicole's eyes closed and her head fell back in ecstasy as his lips nuzzled the tender flesh there. His breathing was ragged now, mirroring her own; she both heard and felt it hot and insistent against her neck, just as she heard and felt his low growl, a sound suffused with passion. Shivers danced through her. Blood moved thin and hot through her veins and pounded in her throat. She felt limp with need. *Take me,* she thought. *Make love to me. Now. Now.*

Through her love-gauzed daze, Nicole was vaguely aware of a soft clicking sound. She felt Michael tense in her arms, as if hesitating.

"No, please," Nicole murmured. "Don't . . ." Her mind completed the thought: *Don't pull away again. I want you. I want you.*

But Michael's mouth abruptly left her throat. Why?

As Nicole lazily opened her eyes, it seemed, for one brief instant, as if time stood still. And in that instant, she saw three things that confused her.

The first was the light atop the piano; for some reason it was flickering. The second was Michael's eyes. Just inches away, they burned into her with all-consuming desire, and seemed to dance with liquid red flames. The third was Michael's teeth. Through his parted lips, she saw that his canine teeth were long and sharp.

Fangs.

CHAPTER 10

ICOLE RECOILED with shock and fright. When she blinked, to her further confusion, Michael's eyes and teeth became normal again. The subtle clicking sound that accompanied this transformation was overwhelmed by a different, distant reverberation, like the drone of an engine coming to life—and the lights came back on full force.

Michael let her go abruptly, sliding off the piano bench and leaping to his feet.

"The power just went out," he said, stepping backward hastily. "The backup generator just came on. I'd better check on the . . ." He broke off, turned, strode quickly across the room, and disappeared down the stairs.

Nicole stared after him, her pulse still racing. *What in the hell?* What had she just seen? *Red flames? Fangs?*

One second, it had seemed as if a monster was staring down at her—a red-eyed monster with fangs, like the terrifying, cloaked figure in her nightmare. The next, he was Michael again. She'd seen flames like that in Michael's eyes the night before—or *thought* she did—but told herself she'd imagined it. Was she going crazy? Was cabin fever playing tricks on her mind? Or was it was a trick of the flickering light?

The backdoor slammed downstairs. Nicole turned to the front windows and looked outside. Michael must be going back to the barn again, to check on the horses. In a few seconds, she'd hear the sound of his truck engine roar to life, catch a glimpse of the truck emerging from the garage around the side of the house, and see it pull out onto the road, his snowplow at the fore. All of which would reassure her that everything was fine and totally normal.

Snow was still falling gently, but a brief break in the wind enabled her to see quite a distance. The roads Michael had cleared that morning were already covered with more than a foot of new snow. Her gaze was drawn to the side road running from the driveway toward that other building about two hundred feet away, hidden by the trees. Inexplicably, a narrow, ragged channel had been blazed through the newly fallen snow on that road, as if it had been haphazardly carved out by a running man—or a whirlwind.

To Nicole's surprise, through the pine branches and snow gloom, she saw a man standing outside that other building. A man in a black parka. He opened a door and vanished inside. Nicole froze in disbelief. *Who was that?* It couldn't have been Michael. Michael left this house a couple of seconds ago. He could never have gotten over there so quickly. He'd barely have had time to cross the side porch, much less travel two hundred feet across that snowy road.

The building couldn't be the barn; Michael had said his barn was down the back side of his hill. Did someone else live across the way? If so, why hadn't Michael mentioned him?

Bewildered, Nicole raced for the stairs, flew down to the mud room, and threw open the door to the garage. Michael's truck and Range Rover were still there. She dashed out the backdoor onto the covered side porch, where freezing cold air slapped her in the face. It was so cold it hurt to breathe.

The drone of a generator came from behind a partition next to the porch, but Michael wasn't there. Shivering, rubbing her arms, Nicole glanced in every direction, scanning the forest, gazing out through the cascade of ever falling snowflakes. There was no sign of Michael anywhere.

Nicole darted back inside the house, stunned. It must have been Michael, after all, whom she'd seen entering that place— whatever it was—across the way. *But that's impossible*, she told herself. *No human being could have moved that fast.*

No human being . . .

As Nicole heard the words in her mind, the hair stood up on the back of her neck. A cold fear rippled through her veins.

When you have eliminated the impossible, whatever remains, however improbable, must be the truth.

All at once, every confused thought she'd ever had about Michael, everything she'd wondered and puzzled over, came together in a rush in her mind:

He never ate or drank. He was never tired or chilled. The bags of blood. The eyes that flamed like torches. The fangs. The journals in his study, all in the same handwriting—*the same handwriting*, she suddenly realized, *as the man who'd signed her book.* The man in the photos . . . for more than a century and a half, *he had never aged.*

With growing horror, Nicole realized what he must be.

Michael was a vampire.

NICOLE'S MIND REELED, trying to reject the notion.

It was impossible.

Beings like that were the stuff of fantasy and legend. They didn't really exist.

But a phrase Michael had uttered the night before came back to her in a flash:

Even legend is founded in a kernel of truth. However impossible, this was *real*, it was happening.

Terrified, she now understood why he'd saved her life in the first place, what the past two days had been all about. She was, indeed, the fly in the spider's web. He'd just been keeping her until he got hungry. The look in his eyes a few minutes ago had revealed what he'd wanted.

He'd wanted her blood.

Panic seized her, the only thought in her mind to run for her life. Now. This very instant. While he was gone. It might be her only chance to escape.

Nicole's mind raced. If the legends were true—*My God, could they really be true?*—then he could overtake her in a second and could overpower her without effort. She had to get away fast and pray that he wouldn't notice until she was far out of his reach.

But how to do it? Where to go?

He'd said his closest neighbor to the east was twenty miles away. She couldn't take one of his vehicles, even if she could find the keys; the highway was closed and covered with snow. It was freezing outside and snowing hard. His snowshoes were still there; apparently he hadn't needed them. But even with snowshoes, how far would she get? There was only about an hour of daylight left, two at most. It would be exhausting to tramp through all that fresh snow, and it'd be dark before she knew it.

Then she remembered. She'd noticed them in the garage, out of the corner of her eye.

Yanking open the door to the garage, she saw them—a pair of cross-country skis and poles hanging neatly on the wall. On a shelf beside them rested a pair of black cross-country ski boots.

She could ski out.

Although Nicole was an accomplished downhill skier, she had never tried cross-country. But she'd seen how it was done. His boots would be too big, but she could make them fit.

Heart racing, Nicole hauled the equipment into the mud room, then sped upstairs to the bedroom. In a frenzy, she tossed out everything unnecessary from her small backpack and stuffed in her purse, water bottle, camera, an extra sweater, and several pairs of socks. Frantically she redressed in her ski clothing: ski pants, turtleneck, and sweater over thermals. After donning two pairs of socks, she pulled her warmest ski hat down over her ears.

From the laundry room, she retrieved her parka and scarf and put them on, then darted back to the mud room where she stuffed socks into the toes of Michael's cross-country ski boots and slid her feet inside. They were still too big. Pulling on a third pair of socks did the trick. Nicole rapidly laced up the boots, shrugged her backpack over her shoulders, put on her ski gloves, and dragged the skis and poles outside to the driveway, which was a foot deep in snow.

Desperately she glanced at the building hidden in the trees across the way, but Michael was nowhere to be seen. *Wherever you are, please stay there*, she prayed.

The wind was picking up. Even with all her warm clothing, her hat pulled low, and her scarf covering her face, she was cold. Quickly, Nicole studied the ski bindings: unlike downhill skis, these only clipped onto the shoe at the toe. She stepped into them. The latches clicked in place. Leaning forward, she dug the ski poles into the snow, sliding one leg forward and then the other. It was very different from downhill skiing—like pulling herself through the snow and gliding. *He must fly like the wind on these*, she thought. For her, it was a lot of work. It took a few minutes to get the hang of it, but soon she was off, skimming across the snow.

Nicole crossed the snowy driveway and coasted down the long, winding road that led downhill. The ski edges felt different, and maneuvering was a bit more awkward than usual due to the boots' toe attachment, but Nicole managed to make it down the sloping road with relative ease. All the way, her heart pounded furiously and she kept looking back over her shoulder, afraid that Michael might be following her; but he wasn't.

When she reached the highway, she hesitated briefly. It was covered in at least three feet of snow. She scanned the embankment along the other side, looking for her car. If it was there, it was entirely buried.

Should she cut off the road into the trees so that Michael couldn't see her? No; that was crazy. She could easily lose her way in the woods, even if she tried staying close to the road, and the terrain was so uneven, it would greatly slow her down. Better to stick to the open road and just pray that he wouldn't come after her.

Nicole plunged onto the main highway. To her dismay, her skis promptly sank down a good eighteen inches into the snow. Using her poles for balance, Nicole pushed her skis forward, packing down the snow as she went, but to her frustration it was very slow going. With each forward slide, a heap of snow cut over the top of the ski, coming up against her legs and weighing her down. She had to lift each ski up to disperse the accumulated snow, slide it forward again, create a new hole, then repeat the process all over again.

It was utterly exhausting. With every movement of the skis, Nicole felt as if she were climbing a mountain and then sinking back down again. Still, she urgently forged on, sinking, sliding, pulling, moving forward at a snail's pace.

It was so very cold. The small patch of skin around Nicole's eyes that was exposed to the elements felt frozen. Her eyes stung from the flakes driven by the biting wind. Every breath burned her lungs, and she soon found herself gasping.

After spending several days in the mountains, she would have thought she'd become accustomed to the altitude by now; but apparently not. Her fingers inside her gloves felt like icicles. Even her feet, with all those socks and insulated boots, began to grow numb. Her leg muscles began to shake with fatigue and she felt herself perspiring, which for some reason made her feel even more cold—and the harder she worked, the colder she got.

To her dismay, daylight was fading. The wind was whipping in a frenzy now, the air once more a mad confusion of misty, swirling whiteness. Nicole couldn't see more than ten feet in any direction. Her teeth began chattering. She felt lost, disoriented. Was she still on the road? Was she heading in the right direction? Her entire body felt like a Popsicle. She was shivering, utterly worn out, nearing the end of her resources.

Silently, she berated herself. *Idiot. What made you think you could do this?* She could never cover twenty miles on these skis. She'd be lucky if she made it another ten yards before collapsing. She felt bad for her mother and sister and nieces, who'd be distraught and confused when they learned what had happened. What was Nicole doing out on that road in a blizzard? Why didn't she stay inside where it was safe and warm?

Safe and warm. Ha! Nicole moved in a daze, her mind whirling as fast as the falling snow, images from the past two days flashing through her mind. Michael's smile. His hands on her body. His hands on the piano keys. His kiss. His red eyes. Fangs. *Vampire.* No wonder she'd been so sexually attracted to him. He must have put her under some kind of spell. Had anything he told her been true? Was he really Patrick Spencer? She was the one who'd made that assumption. Had he simply agreed, after she avowed herself a fan? Was it just a clever lie to lower her guard?

A faint voice drifted by on the wind. A man's voice. It seemed to be calling her name. Who would be calling her? *No, no. Please. Not him.*

Nicole slogged on, not daring to look back. There was the voice again, closer now, urgent and admonishing:

"Nicole! For God's sake, stop! Come back!"

Her pulse raced in terror. Her head spun. She wouldn't stop. Couldn't. So exhausted. Pull. Slide. Slide. Lift. Lift. Wash. Rinse. Repeat.

Suddenly two strong hands were grabbing her by both arms and Michael was standing on top of her skis, looking at her with frantic blue eyes.

"What the hell are you doing? Where are you going?"

"Away." Her voice was hollow, as if it came from a deep void.

"Why? What's wrong?" He sounded completely baffled.

"Let me . . . go." She struggled to free herself from his grasp, but it was no use. She didn't have the strength.

"You'll freeze to death out here. You're blue already."

"Better than . . . dying at . . . your hands."

He started, completely taken aback. "What did you say?"

"I know what you are!" she hissed at him, exhausted, shivering.

His hands gripped her more tightly. "What are you *talking* about?"

"I saw them," she said, gasping. "Red eyes. *Fangs.* Journals. In your study. *Your handwriting.* Pictures. In the hall." Her teeth chattered so hard she thought they might break. "A hundred and fifty years. *They're all you.*"

"Nicole, you're delirious. You—"

"The other building. You moved so fast. Don't deny it. *I saw. You're a vampire.*"

Michael stared at her for a long moment, silent fury building in his gaze. Then, as if in resignation, he shook his head and heaved a deep, guttural sigh. In one fluid motion, he swept her up into his arms, skis, poles, and all. Nicole cried out in terror, trying to pummel her fists against his chest, but she didn't have the strength to fight a gnat.

All at once a great, freezing wind rushed past her body. Snow was in her eyes. Nicole's senses reeled. The world was a blurred kaleidoscope of white, green, gray, and black. They were moving so fast, they seemed to be flying.

Flying.

Back across the snowy highway. Up the road. And into the house.

THE MINUTE HE SET HER DOWN on the living room floor before the fire, she crumbled in his arms, still raving about vampires.

He whirled off her snow-encrusted backpack, hat, gloves, and scarf, and gently lowered her to the carpet, where he un- zipped and took off her parka.

"No," she said, her teeth chattering, her hands flailing at him weakly. "Don't—"

"Nicole, I'm trying to help you," he cried, catching hold of her wrists to restrain her. Acutely aware of the powerful emotion he'd invested in those few words, he paused and took a breath, struggling to rein in the wealth of feeling that burned within him.

He was a fool. He should never have let himself get so carried away earlier. Now Nicole had guessed the truth and was scared senseless—so scared that she'd run off into the snow to escape him, even though it had meant certain death.

Words could not express his distress and agitation when he'd caught sight of her skiing down that road, clearly at the end of her resources.

"I have to get you out of these wet clothes," Michael insisted firmly. "Your sweat froze. You're suffering from hypothermia. If I don't warm you up, you could die."

As he untied and yanked the boots off her feet, she tried to kick him—incredible, he thought, considering how worn out she was. "Lie still. Calm down."

The woman was resourceful; he had to give her that. Michael issued a silent thank-you to the powers that be for making him check the garage when he'd found her missing. To take off like that on his cross-country skis, it was either brave or stupid, perhaps both. He tossed the shoes aside and removed her socks. As he suspected, her feet were as blue as her hands and felt like ice.

In the blink of eye, he retrieved a bath towel and the huge down comforter from his bed, and was back at her side slipping the blanket beneath her. Despite her exhaustion, Nicole tried to fight him as he pulled off the rest of her clothes—pants, sweater, thermals, bra, underwear—but he was too fast, and they were all gone before she could take a breath. For the briefest of seconds he paused, struck by her breathtaking beauty as she lay before him in perfect nudity, her long, red-gold hair swirling around her like a flaming net. She was a vision. A goddess. Venus on the half shell. She was also half frozen, quaking like an aspen in the wind, and her jewel-like green eyes were wide with fright.

"Please," she said, attempting to cover her bare breasts with her arms, her long legs curling up and trembling.

He knew the best thing would be to warm her with his body heat. His body temperature might not be quite as high as desired, but it was far warmer than hers was at the moment. He instantly nixed the notion. Any contact between their naked bodies would only excite him to a level he dared not cross— and it would no doubt only terrify her even further.

Working fast, he dried her with the towel to slow further heat loss, then wrapped her twice around in the soft down comforter, folding it under her feet like a sleeping bag. Kneeling beside her, he drew her swaddled body into his arms. She trembled against him beneath the blanket. Whether it was from cold or terror or physical fatigue or all three, he couldn't be certain.

"Please," she whispered again. "Please don't—"

"Whatever you're afraid I'm going to do—don't be," he vowed solemnly, his mouth against her ear. He massaged her arms and back vigorously through the blanket, trying to get her blood flowing. "I won't hurt you. I just want to help you."

"Promise?" she whispered.

"I promise." A wealth of tender emotions rose within him. If only she weren't so afraid. At last, he felt the tension leave her limbs as she gave up the fight. He laid her down gently on the carpet and gazed earnestly into her eyes.

"Now promise *me* something: that you won't move. We have to get your core body temperature up. I'm going to build up the fire and get you something hot to drink."

He tossed more wood onto the fire, then dashed to the kitchen, where he heated up a mug of water. When he returned, she was lying just where he'd left her, shivering inside the comforter. He winced inwardly when he saw that her eyes were still filled with apprehension.

Sitting down cross-legged beside her, he lifted her into a sitting position, supporting her back firmly against his right arm. With his free hand, he held the mug to her lips.

"It's hot water. Drink it. It will help warm you from the inside."

She obediently took a sip. He slowly fed her the rest of it, pausing only when she was overcome by a wave of chills. As the mug emptied, her shivering decreased significantly. Finally it stopped. Her eyelids began to droop, and she sagged against him as if on the verge of sleep. With apparent difficulty, she opened her eyes again and whispered groggily:

"Say it."

"Say what?" he asked gently.

"Say that you're a vampire."

He hesitated. He'd spent five lifetimes denying it. He had a dozen ready explanations that had always been accepted without question on those rare occasions when it had been required in the past. It wasn't something people *wanted* to believe. He'd usually been able to retreat as fast as his canines retracted and had never encountered those individuals again.

There was no chance of retreating from her, however. If he chose to, despite the mind-blurring speed with which he'd brought her home and the things she claimed to have seen, he might be able convince her that she'd been delirious and had been imagining things. But he didn't want to. Didn't want to lie anymore. Not to this woman, regardless of the consequences.

He met her level gaze. "Yes. I am a vampire."

CHAPTER 11

NICOLE AWOKE IN A WARM, cocooned haze. She was lying on the living room carpet by a crackling fire, wrapped in a down comforter, her head resting in Michael's lap. His fingers were gently stroking her shoulder. The clock on the mantel ticked. It was after seven. Through the windows, she saw that it was dark outside.

All at once everything that had happened, from the moment he'd kissed her at the piano, to the moment just before she'd fallen asleep, when he'd uttered those four incredible words—*I am a vampire*—came back to her in a flash. Her pulse began to pound. She wasn't crazy. She wasn't imagining things. *Michael was a vampire.* And she was back in the vampire's lair.

Sitting up abruptly, Nicole scooted her body quickly away from his, at the same time freeing her arms from the restraint of the comforter and hugging its sumptuous folds more tightly around her breasts. Instinctively, she ran a hand over her neck and throat, searching for any sign of a wound or bite. To her relief her flesh was clear, unmarked.

Michael studied her with a flicker of disappointment. "Did you really think I'd bite you?"

"What else should I think? You're a vampire. You drink blood, don't you?"

"Yes."

Nicole told herself to remain calm, not to show her fear. She was sitting here, naked except for a blanket, trapped like bait in this house with a blood-thirsty, lightning-fast monster and nowhere to run.

Except, confusingly, he didn't look like a monster at all.

He looked as handsome as ever, and she read both compassion and kindness on his face. Was the look deliberate, just a clever trick?

"Why did you drag me back here?" she asked. "Are live victims that hard to find in this neck of the woods?"

He bristled at that as if offended, the compassion leaving his eyes. "Would you truly prefer that I had left you out there? Is being with me not a better alternative to dying?"

"That remains to be seen. If you really mean me no harm, then take me to the next town right now. Since you can zip along at the speed of light, that should be no problem for you, even with this storm."

"I wish that were true, but traveling that fast is very depleting. I can only do it in short bursts, a minute or two at a time."

"Oh." Nicole frowned. "So let me guess: the blood in your fridge—it's backup in case you can't find enough people to feed on?"

"No. That blood is my only nourishment. I gave up feeding on people and animals a long time ago."

A shiver ran through her, even though she was warm. "Then why, when we were sitting on that piano bench, did you look at me like I was about to be lunch?"

"I didn't say I'd lost the *desire* to feed from the living, Nicole," he said, angry now. "I said I *gave it up*."

"Why did you give it up?"

"Because I was tired of hurting people. Because it's too hard to stop. I *could* have bitten you at any time. I could have drained your blood in minutes or killed you instantly with the mere twitch of my hand."

A gasp escaped her throat and Nicole swallowed hard, hot tears threatening behind her eyes. "Thanks for the warning. I'll keep that in mind."

Michael frowned, looked like he wanted to kick himself for his last remarks. "I said *could*, not *would*." He strained for patience. "I'm not going to kill you, Nicole, anymore than I intend to bite you. If I had been determined to drink your blood, don't you think I would have done so long before this?"

She hesitated. He'd certainly had plenty of opportunities to bite her ever since the moment she first arrived, unconscious and bleeding—not to mention the times they'd been in intimate contact. And she'd just slept in his arms without apparent harm.

Nicole's mind raced in confusion, recalling all that he'd done for her just now. She knew how dangerous hypothermia was and how close she'd come to losing her life. Once again, he'd saved her. How was she supposed to reconcile his tender care of her with the threat of what he was and what he *could* do?

"I suppose you would have," she admitted begrudgingly, "and I suppose I should . . . thank you. For rescuing me. And taking such good care of me. Again."

"You're welcome. I'm sorry you felt it necessary to run." Still sitting on the floor across from her, Michael settled back against the base of an easy chair and stretched his long legs out in front of him. "How do you feel?"

"How do you think I feel? Scared. Confused. Anxious. Astonished."

"Don't be."

Nicole rearranged the down comforter around her, hugging her arms across her chest. A tear spilled down her cheek. She wiped it away. "You say that so matter-of-factly. As if it's every day I find out the man I'm snowbound with is a vampire."

"I realize this isn't easy for you."

"No. It's not." In the space of a few hours, a long-held truth had just been turned upside down; a frightening myth had become reality.

"Whatever you've read in the past," he said kindly, "whatever stories you've heard or what you *think* that term means . . . I implore you to keep an open mind."

"Okay." She willed herself to be calm, to believe that she was in no danger, despite those frightening statements he'd just uttered: *I could have drained your blood in minutes . . . Because it's too hard to stop.* "My mind is open. Help me to understand who and what you are."

"You know who I am."

"No, I don't. You said you're Michael Tyler, the man behind Patrick Spencer, but—by the way, is that really true?"

"Of *course* it's true."

"How can I know? You've lied about so many things."

"I had to lie. You must know that."

"You can tell the truth now. It wasn't some distant ancestor who homesteaded this place; it was *you*—right?"

He nodded.

"My God." Her voice was a whisper. "This is so hard to believe . . . How old are you?"

"Old."

"How old?"

"Does it matter?"

"I'd like to know."

He twisted his fingers in his lap, reluctant to answer. "I was born in the early eighteenth century."

Nicole went quiet for a moment, struggling to digest that incredible fact. "Is Michael Tyler your real name?"

"It is now."

"And before that, it was William?"

"Among other names."

"What was your name at birth?"

"Adam Robinson."

She raised an eyebrow. "Like the doctor in your Civil War novels."

He shrugged. "It's a good name."

"Those books in your study, signed by Charles Dickens— he signed them for *you*, didn't he?"

"Yes."

"You *knew* Charles Dickens?"

"I was his physician at one time."

"His *physician*? You're a doctor?"

"I was."

She gazed at him in wonder. So many things about him made sense now. "Why did you move here?"

"To avoid people. To avoid temptation."

"And you raised and trained horses?"

"For years."

"And what else? Built furniture? Played the piano?"

"Yes. It's only recently that I started to write novels. To my surprise, I turned out to be good at it. People kept buying my books. So I kept writing."

"How do you get away with it?"

"Get away with what?"

"If you've lived here all these years and you don't age, why hasn't anyone noticed?"

"For a long time, there weren't enough people around to notice. I live off the beaten path. I didn't go into town very often. As the population in the region grew, I started dying my hair gray every thirty years or so, and always kept a low profile. When I felt I couldn't fake it any longer, I'd travel for a few years, spread word that my 'father' had died, and return as the brown-haired, long-lost son of the previous owner. For the few old-timers who recognized me, I chalked it up to a remarkable family resemblance."

"Clever," she conceded. "So what other . . . powers do you have, exactly? Can you read my mind?"

"No."

"Can you vanish through a crack in a wall? Appear and disappear out of mist or dust?"

"Nothing quite as impressive as that."

"Can you turn into a bat or a wolf?"

A brief laugh rumbled up from his chest. "No. I have only one earthly form, and you see it before you. As far as I can tell, biologically I'm not that different from you. I'm still a human being, just . . . changed. Some of my senses, like sight, hearing, and strength, have been altered or heightened. But I still drink, breathe, sleep, sweat, and bleed, just as you do."

"You sweat? You bleed?"

"I do."

"And you're immortal?"

"I don't think so—not in the literal sense. I don't age and I don't seem to succumb to illness, but if I'm like the other, similar beings I've met, then I can be injured, and I can die."

"You mean like a stake to the heart and . . . ?"

"That's a myth. No stakes or beheadings are required. A vampire—at least all the ones I've known—can bleed to death from any untended wound just like anyone else."

"Have you met many others like yourself?"

"Perhaps a dozen. None since I moved here."

"*None?*"

"None."

"What about sunlight? Does it harm you?"

"I can tolerate it for a few minutes at a time, but too much exposure to solar radiation weakens me and could eventually kill me."

"Do you sleep in a coffin?"

"*No.*"

"Can you put people under a spell?"

"What?" He was taken aback.

Was there a delicate way to put it into words? "You know.

The whole . . . sexual attraction thing that I . . . that we . . . Can you . . . did you . . . ?"

"No," he replied forcefully, obviously perturbed. He quickly got to his feet. "That's enough questions for now. I'm sure you'd like to get dressed, and maybe have something to eat."

He crossed to her and held out his hand. She took it and allowed him to help her stand up. "One last question."

He looked at her, patiently waiting.

"Have you ever killed anyone?"

"Yes. Far more people than I'd like to admit. And I assure you I'm not proud of it."

FAR MORE PEOPLE THAN I'D LIKE TO ADMIT. The words rang in Nicole's ears, making her stomach seize as she shut the bedroom door and got dressed, pulling on jeans, a T-shirt, and sneakers.

Michael had also admitted that he could kill her instantly with a twitch of his hand.

I didn't say I'd lost the desire to feed from the living. I said I gave it up. Because it's too hard to stop.

She'd thought Michael's fierce desire for privacy and reluctance to have her here was because he was Patrick Spencer, reclusive author. In truth, it had little to do with that at all, and she began to understand why he'd been so irritable the past two days. For a vampire who'd sworn off the blood of the living— yet apparently was still tempted—it must have required a great deal of self-restraint just to be in the same room with her.

At least Nicole knew where she stood. She had liked Michael, had been attracted to him from the very start, and it had nothing to do with a vampire spell. It was because he was a good, charming, intelligent, sensitive, and very talented man, who also happened to be a vampire. She believed, now, that he didn't wish her harm. He'd saved her life twice. So far, he'd managed to keep his thirst in check. There was no reason to think he wouldn't continue to do so.

Nicole would have to be on her guard, she told herself, but she didn't have to be terrified for her life every second. The realization brought a sigh of relief.

In this new frame of mind, Nicole made her way to the kitchen, where she found Michael staring dubiously at the contents of the refrigerator.

"I wish I could offer you something interesting for dinner," he said.

"The fixings *are* pretty slim at this establishment," she replied with a little smile. "Don't get me wrong. I'm very grateful for your cleaning woman's contribution. But by the time I get home, I don't think I'll be able to look at enchiladas again for a year."

"If you think your diet is boring after only two days, think what it's like for me. I've been eating the same damn thing for more than 260 years."

Their eyes met and they both laughed.

"If you'd like," he added, "I could go out and hunt you a rabbit."

"No thank you." The calm, congenial look on his face put her even more at ease. Michael seemed to take that in and looked pleased by it. "So you really can't eat or drink anything but blood?"

"Sadly, it's all I can digest."

"That's too bad. Because I made you a very nice carrot and apple salad for lunch," she teased, taking out the dishes she'd concocted and setting them on the counter.

"How thoughtful." He took out a plate and silverware for her, then filled a glass with water. "I'm pleased that you were able to be so inventive with the supplies on hand."

As Nicole heated another serving of enchiladas and helped herself to the other food, a thought occurred to her. "All those carrots and apples—they're for your horses, aren't they?"

"Yes."

"Ditto for the sugar cubes?"

He nodded.

"And the oatmeal . . ."

"Rolled oats. Also for the horses. I brought it all up yesterday before you regained consciousness, to make sure you had something to eat."

She grimaced in disbelief. "Oh my God. I ate horse food?"

"It's the exact same thing you'd find in a Quaker Oats box. I just buy it in bulk."

"Whatever. *It's horse food.*"

"It's keeping you alive, isn't it?"

She sighed, unable to argue with that. They sat down at his kitchen table and she began to eat. Michael leaned back in his chair, studying her.

"This is a little weird," Nicole said in between bites.

"What?"

"You watching me eat."

"I just like looking at you. Would you rather I leave?"

"No." She waved her fork in the air. "But feel free to get a . . . bag of blood . . . or whatever . . . and join me."

"Thank you, but I took care to eat yesterday even though I didn't need to. So I've had an excellent sufficiency."

"Well, thank goodness for that." The image of Michael downing a bag of blood was disturbing, and she banished it from her thoughts. Another image quickly followed: of Michael's sharp fangs piercing the flesh of her tender throat. It was equally disturbing, but for some reason no longer quite as terrifying as before. Her cheeks grew warm. Quickly, she said:

"Speaking of which. How do you get those bags of blood you keep? Do you really pretend to be a hemophiliac?"

"No. I get them from my clinic."

"Your clinic?" she said, surprised.

"I own a small medical clinic in Kremmling, about thirty-five miles from here."

"You own a medical clinic?"

"I founded it in the 1970s so I'd have access to a steady supply of human blood."

"How did you afford that? I mean, I know you have lots of money now. But back then—"

"When you live as long as I have, even very modest investments tend to compound. And I got a bank loan."

"And they give you permission to take home human blood?"

"Not really. My staff runs the place. There's only one job I take personal charge of: the shipping of units of blood every month—which I pay for from my own personal funds—to a sister clinic in Mexico. It so happens that the sister clinic doesn't exist. I take the blood home myself."

"What a complex undertaking, just so you can eat."

"Believe me, if I could have human blood shipped directly to me, I would. Unfortunately it isn't allowed."

"Couldn't you just live on the blood of animals?"

"I did, for a very long time. It tastes vile to me. So I came up with a different plan. A way to nourish myself that didn't harm anyone."

"Oh." There was a brief lull in the conversation. Nicole asked, "How did it happen?"

"How did what happen?"

"How did you become a vampire?"

He opened his mouth as if to reply, then apparently changed his mind and looked away. "I think it's best to leave that topic unexplored."

"Why?"

"It's not the most . . . pleasant of stories, and I don't . . . It happened so long ago. It's better left in the past."

Although disappointed, Nicole said nothing, eating the rest of her meal in silence. After finishing the last bite, she asked, "Who lives in that other building across the way?"

"What?"

"The place I saw you go into earlier, beyond the trees. Who lives there?"

"No one."

"But it belongs to you?"

"It does."

"What's it for?"

"It's where I go when I want to relax, vent some steam, or just . . . get away."

"What do you do in an empty house?"

"I didn't say it was empty."

"Why are you being so vague?"

"I don't mean to be vague."

"What are you hiding?"

"Nothing. It's just that . . . since construction was completed, no one but me has ever set foot in there." He looked at her. "Would you like to see it?"

His sudden offer came as a surprise, and for some reason it made her a little nervous. "I don't know. Would I? I guess it depends on . . . what you keep inside."

"Something you said yesterday makes me think you might appreciate it." He stood up. "Let's go take a look."

Her eyes widened in alarm and strayed to the window, through which nothing could be seen but inky darkness. "You mean—now?"

"Why not?"

"Wouldn't it be better to wait until tomorrow?"

"They say there's no time like the present." An almost boyish excitement lit his face, and he now seemed eager to share this with her.

"But—it's dark."

"I can see in the dark. And the place has lights."

She was starting to regret that she'd ever brought up the subject. "But it's still snowing. I almost froze to death once today already. I just recovered. I don't want to go out there again."

"You'll be with me. You'll be perfectly fine. You'll barely get a flake of snow on you. Have you forgotten how fast I can move?"

"No, but—"

"I do recommend that you put on your warm outer gear, just to be safe." He headed to the kitchen door, urging her to follow. "Come on. Let's go."

Her parka, hat, scarf, and gloves, which he'd hung by the living room hearth, were all warm and dry. With some reluctance, Nicole put them on. Michael slipped into his coat with lightning speed, and before she could resist, he drew her to him, scooped his hands under her bottom, and lifted her body up against the hard wall of his chest.

"Michael! Wait—"

"Wrap your legs around me. We'll be more aerodynamic this way."

Nicole did as bidden, encircling his waist with her legs and wrapping her arms around his shoulders. Her heart hammered, whether it was from the fear of heading outside again, the excitement of the unknown, or simply the close contact with Michael's body, she couldn't be certain. He carried her out the front door into the freezing night air of the porch. With the deep cloud cover and falling snow, there wasn't a speck of natural light anywhere.

"Ready?" came his voice, deep and low against her ear.

She nodded, her cheek against his. With his arms tight about her, he took off down the stairs and pitched headlong into the blackness with the grace, speed, and prowess of a cheetah.

CHAPTER 12

*T*HEY WERE FLYING AGAIN. At least Nicole presumed they were flying. All around her was such deep, intense blackness, the only real proof of their movement was the glacial air that whipped against her face and through her hair, and the snowflakes that stung her eyes and cheeks.

Nicole barely had time to blink before Michael stopped, still carrying her in his arms, her legs wrapped around him. Her pulse raced with anticipation and excitement. In the space of a few hours, the entire world had been turned upside down. Was this really happening to her? Was she truly in the arms of a vampire? What was he about to show her?

"Close your eyes," he said softly. That deep voice at her ear, which caused every nerve in her body to sizzle like a red-hot wire, reassured her that this was real; that *he* was real.

"Why close my eyes? It's so dark, I can't see a thing."

"I'm going to turn on the lights, but I'd rather you experience it through your other senses first."

There was such eager enthusiasm in his voice that Nicole felt compelled to comply. "My eyes are shut."

She heard a door opening and closing as he brought her inside. Immediately, Nicole was enveloped by a thick, pervasive warmth and humidity, as if they'd stepped into a temperate steam room, or onto an island in the tropics. Her ears caught the gentle sound of flowing water. Michael deposited her on her feet, his hands holding her reassuringly by the waist. The ground beneath her was soft and springy. Nicole detected a myriad of delectable scents in the air, including the sweet aroma of fresh earth.

"Where are we?" she said wonderingly, her eyes still shut.

He released her silently and stepped away. Nicole heard the sound of several switches being flipped and then his quiet voice telling her to open her eyes. She did, and gasped aloud.

It was a large indoor garden conservatory. Its high, sturdy walls and airy, domed ceiling were constructed entirely of large glass panels framed in white. A path of finely shaved wood chips meandered past beautifully landscaped beds and displays of tropical plants, trees, and flowers in a multitude of colors and varieties. A complex fluorescent lighting system suspended from the rafters lit up the interior as if it were brightest day.

"Oh!" was all Nicole could manage, before retreating into an astonished and reverent silence. The air was so moist, still, and warm that she ripped off her outerwear down to her jeans and T-shirt and kicked off her sneakers and socks. Leaving everything on a bench near the door, Nicole wandered barefoot along the path, reveling in the sensuous texture of the fragrant, mossy wood chips beneath her feet and feasting on the colorful displays on either side.

Michael strolled up and joined her. With delight, she took in the many varieties of orchids, lilies, gardenia, hibiscus, philodendron, coleus, bird of paradise, and polka dot plants growing amid brilliant green ferns, palm, banana, and plumeria trees, and dozens of other plants, trees, and vines that she couldn't name. Artistically placed tree trunks and rocks supported hundreds of small, exotic-looking potted plants and orchids, many of which were in full bloom. Nicole paused to examine a flowering orchid mounted on a chunk of wood that had been cleverly disguised with hanging moss to look as though it was growing from the tree. Ahead, she saw a rock waterfall and a pond teeming with colorful fish.

Nicole turned to look at Michael, so moved that she could hardly speak. His eyes were strangely vulnerable, as if anxiously awaiting her approval.

"What do you think?" he asked.

"You amaze me," Nicole finally managed, her awe spilling out into her voice. "This is beautiful. Incredible. One minute I was in the middle of a harsh Colorado winter night, and the next it's a summer afternoon in Bali."

A smile lit his face, the corners of his eyes crinkling charmingly. "That's the idea. I can't spend much time outside in nature when the sun shines, so I've brought a little bit of nature inside to me."

"How on earth did you build this?"

"I hired an architectural firm from San Francisco, which sent out a special team. It's modeled after the Conservatory of Flowers in Golden Gate Park, but on a much smaller scale of course. The lighting, heating, sprinkler, and drainage systems are state-of-the-art, along with a computerized climate control system that maintains optimum growth conditions."

Nicole shook her head, stunned. "I don't even want to think about how much this cost to build or to maintain."

"It was either this or a summer palace in Abu Dhabi," he said, grinning, "so . . ."

She laughed.

"Seriously, it's just a glorified greenhouse. The plants and trees cost more than the structure. I'd already donated so many millions to charities. Compared to that and to my new house over there, this was just a drop in the bucket."

She'd forgotten about Patrick Spencer's many philanthropic activities. It reminded her once again of the inherent goodness in the man. "With so much glass, I suppose you can only come in at night?"

"And on cloudy days."

That's a shame, she thought. "Who takes care of all this?"

"I do."

"What? But how? It must require a ton of upkeep. You write books. You build furniture and music boxes. You play piano. You keep horses. How do you find time for *this*?"

"I do things a lot faster than other people. I only sleep three hours a day. And—"

"Three hours? You only need three hours of sleep?"

"Sometimes less. *And*, I don't eat. Have you ever considered the number of hours people spend engaged in the purchase, preparation, and consumption of food, not to mention the cleanup time after meals?"

"Not really. But now that you mention it . . ."

"I have a *lot* of free time, Nicole. A person can only do the same things year in and year out for so long. After a while, you go stir crazy. I had to find a new hobby."

Nicole was incredulous. "What I would give for that kind of free time."

Michael looked away, frowning. "There's such a thing as too much time. I'd give anything to taste a strawberry again. To drink a glass of wine. To stroll down a beach on a hot, sunny day. To be able to—" He broke off, heaving a rueful sigh. Then, a small smile resuming, he nodded toward the pond up ahead. "Would you like to feed the fish?"

Nicole said she would. They strolled to the pond and knelt down on the smooth flagstones beside it. A river rock waterfall descended in tiers into a lovely, natural-looking pool surrounded by tropical plants and flowers, and teeming with orange and black-and-white speckled koi. From a watertight box, Michael scooped a handful of pungent, pea-size, crimson-colored pellets into Nicole's upturned palm. "You can toss them on the water if you like, but if you hold them out, the fish will eat from your hand."

Nicole positioned a few pellets in between her thumb and forefinger, then reached out until her hand was resting just below the surface of the lukewarm water. The fish instantly shimmied off in the opposite direction.

"They're afraid of me."

"It's their instinct to be afraid. Just be patient. They'll overcome their fear and come to you in time."

Nicole kept her hand in the water, waiting. The fish darted back and forth in the distance, then tentatively approached, swimming around her hand in a semicircle, as if assessing whether or not to come closer. At last, a bright orange koi glided up to her hand, opened its mouth wide, and sucked the pellets from her fingers.

Nicole giggled in delight. "I've never fed a fish from my hand before."

She held out a second offering and a swarm of fish now followed suit, nudging each other out of the way as they competed for the food.

"I told you they'd warm up to you," Michael said with a smile.

Nicole fed them until the pellets were gone, then waved her hand in the warm air to dry it. Her gaze fell on a potted plant with a profusion of small, dark pink blooms atop long stems. The flowers had an unusual shape, with two slender, outstretched petals protruding from the center, resembling tiny birds in flight. "What kind of orchid is that?"

"A *Porroglossum*. It's from the Greek, meaning 'far, far off' and 'tongue.'" Michael broke off a small branch from another nearby plant, stripped it of leaves, and handed it to her. "Touch the tip of this to one of the flowers and watch what happens."

Nicole obliged. To her surprise, the lip of the flower quickly snapped shut as if operated by a mechanical hinge.

"It's like a Venus flytrap!"

"Fascinating, aren't they?"

"I've never understood why some plants trap bugs. Do they kill them?"

"The Venus flytrap *is* carnivorous. It's the only species in the genus *Dionaea*. Instead of absorbing nitrogen and other nutrients through its roots like other plants, it secretes an enzyme that digests its prey into usable nutrients. But the *Porroglossum* isn't like that. It's just an orchid with a unique lip mechanism designed to promote pollination. It only traps insects temporarily, to help ensure that the pollinia inside the flower will be removed and later transferred to a receptive surface. The lip opens after thirty minutes or so to release the insect unharmed."

"Well, that's a relief." Nicole was suddenly, self-consciously aware of a kind of metaphorical connection between her relationship with Michael and the liaison between insects and this uncommon and remarkable plant. "And what's that one?" she asked quickly, indicating an impressive black-russet bloom with a velvety napped texture and long tendrils.

"Do you like it?" There was a teasing glint in Michael's eyes as he studied her, but they also held so much affection that her heart gave a little twinge.

"I do."

"It's called the Dracula orchid."

"Are you serious?"

"Perfectly serious."

"Well, it's aptly named," Nicole said, unable to tear her gaze away from his handsome face. "It's very dark and dramatic and . . ." *beautiful . . . Like you,* Nicole wanted to add. Her face grew hot. An automatic mister came on overhead and she was grateful for its delicate, cooling spray. She stood up, trying to calm her beating heart by inhaling deeply the moist, humid air with its delectable, earthy scents. "I can't believe this place. It's so peaceful. It's like Eden. I can see how it would bring you hours and hours of pleasure."

He nimbly rose from the ground to stand beside her. "I hoped you'd like it. You did say you enjoyed gardening." He started down the path and she walked alongside him.

"I've loved playing in the dirt since I was a little girl. My mother says that at age three I could describe the face of a ladybug and a caterpillar. My first memory is digging up a flower in our garden with a little toy shovel."

"Why did you dig it up?"

"I think I wanted to see what was beneath the soil, what made the flower grow. To my delight I found a big, squiggly earthworm, and then a bundle of roots. I was intrigued by the roots and wondered what they were for. Of course by the time I got around to asking my mother about it, the plant had died, and I was devastated."

He laughed. "An interesting lesson. What else did you like to do when you were a little girl?"

"I liked taking care of animals. I had a snake and a hamster and two cats and a lizard. And I loved reading and math and science. I got so far ahead that I ended up skipping fourth grade."

"So you were a child genius?"

"Hardly. I just read a lot. I don't recommend skipping grades to anyone. I was a year younger than all my classmates which was socially problematic at times. I got through it by focusing on schoolwork. I got straight A's every semester of my life. I did science fair projects every year from elementary school up through junior high school, focusing on natural wonders at first and then progressing up to medical themes."

"Medical themes?"

"I was fascinated by the circulatory system, the smell and hearing systems, and what makes the body tick. In fifth grade

I took first place in my school and second place in the district with a project about the human heart."

"Bravo. It sounds to me as though you would have made an excellent doctor."

Nicole felt color rise again to her cheeks. Inadvertently, she'd moved into dangerous territory. "I did think about becoming a doctor for a while," she admitted honestly, "but— I changed my mind. How about you?" she asked, quickly changing the subject. "When did you decide you wanted to be a doctor?"

His smile faded and he didn't answer right away. "It was so long ago, and the memory is so faded, sometimes I'm not sure if it actually happened to me or if I dreamed it." He shoved his hands in his pockets as they walked. "Like you, I was very young at the time. Nine years old, if memory serves."

"What year was it?"

He paused, doing the mental calculation. "1721."

"1721?" Nicole repeated in amazement.

"I told you—"

"I know, I know, you said you were born in the eighteenth century. I couldn't quite wrap my brain around that before. Okay. It's 1721. Go on. Where did you live?"

"I grew up in the county of Lincolnshire. My father was a farmer."

"A farmer? I thought you said he was a carpenter?"

"In truth, I learned carpentry skills much later. I had seven brothers and sisters—there was always a baby in the cradle at our house—but my favorite was my brother Patrick."

"Patrick?" Nicole repeated.

Michael's silent, meaningful nod confirmed it to be the origin of his pseudonym. "Patrick was just a year younger than I was. He was like my twin, my second self. We did everything together. When he was eight years old he became ill with a high fever. My parents didn't have the money for a doctor, and by the time they finally did send for one it was too late. Patrick died."

"Oh! I'm sorry."

"It wasn't until years later, when I became a doctor myself—and saw how limited the knowledge and resources of the profession actually were—that I came to realize my brother would have probably died that day even if a medical man had been in attendance. But I didn't know that then. I was overcome with grief. I decided that when I grew up, I'd become a doctor. I'd learn how to heal the sick, and I'd treat people who couldn't afford to pay."

"A wonderful goal. Did you achieve it?"

"Eventually. It wasn't an easy road. We were so poor. My father needed every hand he could get to run the farm. I didn't mind the farm work. I loved taking care of the animals—the horses in particular. I liked tilling the soil and seeing the crops grow. It instilled in me a love of nature that has stayed with me to this day. But I'd made up my mind: I wanted to become a doctor. I knew my father could never afford to send me away to school. No one in my family even knew how to read or write. So I appealed to the reverend at our church. I was very fortunate. He took a liking to me and offered to finance my education, all the way from grade school through Trinity College, Cambridge. I apprenticed with a physician for a few years, and then moved to London where I started my own practice."

"So your books about Dr. Barclay—"

"In large part, they're based on my own experiences, yes. I attracted a roster of wealthy and generous patients. That income enabled me to send money home to my parents, and to realize the dream that had motivated me from the start: to fund a small clinic where I could treat the poor in the overcrowded parishes."

Nicole wanted to ask Michael more about that, but he seemed to be finished with the subject (or was he avoiding something?). He suddenly picked up a nearby plant, saying, "This needs to be repotted. Come on, I'll show you my hothouse."

Michael brought her into the small, glassed-in room he called his hothouse. A rush of even warmer, moister air hit her as they stepped inside, where many dozens of potted plants in various phases of bloom sat on long, wooden tables or hung from racks suspended above their heads.

"I rotate these plants into the garden when they're at the height of bloom," Michael explained, as he set to work repotting the plant in question.

His repotting process turned out to be far more painstaking and meticulous than her own, revealing a skill and attention to detail that Nicole couldn't help but admire. Michael began by spreading out newspapers on a wooden work surface, then donned sterile gloves and flame-sterilized a pair of shears with a canister of propane.

"Now I see why so few of my houseplants survive," Nicole said with a grin. "I usually just pop a plant into a bigger pot and hope for the best."

"A little extra care goes a long way," Michael said.

After inspecting, removing dead leaves, and judiciously trimming the plant, Michael gently removed it from its pot, holding it in one hand while he pulled away moss from its delicate root system and inspected it for signs of rot or other problems. Finally, he carefully wrapped the roots in fresh moss and placed the plant snugly into a new pot.

Watching him work, Nicole was struck by a sensation of timelessness, of observing a procedure that had remained fundamentally the same for many thousands of years. At the same time, as she took in the caring expression on Michael's face, she was aware of another sensation building within her, and her heart did a little somersault.

How, she wondered, could she have ever feared the extraordinary man before her? When she'd woken up that morning, she'd still thought vampires were a myth. Was it possible that every frightening thing she'd ever read or heard about vampires was a myth as well? This man cared deeply about people. He wrote books she adored. He was skilled and artistic. He made things with his hands. He nurtured things, brought them to life, and made them grow. Michael *created life*; he didn't destroy it.

The truth hit her all at once with a swelling shock, like the rising crescendo of an aria, a truth she couldn't deny. There was only one word to define the feelings welling up inside her, which were stronger and more deeply felt than any she'd ever before experienced. Love.

Was it possible to be in love with someone you'd known for only two days? It must be, Nicole thought. She was in love with Michael, had been falling in love with him a little bit at a time ever since she'd woken up in his living room the day before. Knowing who and what he was, she couldn't possibly voice those feelings aloud; not yet, at least; not until she knew how he felt about her.

Her reverie was interrupted when Michael turned abruptly, as if sensing her study of him. His eyebrows lifted as he dropped the gardening gloves onto the table, his eyes colliding with hers.

"If you keep looking at me that way," he said softly, "I'm afraid I won't be able to keep up my defenses much longer."

"What defenses are those?" Nicole asked, her blood quickening in her veins.

"The ones I've been carefully building up to keep from pulling you into my arms."

Nicole swallowed hard. "Maybe we don't need all those . . . defenses anymore."

"Don't we?"

"No." She moved closer. "Michael: you told me that I shouldn't fear you. I believe it now."

"Do you?"

"Yes. I see who you are. I'm not afraid anymore."

For some reason, there was hesitation in his eyes; but he took her hand, brought it to his lips, and kissed it. His breath was warm against her fingertips. "Nicole." He whispered her name like a caress, then drew her to him and pressed his lips lightly to hers.

Nicole encircled him with her arms, returning the kiss with gentle affection. As the kiss lengthened, it grew more passionate. Nicole felt tiny sparks igniting in every corner of her body. She heard Michael's deep, staccato breath, the mirror of her own quickening respiration.

There was profound longing in his eyes as he stepped back, one hand sliding up to caress her arm, the other brushing back a lock of hair from her forehead. "I think we'd better stop now."

"Why?" she asked. "Don't you want to . . . ?"

"Nicole: there is nothing I'd desire more than to make love to you."

"Then let's make love."

He shook his head. "It's not a good idea for us to be intimate."

"Why not?"

"Because I want to keep you safe."

"Safe? But I am safe. You said you won't hurt me."

"I would never hurt you intentionally, my darling. But that doesn't mean it couldn't happen."

"I trust you."

"I don't trust myself." With a grim look he turned, shoved open the hothouse door, and strode back out into the conservatory.

Nicole raced after him, the slightly cooler air of the garden area coming as a relief after the hothouse. Her bare feet pounded on the soft wood chip path as she caught up to him. "Michael: the man who made this beautiful place would never hurt me."

He said nothing, just kept walking.

"What are you worried about? Is it because physically you're so much stronger than me?"

"That's part of it," he admitted tensely, "but not the biggest part."

"Then what is it?"

"Can't you just take my word for it when I tell you that I can't—that I shouldn't touch you that way? That—"

"No! I won't take your word for it. What I feel for you is too strong, and I know you feel it, too. If you can't kiss me—if you can't love me—then I want to know the reason why."

Michael whirled to face her, his blue eyes blazing, hands tense and clenched. "You want to know why? I'll tell you. Your instincts before—they weren't wrong, Nicole. You have every reason to fear me."

"*Why?*" she said again.

"If you knew more about me, you'd understand." Heaving a deep sigh, he added, "You asked me how it was that I became a vampire. I can see now: it's time that I told you."

CHAPTER *13*

"I WAS THIRTY-FIVE YEARS OLD, working as a physician in London," Michael said as they slowly meandered along the path. "Between my private practice and my clinic, I'd kept so busy over the years that I'd had little time to socialize. But that year I met and fell in love with the daughter of a shipping merchant."

"Did you marry her?" Nicole asked.

"We were engaged to be married. I had never been happier. And then . . ."

Nicole waited. Michael's eyes were haunted as he continued.

"I was on my way home one night after visiting a patient in the poor district, walking down a dark, deserted lane, when I saw a young woman lying on the ground. Presuming that she was sick or intoxicated, I bent down to see if I could help her. When I touched her shoulder, her eyes blinked open and—I'll

never forget it—with a sultry smile she said, 'Hello, my lovely.'
Suddenly her eyes flashed red, her teeth lengthened into fangs,
and before I knew what was happening, she'd pulled me down
beside her, ripped the cravat from my neck, and sunk her teeth
into my flesh. In horror I tried to fight her off, but she seemed
to possess the strength of twenty men. As I struggled, I felt the
blood being drained from my body. I grew weaker and weaker
and thought, I'm going to die. It was a terrifying realization,
yet at the same time I was mortified because I was feeling such
an exquisite sense of . . ." His voice trailed off.

"An exquisite sense of what?"

"Pain," he concluded, a bit too quickly. "I blacked out. I
awoke in her rooms a little while later, lying on a filthy bed
with her sitting beside me. 'Aren't you a handsome one?' she
said with a leer. 'You're a keeper, you are.' I was so weakened
from loss of blood that I could hardly move. She said her name
was Clarissa and that if I wanted to live, she could help me,
but first I would have to drink her blood."

"Drink her blood?"

"Yes. She drew one long fingernail across her neck, then
pressed my mouth hard against the weeping wound. I couldn't
move. I didn't want to drink her blood, but it was that or suf-
focate. So I drank. And drank. I suppose that was the last moment I was truly human."

"Did you die?"

"I don't know. I don't really understand what happened to
me. I don't think any of the vampires I've met since did either.
But one thing is for certain: vampire blood is like a virulent
poison. A large enough quantity, ingested when a person has
suffered a severe blood loss and is on the point of death, seems

to infect their blood and body permanently, leaving a string of transformations in its wake."

Michael yanked off a large, waxy leaf from a plumeria tree and began to dissect it in his fingers as they walked. "I lost consciousness again and when I awoke late the next afternoon, I still had no inkling of what I'd become. My strength had returned. The harpy was asleep, and I fled her lair.

"I stumbled toward home, increasingly baffled by the changes I perceived in myself. I seemed to break everything I touched. All the sounds of the city seemed louder and more distinct. My vision was so acute, I could see every tuft, barb, and vane in the feathers of a bird sitting atop the highest building. But the warm sun made me feel light-headed and nauseous, so sick that I had to rest in the shade of doorways. Finally I was obliged to wait for dusk before I could continue on. At the same time, I was overwhelmed by a simmering rage and a powerful thirst. I drank from a barrel of rainwater but became violently ill. A strange, enticing essence emanated from the people walking by. To my horror, I realized it was their blood I was smelling—but it wasn't blood's familiar scent. It was far more fragrant, potent, and aromatic. I could hear it pumping through their bodies, and I thirsted for it."

Nicole's eyes widened. "Can you . . . hear and smell my blood?"

"Yes."

Nicole glanced away, struggling to quell the uncomfortable feeling that seized hold of her. "You said you gave up feeding on humans long ago," she said slowly, "so I assume that . . . in the beginning . . . you must have drunk blood from people. And perhaps you . . ."

Michael dropped the leaf he'd mangled, his eyes consumed by guilt. "That first night, driven by a compulsion I could neither explain or control, I attacked a man walking alone by the river. I was astonished by my own strength; he quivered powerless in my hands. I think I drank every drop of his blood and still it didn't seem to be enough. The worst part was, when I saw what I had done—that I'd killed a defenseless young man—I felt nothing. I just dropped his body in the river and moved on."

An eerie sense of déjà vu came over her as Nicole recalled the frightening dream she'd had the night before while sleeping in Michael's bed, and her skin prickled in alarm. "You felt . . . nothing?"

"No. I had dedicated my life to tending the sick—yet I had just committed murder, and I didn't care. I felt only emptiness, rage, and confusion. I found Clarissa and I shouted, 'What the hell has happened to me?' She laughed when she told me. She invited me to live with her, saying it wasn't so easy for a vampire to find companionship; that's why she'd made me. I was so filled with blind rage that I . . ."

"What did you do?" Nicole asked.

Michael stopped, crossing his arms over his chest and staring at his feet. "I killed her," he said in a low, ragged voice. "I grabbed a knife from the table, I slashed her throat, and I watched her bleed to death."

Nicole caught her breath, struggling against the confluence of emotions running through her. After a moment, she circled around to stand in front of him, placing her hands gently on his muscular biceps. "Michael. It wasn't your fault. You were under a force far beyond your control that day."

"That day?" He let out an ironic laugh. "You don't understand, do you? It wasn't *one day*. That was just the beginning of a murderous rampage that went on for nearly fifty years."

"Fifty years?" Nicole drew her hands back in shock and dismay.

"That's better," Michael said bitterly. "You *should* flinch at my touch. It's what I've been trying to tell you. I was a madman, Nicole. I had barely a shred of humanity left, just enough to convince me to abandon my clinic, my practice, and my fiancée. I never saw her or anyone in my family again. It wasn't just because I was afraid I'd murder them; it was because I'd lost interest in any kind of human connection. I only wanted two things: sex and blood."

It was the first time she'd ever heard Michael utter the word *sex*. His dark look and tone, and the way he seemed to interconnect it with the key word that followed—*blood*—made Nicole's own blood run cold.

They entered a small, adjoining gallery with a flagstone patio that was adorned with several potted, blooming rose bushes and other plants and trees. Michael dropped onto a wicker chair and bent forward, elbows on his knees, head in his hands as he talked, as if he couldn't bear to look at her. Nicole sank down upright on the edge of the cushioned chaise lounge beside him, listening tensely.

"I rented rooms in a part of the city where I wasn't known," Michael went on. "I lived on the outskirts of society, stealing, making love to women, and drinking people's blood. Blood was like a narcotic; when I drank, I went into a kind of daze. I always wanted more; I couldn't stop. My victims had to die. How could I let them live, with the knowledge of what

I was? Clarissa was right: I found myself very much alone. I was frantic to find out if there were any other creatures like me—I had encountered none in London. So I sailed to the Continent, where I met a few. For the most part I didn't enjoy their company, but it was better than no company at all. I traveled widely, committing the same atrocities that I had in London. I can't bear to look back now and think of what I did. It went on that way for decades. The only reputable thing I did during that time was to read. I had so much time on my hands, I read everything I could find."

"Did you ever make any other . . . beings like yourself?"

Michael leaned back in his chair and shook his head. "No. As angry and miserable as I was, I still couldn't bring myself to doom anyone else to my fate. Finally, one day when I was in Salzburg, I met a European vampire who was different from the rest. He was a handsome fellow. He looked a few years younger than I was, but in actuality he was much older—he said he was born in the fifteenth century. He was cultured, sophisticated, and intelligent, and appeared to have some skills and limitations that were different from mine. He took one look at me and said it was a shame that I was wasting my gift. 'Gift?' I said, rather mockingly as I recall. 'This existence is a curse.' He said he begged to differ. He told me he had learned to discipline himself, to rein in his desires and his thirst—that any vampire could do it, it just took time and required enormous self-control. With nothing *but* time, he said, there were no bounds to the ways in which a man could expand his mind and talents."

"Who was he?"

"I don't know. I think he said his name was Wagner—no relation to the musician Wagner. When I went looking for him the next night, he was gone. But his message stayed with me. I looked in the mirror and decided I couldn't imagine going on in this debauched way forever. I'd had enough, and I determined to fix myself."

"What did you do?"

"I returned to Britain and began a new life. I spent a few years in Scotland where I practiced being around people in moderation—it was very difficult at first—until I could do so without being tempted. I restricted myself to drinking the blood of animals, even though I detested it. Then I moved back to England and lived in the countryside. I tried writing for the first time, although I didn't sell anything. I found steady work by apprenticing myself to a carpenter, where I could labor indoors and at night."

"So that's where you learned your woodworking skills."

"Yes. I enjoyed it immensely. But in the end, it was not my profession of choice. Finally, in about 1825, when I was certain I could be around people and blood without flinching, I began to practice medicine again."

"You practiced medicine again?" Nicole repeated, surprised. "Oh! Now I see. That's how you met Dickens."

He nodded. "Country villages were desperately in need of good doctors, and so were the inhabitants of London when I moved back. None of my previous acquaintances were still alive to recognize me, and not much had changed in medical science since I'd been trained. I had already posed as a normal human for many years with success. Being a physician was—I won't say that it was easy. Every day was a struggle, but I found that I could do it. I admit, there was one widespread practice all the other doctors swore by, but which I saw no point to and refused to administer."

Nicole stretched out on the lounge and lay back with a smile. "Let me guess: bleeding."

"Exactly. Looking back now, I believe I saved a lot of patients."

"I'll bet you did."

"For a long while I was content. I was living a chaste and clean existence, truly helping people, doing the kind of work I'd dreamed of doing as a young man, before I was . . ." His voice trailed off and his eyes grew bleak. "Then one day it all ended."

"What happened?"

Michael stood up again and paced back and forth across the flagstones. "I had a wealthy patient—an attractive married woman whose husband was a lord, an important man in Parliament. She sent for me and as usual I went to her home, up to her bedroom. I suppose she must have fancied me. She admitted she wasn't ill and basically threw herself at me. It had been so long since I'd been with a woman, that I . . . I was unable to refuse. I made love to her, and at the height of passion . . ." Michael stopped and turned away, unable to continue.

Nicole tensed apprehensively, expecting the worst. "Did you kill her?"

"I don't know. I may have. All I remember is that I was overcome by thirst and couldn't stop myself from tasting her blood. The next thing I knew, she was whimpering, as white as a ghost, at the end of her strength, and at that moment her husband walked into the room."

"Oh my God."

"People were shocked and thrilled by vampire legends in England at that time, which had inspired several stories and popular plays. She had seen me transform into a bloodthirsty beast and so had he. I knew my career in London was over—in Great Britain for that matter. So I fled. I gathered every penny I had, packed my most prized possessions, and booked passage on the first ship sailing from London harbor. It happened to be heading for America. And that's how I came to be here."

"What year was this?"

"It was the autumn of 1860. The trip took forty-four days. I fed from the rats and livestock onboard. I arrived in New York semi-starved, with no real idea what I wanted to do. I worked as a carpenter for a while. A few months later, seven southern states seceded from the Union. Four more soon followed. By summer, your country was embroiled in the Civil War. When the news came in about the Union's terrible defeat at the first battle of Bull Run, I wondered if I could help. Did I dare work as a physician again? I told myself that my only lapse in all those years had been when I was with a woman, so perhaps it would be all right. There would be no women on the battlefield. So I offered my services as a doctor for the Union Army."

"Oh!" Nicole said. "I should have guessed that you lived through that, too."

"Everything you've read in my novels was inspired by my experience in one fashion or another. Only the love stories were fiction. Anyway, I served in the army for two years. I managed to hide my unique proclivities from the men in my unit until . . ." He hesitated, looking at her. "Do you remember the scene you mentioned in *The Wind of Dawn*—when Dr. Robinson so 'heroically' killed the Confederate soldiers who descended on his medical tent?"

Nicole nodded.

"That wasn't fiction, and there was nothing heroic about it. Those Rebs weren't there to kill us. They were exhausted and starving and asked me for water. For *water*. I went to get a cup, when one of my patients—a decorated officer and a friend—grabbed his pistol from beneath his cot and shot one of the Confederate soldiers point blank. The Rebs drew what weapons they possessed and descended on the wounded man. I lashed out in fury. When I next looked around, every one of those Rebels lay dead on the ground. I had slaughtered them."

"Surely you don't blame yourself for killing those men," Nicole said slowly. "They were the enemy, and you were defending your friend."

"I do blame myself. Those men didn't have to die. They had nothing but knives and muskets, which I could have knocked away before they had a chance to use them. I could have talked them down; I'd done it plenty of times before. But that's not the worst part. There's more to the story. There was so much blood—the tent was awash in it—and I lost all sense of myself. I dragged the first dead man outside and drank every drop of blood in his body. Once I started I couldn't stop. Like a demon, I fed off all six of those men until I was full and bloated."

"Oh!" was all Nicole could manage.

Michael's face was consumed with guilt, his voice soft and low. "That's why I left the army. That's why I moved out west. I had to disappear again, to start over in a new, less populated place far, far away. When I saw this land, I knew I'd found my sanctuary. It was miles from anywhere. Down the back side of this ridge is a deep, protected valley that lies under cloud cover most of the year, which meant I could spend a decent amount of daytime outside. I homesteaded the property and built a cabin and . . . you know the rest."

"Yes."

Michael stopped a few feet away from the chaise lounge where she lay and looked at her, his expression grim. "Have I shocked and horrified you?"

Nicole swallowed hard. Parts of the story *were* incredibly shocking and horrible. Some inner voice warned her that she ought to recoil in terror from the demon he claimed to be. But her heart spoke louder, refusing to be afraid. Michael struggled on a daily basis to deal with powerful thirsts and dark temptations that she couldn't even begin to imagine—yet it seemed that, today, he had learned to control those urges. "The parts that shock and horrify all happened a very long time ago," Nicole said quietly.

"Some things don't change, even with the passage of time."

"I think they do change." Nicole rose and moved to stand before him, earnestly taking one of his hands in hers. "*You've* changed a great deal, Michael. Yes, you've done terrible things, but you also worked hard to rise above terrible adversity and created a purposeful life for yourself. For most of that life, you dedicated yourself to helping others. You've done so much good, and you're still making a difference: your books bring pleasure to millions."

"It's kind of you to say so. But at heart I'm still that monster who craves blood; a demon who, centuries ago, murdered countless people."

Nicole reached up and rested her hand gently on Michael's cheek. "No. At heart, you're not a monster at all. Not anymore. You're a man. An extraordinarily talented, dedicated, sensitive, caring man. A man with a *good heart*."

Michael's hands slid around to clasp her back, pulling her to him. "Haven't you been listening?" he cried desperately. "Haven't you heard anything I've said?"

Nicole felt as if her very soul would melt under the compassion and yearning she saw in his eyes. "I have. It only helped me see who you really are. I'm not afraid, Michael. I want to prove to you that you're no monster. I want you to prove it to yourself."

"Nicole . . ."

"No more talking," she insisted softly. "Just kiss me."

CHAPTER *14*

NICOLE DIDN'T WAIT FOR HIM to comply. She pressed her lips against his, infusing her kiss with all the affection that welled within her.

Michael's resistance crumbled. He returned her kiss immediately and with rising passion as their bodies came together and clung.

A primitive force seemed to be controlling Nicole's hands and body as she pressed herself to him, swallowing his kisses feverishly, each one only increasing her thirst for more. One hand roamed the hard muscles of his back, the other twisted into his silky brown hair. Soon, she felt desperate to heighten their contact. The clothing that separated them was an intrusion; she yearned to feel his bare flesh against hers.

With trembling fingers Nicole grabbed hold of the hem of his T-shirt and began to tug it upward. Michael finished the job for her, whipping off his shirt in one swift movement. She caught her breath for one brief instant at the sight of the beautiful, naked rise of his chest, the tight-knit muscles of his bare, flat stomach, and his powerfully sculpted upper arms. Then she was in those arms again and he was kissing her, his hands slipping up beneath the thin fabric of her own T-shirt to rove up and down her back. He kissed her long and lovingly, with an intensity that left every muscle in her body limp with need.

Nicole took a step back, panting, and ripped her own shirt over her head. In seconds the rest of their clothing was gone and Michael was lowering her onto the soft cushion of the chaise lounge, his hard, naked body pressed tightly against hers, his mouth coming to hers in a hungry caress.

They didn't speak, communicating only through touch, taste, sight, and sound. As they kissed, Michael's hand glided up to cup her breast, shaping and kneading it, his thumb gently seeking and prodding her nipple. Desire spun through her like electricity. Nicole's hand slipped down to knead the flesh below his navel, and then moved lower, her fingers seeking and massaging, giving him the pleasure that he was giving her. She both heard and felt his soft moan. Then his lips left hers and followed where his fingertips had been, taking her nipple deeply in his mouth and rolling it back and forth with his tongue. Nicole's back arched in answer to the caress. Her blood seemed to be spinning through her veins, her pulse pounding in every pore of her body.

His mouth still at her breast, Michael's hand traveled down her belly to the private sanctum between her inner thighs. With rising pleasure, Nicole received the deliberate attention of his fingertips, her own hands exploring the hard knit muscles of his back and buttocks. Now he was sliding down, and she gasped as his tongue replaced his fingers.

The magic he worked with that tongue sent her into a delirium, filling her with liquid, molten need, bringing her almost to ecstasy. Fiercely she grabbed his muscled biceps, urging him upward, silently letting him know that she wanted him, *now*. In a fraction of a heartbeat he was above her again, spreading her legs with his body, and inside her, filling her, moving above and within her.

Nicole felt the thud of his pulse against her breasts. Her head fell back, exposing her throat to his lips. He planted tiny, hot kisses there, moving down the length of her neck. Then he paused. Nicole heard his ragged breath against her ear and she briefly froze, pulse racing, holding her breath, wondering.

But his teeth didn't touch her tender and pliant flesh. Instead, his mouth quickly returned to hers and he buried himself more deeply within her. Nicole's body answered, quivering with anticipation and then shuddering deeply each time he slowly thrust himself into her. Together, they moved to an unearthly rhythm. Deep down inside her womanhood she ached and throbbed. Her mind emptied. She could think of nothing but the need to give herself to the rising fire within her. Just as she heard his passionate exclamation, she gasped with pleasure, her body exploding into a million fragments of white hot sensation.

AFTERWARD, THEY LAY CLASPED in each other's arms on the chaise lounge, faces almost touching, the moist air of the conservatory enfolding them in its luxurious warmth. Michael's blue eyes as they held hers were luminous, regarding her with wonder as he gently traced the length of her arm with his fingertips. At last, he said softly:

"Do you know what I ask myself every time I look at you?"

"No, what?" she asked breathlessly.

"I ask myself: is she real? Or is she just another one of my fantasies?"

"I'm as real as you are."

"Nicole, you are so lovely in every way, you couldn't be more perfect if I had conjured you out of thin air." Michael caressed her cheek with the back of his hand. "I can't stop touching you. I've lived so long in my imagination, I still can't believe that . . ."

"It's never been like that for me," Nicole whispered with similar wonder. "And," she added with a soft, slow smile, "may I point out that you didn't bite me."

"No. I didn't."

"That's a little victory for you, isn't it? That you could make love and not lose control?"

"I suppose it is."

Hesitantly, she asked, "Were you tempted?"

"Yes."

Her brow furrowed with concern as she looked at him. "How tempted? Was it . . . difficult for you not to . . . ?"

Michael moved on top of her, his eyes smoldering as he wrapped her more tightly in his embrace. "Shall we try it again and find out . . . at a more leisurely pace this time?"

LATER, AFTER THEY DRESSED, Michael brought her home from the conservatory in the same manner in which they had arrived.

He felt Nicole shiver in his embrace at the first blast of frigid air outside, but soon remedied that by delivering her speedily to the toasty, dry warmth of the house.

Setting her down in the mud room, Michael shut the door with his foot, his arms still around her, gazing enraptured into those bright green eyes, not wanting to let her go.

"What?" she said, her smile meeting his.

"Nothing. I'm just . . . memorizing the moment."

He was still reeling with elation from the beautiful, incredible thing that had just happened between them. He'd told Nicole everything and she hadn't been afraid; she'd still wanted him. Centuries ago, when he'd come to terms with his nature and made his choice of how to live, he'd given up the hope of ever being able to love a woman again. Nicole had helped him see that it was still possible. He'd just made love to her twice, and he hadn't harmed her. It was like a miracle.

Michael couldn't stop smiling as they hung up their heavy winter garments, couldn't take his eyes off her as they made their way upstairs. He could admit it now—if only to himself: Nicole was everything he'd ever dreamed of in a woman. He loved her, had loved her from the first moment he saw her, and every moment in her presence since had only reaffirmed it. Was it possible that his love for her was responsible for silencing the demon that was inside him? Would it remain silent a little while longer, so he could enjoy and love her while she was here?

He knew she would only stay two more days; he couldn't expect more than that. He knew, too, that she was still holding something back from him. Something haunted her from her past, and he suspected that it had to do with her fear of blood. He hoped that eventually she would open up to him.

Taking Nicole by the hand, he brought her to the curio cabinet where he displayed his music boxes.

"You asked about this yesterday," Michael said, opening the cabinet and taking out the box she'd admired—the one inlaid with the red rose design and a scroll of music. "I thought you might like to look at it."

Michael wound up the music box and handed it to her. Reverently, Nicole studied the detailed, colorful mosaic of the lid, running her fingers over its lacquered surface.

"It's truly beautiful. The red rose is perfectly done—it looks so real, I can almost smell its fragrance."

He smiled, flattered, and watched as she lifted the lid. Inside, the high-quality brass cylindrical mechanism began to play its tune.

"It's lovely," Nicole said, listening, "but I don't recognize it."

"Don't you? It's one of my favorite songs. Come, I'll play the CD for you."

They retreated to his study, where he built a fire in the hearth. Retrieving a CD from his collection, he popped it into his stereo and set it to play the appropriate track. It was a tender, old-fashioned Scottish song, sung by a gorgeous tenor to the accompaniment of a full orchestra.

O, my Love's like a red, red rose,
That's newly sprung in June.
O, my Love's like the melody,
That's sweetly played in tune.

As fair art thou, my bonnie lass,
So deep in love am I,
And I will love thee still, my dear,
Till all the seas run dry.

174

The song went on with simple but heartrending elegance, describing a love that was fresh and everlasting. As Nicole listened, Michael strode up and wrapped his arms around her from behind, pressing his lips against the radiant abundance of her long, flaming hair. Her waist was so small; she felt so delicate, feminine, and breakable beneath his hands. Nicole leaned her head back against his shoulder and sighed as the music and lyrics of the full-bodied, melodious tune filled the room. He'd heard it at least a thousand times, yet it was so beautiful and heartfelt that it always gave him a rush of pleasure. Nicole seemed to share his reaction, for when the song ended, he saw tears brimming in her eyes.

"What an exquisite song," Nicole said, clasping her arms over his. "I can see why it's your favorite. Who wrote it?"

"The poem was written by Robert Burns, a Scottish poet, in 1794," Michael said, kissing her shoulder.

"I've heard of him. He's famous. Didn't he write the song 'Auld Lang Syne'?"

"He did. Burns was so struck by the words to 'Red, Red Rose' when sung by a country girl that he wrote them down. Not being pleased with the air, he asked me to give it to his friend Pietro Urbani, a Scots singer, and see if he'd set the words to music in the style of a Scots tune, which Urbani did accordingly."

Nicole spun slowly in Michael's embrace until she faced him, her arms encircling his waist. "Burns *asked you to.* . . ?" She stared at him. "Are you saying you actually knew the poet Robert Burns?"

"I met Burns during the first year of my . . . rehabilitation, shall we call it," Michael answered, "when I spent some time up in Scotland."

Nicole let out a laugh that seemed to be half incredulity, half delight. "What was he like?"

"He was about my age—or the age I appeared to be, anyway. He was a good-looking chap, very spirited and intelligent. His eyes literally glowed when he spoke with feeling or interest. He talked about his love of poetry and about his muse. Sadly, he became ill and died soon after he wrote that poem. But it was Burns who first inspired my interest in writing."

"Well then, the world—and I—owe a greater debt to Robert Burns than we ever knew," Nicole said.

Her smile as she gazed at him was such a mix of wonder, affection, and admiration that Michael's heart turned over. He kissed her, then spread small, slow kisses across her cheeks and nose. As he tenderly brushed back the hair from Nicole's forehead, his eyes fell upon the butterfly bandage concealing the cut on her temple, which still looked angry. "Does that hurt?"

"A little," she admitted.

"I could heal it for you right now, if you wanted."

"Heal it? What do you mean?"

"There's an antimicrobial protein in saliva—it's called histatin—"

"Yes, I know—it's said to aid in the healing of wounds."

He was surprised she knew that, but then remembered her interest in medicine, and that she'd once considered becoming a doctor. "That's why cuts in the mouth heal so much faster than other injuries."

"And why animals lick their wounds."

Michael remained silent, eyeing her meaningfully, waiting for her to make the connection.

"So what are you saying?" she asked. "That your saliva—?"

"Like everything else in my body, the healing properties of my saliva are heightened. If you'd like, I can . . ."

Nicole laughed again. "You are just one surprise after another. I never know what to expect next from you." She beamed at him and said with a melodramatic flair, "Okay. Yes! Please, doctor! Heal me."

Gently, Michael removed the butterfly bandage near her hairline. "This might sting a little at first, but that will pass."

He lowered his head and lightly pressed his tongue to the wound. As he lapped against the severed ridges of her tender flesh, he felt her tense. Then a quiver ran through her body, she gasped, and her hands slid up to grip his shoulders, as if to steady herself. He continued to lick her wound with infinite slowness, feeling the subtle but steady changes as they occurred beneath his tongue.

"It did sting at first, but now it feels really . . . *really* . . . nice," she whispered.

Her limbs and body grew heavier in his arms as she relaxed. "Now it tickles," she giggled.

At last he pressed a firm kiss against her smooth, moist flesh, and drew back slightly.

"Don't stop," she murmured sleepily.

"But you're healed," he said, gazing at her tenderly.

Nicole opened surprised green eyes, mere inches away from his. "I . . . am?"

"You are."

She touched the clean, healed spot where the wound used to be. "That's a pretty neat trick."

"It comes in handy at times."

A thought seemed to occur to her. "If your saliva has such unique properties, is that why, whenever we kiss . . . and a little while ago, when we . . . when you . . . *you know* . . . Is that why it felt so . . . so amazingly, incredibly, indescribable?"

He smiled. "I don't know. Perhaps it was."

"Wow," Nicole said breathily. "Wow."

It was very late now, and Nicole suddenly looked so sleepy that Michael led her to the couch in front of the fireplace, where they stretched out, face-to-face in each other's arms. His fingers searched tenderly in her heavy curtain of hair, finding and exposing her ear. In a low tone that did nothing to disguise his adoration, he quoted:

"'My love's like a red, red rose, that's newly sprung in June.'"

He kissed the bare flesh of her neck and felt her body tremble. "'My love's like the melody that's sweetly played in tune.'"

Pulling aside her T-shirt, he delicately brushed his lips across the sensual slope of her upper shoulder. "'As fair art thou, my bonnie lass, so deep in love am I . . .'"

Michael bent his head to hers and gave her a languorous kiss. "'And I will love thee still, my dear,'" he whispered, "'till all the seas run dry.'"

Nicole came fully awake in his arms, her green eyes luminous as they gazed into his. They began to make love.

Joy surged through him. For so long—an eternity—he had been with a woman only in his mind and dreams. But she was here and real. With hands and lips, he worshiped her. They shed their clothes with unhurried grace, pausing to gaze at each other, admire, and smile. She was perfect in her nudity. Perfect. Beautiful. Physical desire, so long denied, rioted in his veins.

Murmuring his praise, he turned her to him and slid down on the couch, past her hips, letting his hands glide over every curve of her slender body. The provocative form of her inner thighs was captivating. Tenderly, he nestled his face into the warm cloud of that feminine softness. He heard her gasp and call his name. The texture and taste of her was intoxicating. He took his time, felt her legs tremble violently beneath him as her fingers clenched his arms.

He moved up to take her, but Nicole suddenly spun in his embrace and rolled to a sitting position, trapping his legs beneath her on the couch. He tried to drag her to him but she stopped him, placing a silent fingertip to his lips. Settling atop him like a sylph or siren, she slowly planted kisses over the curves of his chest, then worked her way down his side, softly touching her lips and tongue in between each rib as she traveled ever lower, past his hips now. He felt the contact burn in hot channels throughout his body. Her breasts, as she moved, were an unconscious caress and he felt himself tighten more urgently beneath her, his breath sharpening in little staccato gasps as she embraced him with her mouth.

Michael reached down to thread his hands into her luxurious hair, urgently raising her head back up to his. "My love," he whispered thickly, "I don't know how much more of that I can take."

Nicole beamed down at him radiantly as his fingers fanned over her breasts in deepening strokes, his thumbs languorously stroking her nipples in circles. He heard her breath quicken in her throat. His entire body felt hot, like molten putty.

Michael's hands glided around to her willowy, arching back and pulled her close, until the sweeping, moist heat of her pressed tightly against him. Their mouths searched for and found each other; then he planted fervent kisses across her cheek to her neck. The flaming passion within his body only heightened his awareness of the throbbing pulse in the throat beneath his lips. Oh, how he wanted her. He wanted all of her. *All of her.*

He could hear Nicole's red blood pulsating through her veins. Its warm, delectable scent assailed his nostrils, and with it came the familiar, threatening heat behind his eyes and the ache in his jaw. He longed to try that blood, to test its flavor. He yearned to suck the essence from her body and experience the ecstasy that always accompanied it. *Just a taste*, he thought; *just a taste.*

But no; *no.* Michael briefly closed his eyes and sternly, deliberately forced the thoughts away. He wouldn't. He couldn't. Loving her this way was all that was permitted; and it was enough.

With deliberate slowness he guided her hips to join their bodies, easing himself into her melting warmth. Moving within her, gazing once more into the vivid greenness of her eyes, he concentrated on every vibrant sensation of pleasure building inside him. This was not just making love, he told himself; it was an act of love, a physical expression of all that was in his heart, something he had never in his entire existence experienced before tonight.

As she cried out in ecstasy and a bright flare of sensation engulfed him, the miracle of it rang through him as if it were the brilliant, climactic resolution of a symphony.

CHAPTER 15

SUNSHINE CREPT IN around the edges of the draperies, imbuing the study with a warm, gentle light. Nicole awoke to find herself alone on the couch. Her head rested on a throw pillow and she was covered by a warm blanket. She must have fallen asleep in Michael's arms. Where was he?

A heat rose to Nicole's cheeks and an exhilarating shiver ran through her as she recalled their lovemaking the night before. Had she really just spent the night making love with a man—a strong, intelligent, tender, caring man—who also happened to be a vampire? It all felt unreal; yet it had been more meaningful and powerful than any act of love she'd ever experienced before.

The clock above the glowing hearth announced that it was 12:17. Half the day already gone—but no wonder. The previous day had been very, very long, and they'd been up most of the night. There was a lovely stillness in the air. She realized she could no longer hear the gentle drone of the backup generator; the power must have been restored.

Nicole stood, wrapping the blanket around her nude body as she went to the window, where she pulled back the draperies. Sunlight blared in with such fierce intensity that she drew back, squinting, and half-covered her eyes with her hand. Even with that limited viewing capacity, the sight that met her gaze was so achingly beautiful, she gasped aloud.

In the years she'd lived in Washington State and all the times she'd gone skiing, she'd seen plenty of wintry, mountainous vistas before, but none quite so spectacular as this.

It was as if she was on top of heaven. The storm was a distant memory. The world looked fresh, clean, and new, as if it had been reborn. The sky was the bluest blue Nicole had ever seen, and the air so crystal clear that she could see for miles. Distant, snow-capped mountain peaks framed a wide valley that went on forever, most of it densely packed with trees thickly covered in snow and dripping with ice crystals that sparkled in the sunlight. In the open patches between the forested hills and valleys, everything was frosted in deep, pure, brilliant white.

Nicole caught her first full view of the road that snaked down in elegant curves from Michael's house to the highway a half mile below. Michael had completely cleared his road, she realized, while she lay sleeping. The highway itself, however, was still blanketed in snow except for one cleared patch where his road intersected it. On the other side of that patch, to her astonishment, she could clearly make out the form of her rental car nestled down in the embankment, sunlight glinting off its battered roof. That car should have been hidden this morning beneath a deep mound of snow. Michael must have unburied it for her—perhaps fearing that when the county snowplows eventually came by, it would be obscured beyond recognition. Considering his aversion to sunlight, he must have done it before dawn.

Nicole's heart turned over at this fresh evidence of his thoughtfulness and caring.

She shook her head in wonder. The miracle of the world outside seemed no less extraordinary than the private miracle that had occurred inside this house and the conservatory the night before. So much had changed in the past twenty-four hours. *She* felt changed, as if she, too, had been reborn.

The sunlight's glare on the snow below was so bright that Nicole had to turn away from the window. It was also a visible reminder of how fleeting her time was here. Michael had said it would probably take two days after the storm ended for the snowplows to come through.

Two days. After that, she'd be able to leave anytime. The thought filled her with such sadness that a lump welled up in her throat.

One thing was as clear to Nicole as the wide-open vista below: she loved Michael with all her heart. Could she tell him? Would he welcome such an admission, or see it as a burden? She sensed that he had deep feelings for her; although he hadn't said so straight out, he'd revealed it with every look and gesture during their lovemaking, and when he'd quoted that beautiful song to her the night before.

Their affair had progressed at the speed of light—but that should be par for the course with a vampire, shouldn't it? Nicole's mind leaped ahead with similar speed, trying to imagine a future that would include him in it. Would she live here? Would he want her to? How would that even work? She would grow older every day, but he would not. An image formed in her mind of herself, old and gray, sitting beside Michael, still young and beautiful.

The image was so upsetting that Nicole immediately cut it off, shaking her head to clear it. She had no idea if Michael would even want her in his life, had no idea what *she* wanted, or if a future between them was even possible.

She wouldn't think about it. For now, she was here. They were together. And she was going to do her best to enjoy every minute of it.

Nicole heard Michael's truck pull into the garage and the engine shut off. She dashed across the house into the master bathroom, cleaned up, and dressed quickly in jeans and a long-sleeve shirt. She'd just finished pulling on her boots when Michael entered the bedroom and crossed to her.

"Sleep well?" he asked. He was wearing his usual blue jeans, cowboy boots, and a black button-up shirt with a subtle cross-hatch pattern. The dark color was an attractive complement to his fair complexion and handsome face.

"I did." With a smile, Nicole walked into his arms. "Michael, it's so gorgeous out! To think that you see that view every day."

He kissed her long and hard, then drew back to look at her affectionately. "It is something. I spent far too many years living in the protected valley on the other side of my hill. When I built this house, I was glad to finally take advantage of the view."

"It's so beautiful it made my eyes hurt."

He laughed and kissed her again. "Do you need to make a phone call or check the Internet? My satellite dish is up and running again."

"Oh." Two days ago, Nicole would have been itching to call someone or check her email, but she had no interest in either one. "Thanks, but I'll tell you what, after two days inside, I'm dying to take a walk. I don't suppose that you—"

Michael abruptly shook his head. "I have to wait for an overcast day. I can only go out in sun this bright under the protection of a vehicle. You're welcome to take a walk on your own, but I'd advise you to stick to the cleared roads. It's not easy to trek in new snow, even in snowshoes. And the wildlife tends to come out after a storm, looking for their next meal."

"What kind of wildlife?"

"The rabbits come out hunting for pine cones and pine needles. Then the foxes come out hunting for rabbits. Sometimes an elk or deer or mountain lion wanders down into the valley."

"A mountain lion?" Nicole shuddered. "That's okay, I'll pass on a walk. Thank you so much for unburying my car."

"I figured I'd better, otherwise they'd never find it. It's pretty much stuck in that ravine. I'm afraid they'll have to tow it out."

"That's what I told them when I called."

He frowned suddenly and let go of her, taking a step back and staring at the floor. A hush fell. Nicole wondered if he was thinking the same thing she was thinking: that when the tow truck came, she would be on her way.

"So," he said finally, his eyes flicking back up to hers with what looked like a forced smile. "I think it's high time that I introduced you to my horses."

ALTHOUGH IT WAS WELL PAST NOON, Nicole's stomach wanted breakfast. She downed a quick bowl of oatmeal, grabbed an apple, donned a sweater and her winter gear, and followed Michael to the garage where they climbed into his pickup truck. He turned on the heat full blast and they roared off down his freshly cleared road in the opposite direction of the highway, toward the back side of his property, which Nicole had not yet seen.

Nicole munched on the apple as they drove. Looking back over her shoulder, she could see and appreciate his house in its entirety for the first time. The huge, stunning domicile with its multipeaked roofline, stained wood siding, wraparound porches, and tall picture windows glinted majestically beneath the afternoon sun, surrounded by snow-draped pines. When the truck crested the ridge and began to head down the winding road on the other side, Nicole's eyes widened and she caught her breath at another vista, this time of uninterrupted, stunning natural beauty. An oblong, snow-covered valley was ringed by forested white mountains on all sides. A frozen stream wound through the valley, ending at a lake that glistened in the sun at the base of one of the mountains.

"How much of this is yours?" Nicole asked, gazing out the window in awe.

"Everything inside those ridges," he said, pointing to the mountains around them. "I own the valley all the way up to the lake, and everything behind us back to the main highway. It's a little over two thousand acres, or about three square miles."

"Three square miles? That's incredible. It's all so beautiful."

Nicole drank in the view as they traveled to the bottom of the road, passing an old log cabin nestled up against the back side of the hill at the mouth of the valley, in the shelter of the trees. "Do you use the old cabin anymore?"

"I have a ranch hand who lives there about eight months a year, late spring through autumn. In the winter, everything's so frozen up, he goes back home."

Not far from the cabin, two huge barns stood side by side against the hillside. They weren't painted the typical red or green of other barns Nicole had seen. These were rustic-looking with peeled log exteriors that blended in harmoniously with the scenery and the countryside. One of the barns appeared to be over a century old, while the other one looked almost brand-new, with freshly stained logs and shiny new metal around its frame doors and windows. Attached to the newer barn was an immense covered and fenced structure that Michael explained was an outdoor arena.

The snow-capped, peaked roof of each building was strung around the edges with dagger-sharp icicles hanging in a sparkling row like a queen's necklace. A large covered portico connecting the two barns out front protected a paved area from sunlight, snow, and rain.

As Michael drove up under the portico, Nicole asked, "Why do you have two barns?"

"That one's my hay barn," he said, indicating the older building. "It's been here in one form or another since I first homesteaded the place. I grow oat hay and barley in the meadow, hire a team of workers to harvest and bale it, then store it there with my tractor and other equipment." Michael parked the truck and shut off the engine. "In the old days, when I was breeding and training horses by the truckload, I used to turn my horses loose in the pasture in winter."

"You turned them loose? Didn't they run off or freeze?"

"The valley penned them in and protected them from the worst weather, and they grew three inches of hair on their bodies."

"I didn't know horses could grow long hair," Nicole said with a laugh.

"Oh yeah, they looked like woolly bears. I used to feed and water them in the old horse barn that stood here. But I gave all that up a while back, when I started writing books. Now I just keep two quarter horses for pleasure and riding. A few years ago I decided to tear down the old horse barn and put up this one, along with the new riding arena." Michael opened his cab door. "Wait there, I'll come around to you. I de-iced the area this morning, but it still might be slippery."

As Michael walked around the front of the cab to her, Nicole cautiously stepped down onto the frozen pavement and took a deep breath of the icy cold air. It smelled fresh and clean, imbued with the heady scent of pine. "Mmm. I love that smell. I wish I could live up here forever."

As she spoke the words, Nicole saw Michael dart a sharp look in her direction. A dismayed blush stole across her cheeks. It almost sounded as if she'd issued a very forward proclamation to become his vampire bride—but she hadn't intended anything of the sort—had she?

Michael held out his arm to her. Nicole couldn't read his expression. Was he upset? Annoyed? Abashed into silence, she slipped her gloved hand into the crook of his elbow and let him lead her across the driveway to the newer barn.

The huge barn doors seemed to be frozen shut. Michael slid one open with an effortless, one-handed shove. Inside, the pleasant smells of hay and horse immediately enveloped her. The barn was surprisingly warm, which Michael said was courtesy of the big natural gas heaters hanging from the ceiling that kept it at a steady 55 degrees. The interior was entirely insulated, he explained, pointing out the hayloft up top, the tack room, and the grooming area with its hot water heater and wash rack unit.

There were four box stalls with open Dutch doors, from which two beautiful horses draped in quilted blankets were looking out at them with interest. The stalls had eight-foot walls, paneled in wood on the bottom half, and topped by black metal bars like a wrought iron gate. The horses began to nicker quietly as Michael approached with Nicole at his side. Michael removed his parka, hung it on a peg, then stopped outside the first stall, where an elegant, sorrel-red male horse stood on a bed of hay.

"This is Posse," Michael said. The beast shot his head up and darted a wary look in Nicole's direction, nervously moving his feet, wrinkling his nose, and flattening his ears with an angry snort. "It's okay, boy," Michael said softly, stroking the horse's face. "She's a friend." Nicole longed to pet him, but the horse continued to eye her with suspicion, now baring his teeth.

"He doesn't see many people other than me and my ranch hand," Michael said. Gently placing both hands on either side of the animal's head, Michael stared silently into its eyes. The horse's ears extended forward, as if he were listening. For a long moment it seemed, uncannily, as if man and horse were wordlessly communicating. Gradually the horse's ears relaxed, his eyes closed partly, he let out a low, contented sigh followed by a slight shudder, and he lowered his head, nuzzling it affectionately against Michael's chest.

"That's better," Michael said. Glancing at Nicole, he added, "If you'd like to pet him, he's okay with it now."

"He's 'okay with it now'? What did you do?"

"I talked to him."

"But you didn't *say* anything."

"Yes, I did. I just didn't say it out loud."

Dumbfounded, Nicole tentatively reached out and stroked the front of the horse's face. He calmly accepted her touch. "So you just . . . think at him?"

"I call it mingling with the mind of the horse. It's particularly handy for riding at night—which is often the only time I can go out. Horses have excellent night vision, but mine is better. After 150 years, I know the trails around here like the back of my hand. Together, we can cover ground at breakneck speed in pitch-darkness, in territory you normally could never ride after sunset."

Nicole, at a loss for words, tried to grapple with that extraordinary notion. "Can you talk to other animals?"

"Just horses. They're very intuitive creatures. I think they sense that I'm more of a predator than a typical human, so it's a skill I've had to develop over time. I've had a couple of centuries of practice to get it right."

"You're like the Horse Whisperer without the whispering."

Michael laughed. "Posse and I have an understanding," he went on, scratching the horse on the neck. "I don't let anyone else ride him, and he won't take apart his automatic waterer anymore."

"Take apart his what?"

Michael pointed out a mechanical device in the horse's stall that consisted of a little flap over a small bowl of water. "When I first put the automatic heated waterers in their stalls, Posse completely disassembled his and then laid out all the parts neatly on the straw in front of it. He'd created a problem for himself because now he couldn't get any water—but every morning for about a month I'd come in and find it disassembled. Finally he told me he was doing it to piss off my ranch hand—who, by the way, is a great guy—and that he didn't want anyone but me riding him."

Nicole smiled. "Sounds to me like Posse's a genius who knows how to get what he wants—and lucky to have a master who understands him."

Michael introduced her next to his other horse, Pockets, a beautiful, seal-brown quarter horse with a black mane and tail and black legs with two white stockings.

"She's an eighteen-year-old mare, and a very gentle soul," Michael said as he opened the stall door. He and the horse affectionately greeted each other. Michael then gazed briefly and meaningfully into the horse's eyes, stepped back, and waited as the animal walked obediently out of the stall and stopped before him. The beast took a brief, interested look at Nicole, then turned back to Michael and lowered her head slightly.

Michael took off Pockets' blanket and lifted her legs one at a time, quickly cleaning her hooves with a hoof pick. Nicole watched appreciatively. Michael had such a warm and easy connection with the horse. As he moved on to brush the horse's back and sides, Nicole couldn't help but recall the way those same hands had felt on her own body the night before.

"Don't be shy."

"What?" Michael's voice broke into Nicole's thoughts and she blinked, the memory scattering as her cheeks grew warm.

"Pockets loves to be petted," Michael said.

"Why did you name her Pockets?" Nicole moved closer and stroked the front of the horse's face.

"It's short for Hip Pockets. I'll show you why." Michael grabbed a halter from a peg outside the stall and slipped it over the horse's head. "Wait here. I have to get something from the cellar." He dropped the lead rope to the floor and strode off.

"Wait, what should I do if she—?" Nicole began in alarm.

"Don't worry," Michael called back over his shoulder. "My horses are taught to ground tie. Not for my sake—we communicate just fine without it—but it helps my ranch hand, and you'll find it useful. Once that lead rope hits the ground it means *stand still*, as if she's tied to a rock or a tree, just like you'd teach a dog to *stay*." Before disappearing through a door, he added, "Scratch her neck. That's one of her favorite things."

As Nicole grazed her fingertips against the horse's neck, the horse dropped her head and pushed up happily against her. "You are so sweet," Nicole said, looking into the horse's soft, doe eyes, and feeling the velvet on her nose while she breathed on her hand.

They shared a peaceful, quiet moment together, which changed the second that Michael returned with a big bunch of carrots in his hand. At Michael's approach, Pockets jerked her head excitedly in his direction, whinnying and wiggling her teeth and lips.

"Here's how she got her name," Michael said, smiling. He shoved a carrot into the back pocket of his jeans and turned around. The horse leaned forward and, with teeth and tongue, expertly removed the carrot from his pocket and chowed it down.

Nicole laughed.

"She's been doing that since she was a filly. She's a carrot-aholic." Michael broke off a chunk of carrot and handed it to Nicole. "Keep your fingers pressed tightly together, so she won't mistake one for something good to eat."

Nicole offered the treat to the horse, who eagerly fed from her hand. Nicole enjoyed the nuzzling sensation.

"Have you ever ridden before?" Michael asked.

"Just once, when I was kid. I rode a pony at a fair."

"Well," he said with a smile, "you are now going to learn to ride a *horse*."

CHAPTER *16*

A CITY GIRL BORN AND BRED, Nicole had always been a little envious of the horsemen and horsewomen depicted in books or movies, who seemed so content and comfortable around their animals. Still, the prospect of riding a horse made her a little nervous.

Under Michael's direction, the experience proved to be unlike anything Nicole had expected or imagined.

"I use a special kind of bridle which I braid by hand from rawhide," he explained, slipping the lightweight woven bridle over the horse's nose and head. "My father taught me how to make these when I was a child. Many Native Americans used a similar device. They call it an Indian Hackamore."

"There's no bit," Nicole observed in surprise.

"I don't believe in bits. Would you like it if someone stuck a hunk of metal into your mouth and banged it against your tongue and gums?"

"No," Nicole admitted, "but people have been using bits on horses for ages, haven't they?"

"That doesn't make it right. A well-trained horse doesn't need one. Most people steer a horse by pulling on its mouth instead of intuitively feeling and telling the horse what they want to do."

"Not all of us have telepathic communication skills," Nicole pointed out.

"Any human being can learn to communicate to a horse with their body—to become one with the horse. I'll show you how it's done." As Michael slid open the doors to the adjacent arena, cold air filtered in.

"Aren't you going to put a saddle on her?" Nicole asked.

"I have saddles," Michael shrugged, "but I rarely use them. Riding with a saddle is like riding a bus. You're not actually *driving* the bus, you're just sitting on it as a passenger. If you really want to *ride* a horse, you have to feel the horse with your legs. You have to ride bareback."

Nicole stared at him. "Bareback?"

"Trust me. You'll love it."

Nicole was dubious as they entered the immense, covered outdoor arena, which had a lofty ceiling and a sandy floor enclosed by a five-foot-high circular fence. Scattered piles of snow had accumulated against the walls in certain areas, blown in by the wind, but for the most part the space was pristine. She could see their breath in the frosty air as they talked, but her sweater, hat, ski jacket, and gloves kept her warm.

"I used to be constrained to do all my riding at night or on overcast days," Michael said. "Sometimes even that was a problem. They have a saying up here: if you don't like the weather, wait five minutes and it'll change. It's true. There've been plenty of times where I went out riding under the safety of a deep cloud cover, and then, miles from home, the clouds suddenly blew away and the sun came out as if God had turned on a floodlight."

"Oh no! What did you do?"

"I raced for cover under the trees and had to wait for nightfall. It was a pain. Now I can ride whenever I want, day or night, rain, snow, or shine. So, do you want to go first?"

Nicole abdicated that privilege to him. Michael leaped up nimbly onto the horse's back in one swift motion, as easily as if he'd swung his leg over a rail.

For the next quarter of an hour, Nicole sat on the fence and watched with delight as Michael exercised the horse, at first simply walking, trotting, and cantering around the arena in one direction or another. Michael rode with a kind of understated elegance that was a pleasure to see. His legs hung naturally at the horse's sides, his knees only slightly bent, his shoulders to the back of his hips to his heels in a perfectly straight line. No matter how fast or slow he rode, he maintained a graceful, relaxed, but straight profile. The amazing thing to Nicole was that, even without a saddle or bridle, he always seemed to be in perfect control, leaving the reins lying loosely over the horse's neck and using only his legs—and presumably his thoughts—to give her direction.

Michael demonstrated a couple of tricks, bringing Pockets up onto her hind legs and dancing, to which Nicole responded with cheers and applause.

Then the real fun began.

"Don't move from that rail," Michael sternly instructed Nicole.

Michael leaned forward and wrapped his arms around the horse's neck. Pockets broke into a gallop, tearing around the arena at breakneck speed, which escalated—to Nicole's astonishment—into a blur of motion. Nicole had never seen anything, be it man, beast, or machine, move that fast. It was like a bolt of lightning, like liquid color racing around in a circle at the speed of light. When they slowed and became visible again, they returned to Nicole's side at a trot. She was speechless.

"Your turn," Michael said, his lips twitching with the effort to hide a smile as he casually dismounted before her. The horse had barely worked up a sweat.

"What on earth was that?" Nicole cried, when she found her voice. "Is she a vampire horse?"

Michael laughed. "No."

"Then how—"

"It's not that much different than when I carried you to and from the house to the conservatory. Usually, I let my horses carry me. But sometimes—when I want to go really fast—I carry them."

"You carry them?" Nicole repeated in disbelief.

"It's all in the arms, thighs, and knees, and a bit of the mind—a mingling technique that's taken me a long time to master. I transfer my speed and strength to them. They think it's fun, like being on a roller coaster."

"Okay. I have no idea how that works, but seriously, it was amazing. I think we should forget about me riding. How could I follow something like that?"

Michael wasn't about to let her get out of it, though, and neither was Pockets. Probably responding to one of Michael's mental commands, the horse came up and nuzzled Nicole's neck with a happy nickering sound, then licked her throat and cheek until Nicole burst into laughter. The beast then turned, presenting her side flank to Nicole as if waiting patiently for her to mount.

"That's a pretty clear offer, if I've ever seen one," Michael said with a grin.

"All right, let's do this. But I just want to walk. Slowly. Nothing fancy, okay?"

"Whatever makes you comfortable."

"How do I climb on?"

"Like this." Michael put his hands around Nicole's waist and effortlessly lifted her up onto the animal's back. "Take a deep breath and sink down onto the horse. Let your legs hang naturally, don't squeeze. Relax your back, arms, and shoulders, while maintaining good posture."

It was a lot to remember. Nicole did her best to settle astride the horse's back as directed, feeling a little precarious, and surprised by how warm the animal was. Even through the heavy fabric of her jeans, Nicole could feel the horse's moist body heat radiating up into her thighs. As Nicole instinctively gathered the reins into one hand, Michael said:

"Remember, the reins are a crutch people use to communicate with the horse's mouth. Hold onto them, but know that you can communicate through your body. When you want the horse to walk, just open the door."

"Open the door?"

"Gently tense the back of your thighs and tighten your butt cheeks. That signals the horse to move forward. Tell it to walk."

Nicole tried to implement his instructions. Nothing happened.

"Try again," Michael said. "You'll get it."

Once more, Nicole focused on the body parts he'd described. "Walk," she said. To her surprise, the horse moved forward.

"When you want her to stop, take a deep breath, let it out, relax, and say *whoa*. If she doesn't stop, *then* lightly pull back on the reins."

It was more than a little scary to be riding bareback atop this great beast, and disconcerting to have nothing to hold onto. Michael walked by her side as they slowly ambled around the arena, and he taught Nicole how to turn or moderate her speed, using subtle pressures of her legs.

"Keep your arms close to your body," he said, "so everything's as close as possible to your center of gravity. That's perfect. You're doing great."

"Yeah—great. I'm not falling off," Nicole quipped.

After a while, however, Nicole found her balance and began to relax a bit. The horse was very well trained and responded to her commands. Sensing her newfound confidence, Michael leaned back against the fence and told Nicole she could take the horse on a turn on her own.

As Nicole rode slowly around the arena, she stroked Pockets gently on the side of her neck. She could feel the horse's hard spine and muscles beneath her thighs. Every movement of the animal's body seemed to ripple through her, as if they were moving together. Nicole knew she was totally green, that it took people years to become adept riders; yet for the first time, she had an inkling of what Michael meant by the phrase "become one with the horse." It was a wonderful feeling. Smiling at Michael, who was watching from the far side of the arena, she urged Pockets to move a bit faster now, keeping her balance, very quiet and relaxed and controlling the horse in a slow trot.

That's when Nicole heard the sound. It came out of nowhere and was very close by, a sharp, loud crack, like the report of gunfire. *What the hell?* Nicole thought in alarm. *Was someone shooting at them?*

At the sudden noise the horse shied sideways and took off running. Nicole gasped in sheer terror, the pit of her stomach falling out, trying to hold on for dear life with her thighs and heels as she pulled back on the reins. The horse wouldn't stop. It raced across the arena like a rocket. Nicole felt herself slipping from its back. She made a desperate grab for the horse's mane but it was too late.

She was falling, falling into thin air.

Then just as suddenly she was being swept up by Michael's strong arms and held snugly against his chest.

Nicole's mind whirled. Her heart pounded. Michael's lips were at her ear. "Are you all right?" he uttered urgently.

"Y—yes," she stammered, struggling to calm herself.

Michael gently set Nicole down on her feet, and without another word he dashed like a streak of light toward the frantic horse, who was racing around the arena with flared nostrils and terror in her eyes. Suddenly Michael appeared on Pockets' back. The horse reared in surprise. Then, as if by magic, she began to slow down, the fear left her eyes, she dropped her head, and her breathing slowed. Michael trotted over to where Nicole was standing and stopped.

"Sorry about that," Michael said. "She spooked when that icicle broke off."

"Icicle?" Nicole glanced at the huge icicles ringing the roofline of the arena, and understood. "I thought it was a gunshot."

"When the sun's out, the icicles heat up and crack before they fall. Even the best-trained horse will freak at that sound." Michael slid off the horse and took Nicole in his arms. "I should have warned you about it. I'm sorry."

"It's okay, I'm fine. Thank you for rescuing me. It was rather . . . spectacular." Nicole kissed him. "Actually, I wouldn't mind being rescued like that again sometime."

Michael kissed her again. "Let's hope the occasion never arises."

BEFORE LEAVING THE BARN, Michael groomed, fed, and watered the horses, and then cleaned out their stalls. Nicole offered to help, but he insisted he could do it more quickly himself. Indeed, as she stood back in fascination, it was like watching a movie on fast forward. In a matter of minutes, Michael completed tasks that might have taken a normal person a good hour at least. The horses didn't even bat an eyelash at the whirlwind of activity.

"They're used to it," he explained. "They were both born into my hands. They think my ranch hand moves at a glacial pace."

The sun was low in the sky by the time they returned to the house. Nicole was so hungry that for dinner she ate a can of soup standing at the kitchen counter.

"I'll lose weight fast if I stick to this diet," she said, as Michael leaned against the counter, watching her.

"I don't want you to lose weight. You're perfect the way you are."

They went out on the deck of the house and knocked off huge icicles from the roofline in areas where they'd be walking, an activity that devolved into a hysterical, swordfight-like battle wielded by mop and broom handle.

Afterward, Nicole was shivering with cold and dying to warm up in a hot bath. Michael filled the marble tub in the master bathroom, they stripped off their clothes, and sank down together in the soothing hot water.

Nicole closed her eyes and sighed with pleasure as Michael shampooed her hair, massaging her head with his nimble fingers. Cradling her shoulders with one arm, Michael then eased her head back into the warm water, rinsing away the soap suds with gentle hands, her long hair floating around them like tendrils of reddish-gold seaweed.

As Michael scanned Nicole's naked body, he said, "Let me soap you up," the low timbre of his voice and the glow in his eyes seeming to promise a great deal more than sudsing.

Nicole's pulse beat to a new rhythm as she watched Michael soap up a bath scrunchie. He took one of her hands in his, grazed the slippery smooth surface of her slender arm from the top of her shoulder to the tip of her fingers with the soapy sponge, then ran it back up the underside of her arm. As he soaped his way along the inside curve of her underarm, then moved on to linger over her breasts, Nicole let out a little moan of pleasure.

Michael mirrored the exercise with her other arm, then ran the sponge tantalizingly over her legs one at a time, pausing to pay extra attention to each foot, and to the soft, sensitive region of each inner thigh. Nicole's nerves were on fire, yet at the same time she felt as if every muscle in her body had turned to jelly.

"Roll over," he said softly.

Limply, Nicole turned herself over in the water. Michael ran the sponge with tormenting slowness over every curve of her back and her submerged buttocks. Tiny embers ignited beneath her flesh at every touch of the soapy sponge driven by his strong hand. When he'd finished, Michael scooped her up to face him, pulling her close. He was ready to make love and so was she, but Nicole put off the pleasure, seizing the bath sponge and instructing him to lie back against the tub wall.

Now Nicole returned the favor, giving Michael the same treatment he'd given her, soaping him up over the length and breadth of his lean body until they were both breathing hard and quivering from the tension of restrained desire.

Taking Nicole's face lovingly between his hands, Michael brought his mouth to hers, kissing her with fierce need, his hard, wet, naked body pressed against hers. Nicole's heart raced. She was wet, so wet, without and within.

"Please," she whispered hoarsely against his lips. "I want you."

"You have me," he responded, and with one swift movement he was inside her.

They moved in each other's arms like a pair of slippery seals in the steamy water, mouths meeting, parting, meeting again. With his every thrust Nicole felt as if hot, erotic fibers were gathering in her very center and hardening into a tense ball of electric need.

Through a gauzy love haze, Nicole became vaguely aware of another kind of heat, emanating not from her own body but from Michael's. She heard a subtle *click*. Michael's mouth left hers and he took a ragged breath. Nicole glanced up and couldn't prevent a sudden gasp. Michael's blue eyes were burning red, his canine teeth were fangs, and he was looking at her with an expression that could only be called *hungry*.

Nicole held her breath uncertainly. Their bodies were still joined. He wanted her blood; the one thing that, for so many reasons, she was terrified to give him.

If he bites me, if he drinks too much and can't stop himself, I could die, she thought.

Heart pounding, Nicole stared back into his burning eyes. She loved him. She wanted him. She wanted to experience all the ways that he wanted *her*, to give him the pleasure he sought. And she trusted him not to hurt her.

Wrapping a slippery hand behind Michael's neck, she urged him closer.

"Bite me," she said softly.

CHAPTER 17

*H*E NEEDED NO FURTHER INVITATION. With fevered need, Michael lunged for her wet throat. Nicole cried out at the first sharp prick of his teeth piercing her flesh, but just as quickly the pain dissipated, replaced by the warm, arousing, suckling sensation of his lips against her skin.

What she felt next filled her with surprise. It was as if she could feel her own blood slowly emanating from her body and mingling at the point of contact with some delectable essence of his. A molten shiver ran through her as the exquisitely erotic exchange continued. As he drank, he moved inside her. Nicole gasped with pleasure as the twin forces simultaneously spread shock waves of intense, rising sensation within her body. She had never imagined a bliss so delirious as this.

His mouth at her throat and his every thrust within brought her ever closer to the point of rapture. As she hovered on the brink of her sexual peak, Michael's mouth moved up to cover hers once more. His lips and tongue tasted warm, tangy, and coppery. Moving together, they breached the pinnacle of ecstasy, gasping with pleasure as their two souls became one.

"I SHOULDN'T HAVE BITTEN YOU," Michael said, regret in his voice.

They were sitting on the carpet in the great room before the hearth. Nicole wore Michael's soft, luxurious bathrobe with the cuffs rolled up several times, and he had thrown on a pair of sweat pants and a T-shirt. As Nicole ran his brush through her damp hair to dry it by the roaring fire, Michael's eyes fell on the bite marks imprinted on her exposed throat, and she saw him wince.

"I'm glad you did it," she told him. She wondered now why the thought of him drinking her blood had seemed so frightening before. "I liked it. Very much, in fact."

"You're supposed to like it," Michael said grimly. "Here, let me mend the wound."

Gently, he pulled her backward in his arms until she was sitting in the V of his legs. Tilting her head to one side, he slowly, tenderly ran his moist tongue over the tiny wounds on her neck. Even under his light touch, Nicole's pierced flesh smarted slightly, as if that spot were under the siege of a hundred needle points, just as it had when he'd cured the cut on her forehead the night before. Knowing what was coming, she relaxed in his embrace, holding the hairbrush in her lap.

"It's part of the higher plan, I think," Michael went on, his tongue lapping against her sensitive flesh. Soon the barbed, stinging sensation waned and altered into something sweet and ticklish, as if he were stroking her with the tip of a feather. A giggle bubbled up from her chest, followed by a calm, lethargic warmth and a sense of well-being as the tickling finally eased.

Nicole felt her neck; the marks were gone. She gazed up at him with a smile. "Thank you. What higher plan?"

"The blood exchange, I believe, is designed so that people will enjoy it. It's just like sex. Why do you think lovemaking is so pleasurable? It's to ensure the continuation of the species."

"The continuation of the species?" Nicole's pulse skittered as she sat up and turned to face him on the carpet. "What are you saying? I know you were worried that you'd take too much blood. You *didn't*. You stopped. But if you *had* kept drinking—?"

He reached out to gently stroke her cheek. "Don't worry, my darling. I shouldn't have taken your blood; I vowed that I wouldn't, and I promise I won't do it again. But if I drink from you—that, on its own, wouldn't make you a vampire."

"That's right," she nodded. "To become like you, I'd have to be near death and then drink *your* blood, wouldn't I? The way you drank from . . . ?"

"Yes."

"How much blood would I have to drink to . . . ?"

He pulled his hand away, frowning. "Don't ask. Don't even think about it."

Michael took the hairbrush from Nicole's hand and asked her to turn around again. She settled on the floor cross-legged as he brushed the long, damp hair, which flowed down her back like a mantle. For a while neither of them spoke, as the bristles tingled intermittently against her scalp, followed by a gentle tug as the brush pulled through her locks.

Michael said, "May I ask you something?"

"Of course."

"I've told you my history. But when it comes to talking about yourself, you've been very reticent."

"Have I?" she asked, knowing full well that it was true.

"Forgive me if I'm wrong, but I got the distinct impression that you don't find your current line of work very fulfilling. Not to mention that it seems a bit beneath your abilities and talents."

Nicole's cheeks grew warm but she didn't reply.

"When I asked what you did before that job, you didn't answer, and you seem to have been avoiding the topic ever since."

"A lady doesn't like to talk about herself," Nicole said lightly, hoping he would change the subject. But he didn't.

"The first night we spoke, you told me how much you loved children and that you dreamed of working with them one day. Yesterday, you said you once thought about becoming a doctor. What happened to that dream?"

Nicole didn't respond immediately. The fire crackled. The clock ticked. The brush tugged and glided through her hair. Michael remained silent, waiting. Unable to think of a way to gracefully avoid his question, Nicole sighed and said, "Actually I did pursue it for a while. I went to college fully expecting that I'd become a pediatrician."

"You did?"

She nodded. "I graduated from high school at seventeen, got a scholarship to a great university, and began my undergrad studies with a premed focus. I took all the difficult prerequisite classes that are supposed to weed out people. I did very well academically, but . . ."

"But?"

"I really didn't enjoy the people I was with. There was this hypercompetitive component. People actually celebrated when someone else flunked a test or dropped out—and I'm not that way."

"You wanted everyone to do well."

"Yes. In that cutthroat environment, I was miserable. In my second year of college I went to the health center with strep throat and was seen by a nurse practitioner. She was fantastic and had about a hundred letters embroidered on her lab coat after her name. I asked what the letters meant, and she was really kind, told me all about it—that RN was registered nurse, BSN meant she had a bachelor's degree in science and nursing, MSN was her master's, and ARNP was for advanced registered nurse practitioner. At the end of my visit, she said, 'You're premed, aren't you?' And I said yes. 'You hate it, huh?' she asked. I admitted I did. She said: 'You know, there are about a zillion other ways to go into health care without being a physician.' A huge lightbulb came on for me. I realized that I could have a fulfilling career in the medical profession and still work with kids by becoming a pediatric nurse."

Michael's brush strokes continued to pull pleasingly through her hair. "A pediatric nurse? That sounds like the ideal profession for you."

"I thought so too, at the time. Due to the shift work that's common in the nursing profession, it seemed like it would work with my other hope, to become a mother and raise a family of my own. Within a month I'd looked into nursing programs all over the country and applied for a transfer. At the end of my second year I moved up to Seattle to go to nursing school. Even though I'd taken all those premed courses, I had to make up a whole bunch of nursing prerequisites. I took an extra heavy course load every semester and attended summer school so that I could still get my undergrad degree in four years."

"So you did graduate? You became a nurse?" he asked, surprised.

"Yes." She ran her fingers through her hair, which was now almost completely dry, and turned around to face him where they sat. "I took a job at Puget Sound Children's Hospital in the pediatric oncology unit—"

"Oncology?" His eyebrows lifted and she thought she detected admiration in his gaze.

"I worked on a hematology, oncology, and bone marrow transplant floor, responsible for between three and six patients per shift."

"Did you enjoy it?"

"I loved it. The kids would check in and stay for weeks or months at a time. We really got to know people, so when we experienced a loss, it was a huge loss, and it was stressful. But the kids were such fighters. It meant so much to me to be a part of returning children to health, young people who still had their whole lives ahead of them—or in the terminal cases, helping them through a difficult illness with affection and respect. There's a layer in pediatrics that's not present in adult nursing or adult medicine. I think it has a lot to do with the fact that no one tells kids how they're supposed to be sick. They don't really know about the social construction of illness. So when they're sick—and for five years I dealt with some very sick kids—I was amazed that they never wallowed in self-pity. Ever. They just went about their day. It was very compelling to me that in the midst of their chemotherapy and throwing up from the side effects they'd be saying 'Are we almost done yet? I really want to go to the playroom.'"

"What about the parents?"

"They were the ones you had to peel off the ceiling. And that's one of the things I loved about pediatric nursing: that the kid is the centerpiece but you're really taking care of the whole family. You have to tailor your caring and the way you're delivering your nursing to many different family members with many different needs. It was a wonderful balance for me, where I could act like a kid and do goofy knock-knock jokes all day, and then go become an adult when I talked with their mom and dad."

"When I was a physician," Michael said, "cancer was an even bigger mystery than it is today. There was no real way to treat it. The survival rate was negligible. There's still so much about that terrible disease that we don't understand, but at least there have been some breakthroughs. It must be thrilling to know that you have the power now to cure certain cases."

"Yes! So many times, at a party someone would ask, 'what do you do?' When I said 'I'm a pediatric oncology nurse,' they'd just want to walk away. I spent a lot of time telling people, 'it's actually a lot more hopeful than you think.' Granted, bone tumors and brain tumors don't do so well. But a good number of leukemia cases are actually cured, and that's a lot of what we saw in oncology."

Michael hesitated, as if weighing his next words carefully. "I would imagine that, even loving nursing as much as you did, a specialty like oncology must have been . . . very difficult at times."

"It was. I worked at a very renowned center. Kids who couldn't be cured with traditional chemo came from all over the country and the world to have last-chance treatments, and they were expecting miracles from us. That didn't happen very often. That was really hard. And it's never easy when you—" She broke off suddenly, her stomach seizing as the memory came crashing back, and with it all the horror and stress of everything that followed.

She felt him studying her as she picked at the carpet, struggling desperately to reassemble her thoughts. At length, he said, "I've heard a saying: 'Nurses eat their young.' That older nurses make it difficult for younger ones, who really have to earn their stripes. Is that true?"

"There is that perception," she agreed. "I don't know why. I never once encountered that issue, nor have any of the people I know. There was no hazing when I first started. I was never bullied. I was surrounded by extremely supportive and professional people. I had a network of four nurses I had graduated with, and we became very close friends. We all worked weird swing shifts, so we'd get together at bizarre hours, meet for drinks at midnight or for dinner at 9:30 PM before someone started the night shift at 11:00. We helped each other cope. And we loved to ski."

"To ski?"

"We used to make our schedules fit with each other's and get season passes to a mountain resort close to us in Seattle. We spent a lot of our days off skiing."

"That sounds like a great outlet."

"It was—a place I could go to get away from the stress and tension and just let loose, so that I was clear-headed and raring to go when I got back to work."

He smiled. "I'll bet you were a wonderful nurse."

"Well, I don't know how wonderful I was, but I always tried to do whatever I could to make the children's experience in the hospital a little more pleasant, to help them understand and be okay with their diagnosis, tolerant of their treatment, and actually come up smiling. I used to ask what their favorite color was and buy them a bright knit cap or new do-rag in that color to cover their bald heads—that often cheered them up. But some of the children were very introverted and had a lot of trouble opening up and responding."

"Such as?"

"I remember one patient—a darling five-year-old girl with leukemia. She was a Native American from Alaska who spoke very little English. She was shy, in pain, and traumatized, and for weeks she would hardly look at me. I tried to explain to her about the Make-A-Wish Foundation—they grant wishes for kids who've been diagnosed with a life-threatening illness, whether their prognosis is hopeful or terminal—but she didn't understand. I brought in a translator, I bought her toys and a hat and a doll, but she still wouldn't come out of her shell and she wasn't responding to treatment; she was going downhill. I couldn't think of what else to do.

"Then I thought: maybe she could *draw* what she's thinking. So I brought in a pad of paper and some crayons and left them with her. When I came back, she'd drawn a picture of a dog. I called back the interpreter and discovered that the family had a dog back home that she missed terribly. So I pulled some strings and talked to the right people, and by the end of the week, the Make-A-Wish Foundation delivered her dog to the hospital. When we wheeled the little girl outside and she saw that animal, her face lit up with such a big, toothy grin—I'll never forget it. Every afternoon for a week, she got to spend some time outside with her dog. She rallied after that, and she beat the leukemia."

"What a wonderful story," Michael said. "That hospital—and those children—were very lucky to have you as their nurse." He took one of her hands in his and kissed it. "How long did you work there?"

"Five years." Tension filled her. Nicole knew what he'd ask next; waited for it; it was inevitable.

"And after that? You said you live in California."

"Yes. I left Seattle when . . . I left nursing."

"Why did you leave?"

Nicole felt the pressure building up in her chest; her throat felt as if it were closing, and perspiration broke out with sudden force on her brow. She couldn't go there, couldn't bear dredging all that up again. Leaping to her feet, she walked away, stopping by the grand piano several yards across the room. She felt Michael's eyes on her from behind. When he spoke, there was compassion in his voice.

"I realize this is something you don't like to talk about. If anyone can understand what that's like, I do, believe me.

"I can't go back to nursing, Michael."

"Are you happy with the work you're doing now?"

"No," Nicole said, "but—"

"That story you told me, about the Native Alaskan girl and her dog—I think that's far more emblematic of who you are than the boy you couldn't save. When you talked about nursing just now and what you loved about it, there was an excitement in your voice and eyes that came from the depths of your soul. Nursing is what you are meant to do. Go back to it. You are so compassionate and giving. You have skills that can help so many people and make a difference in so many lives. You have to forgive yourself, Nicole. Don't let one mistake alter the entire direction of your life."

Nicole mulled over his words, knowing deep down that he was right. "I could say the same thing to you."

"You could, and you'd be right—except for two tiny details. One: the things I did are so much worse than what you did, they're not even in the same hemisphere. And two: you're a human being. You can learn from your mistakes, and change. You can go back to nursing and be more aware and vigilant. I can never go back. I can't trust myself to always do the right thing. I am what I am, and always will be."

"You're a human being to me, Michael, in all the ways that matter."

"Oh my love," he said, kissing her, "how I wish that were true."

CHAPTER *18*

*T*HEY TALKED FAR INTO THE NIGHT, peppering each other with questions, each one fascinated by the life experiences and perspectives of the other on a multitude of subjects.

"It boggles my mind to think of all the changes you've seen in the world since you were born," Nicole said, as they stood before the living room windows looking out at the night sky, which was brilliantly lit by stars.

"It has been a fascinating journey," Michael admitted, wrapping his arms around her. "But the changes came slowly. When I first moved here, we still got about by train, carriage, and horseback. The biggest and fastest changes have come in the last hundred years, but I've seen a lot of them from afar."

"Have you ever flown on a plane?"

"I hired a pilot a few times to take me up in a private plane. It's spectacular, viewing the world from above, and such a feeling of freedom. I wish I could travel farther and more often, but I don't like the idea of a commercial jet. Too many people in one enclosed space."

"I think you underestimate yourself," Nicole said. "What do you think about computers? Cars? Movies? Antibiotics?"

"All wonderful advances. Others have taken my breath away. Like radio and television and space travel. We take it for granted now, but if you had told me 150 years ago that someday we'd be able to transmit sound and pictures over the airwaves and fly to the moon, I would have said you were mad. I think people have forgotten how to marvel."

"I think we have."

"TV and the Internet have changed everything for me. I no longer feel isolated. I'm linked in to the rest of the planet. I can keep up with world news and every change without ever leaving my little fiefdom here."

Nicole smiled. "Do you know that I haven't once thought about television, or missed it, since I got here?"

He kissed her. "Neither have I."

Later, Michael told her the story of how he met Charles Dickens.

"In the summer of 1858, Dickens undertook his first series of public readings in London for pay. He was a tireless and enthusiastic public speaker but worked at a grueling pace, sometimes giving both a matinee and an evening performance seven days a week. I treated him for exhaustion and a sore throat, and he was so grateful, he saw me every time he was in London thereafter and signed two books for me."

"Did you like him?"

"Very much. He was a great talent, a philanthropist, and a passionate abolitionist. He believed in ghosts, was fascinated by the paranormal, and I think some of his ideals and work ethic rubbed off on me."

They talked more about Nicole's childhood and her family. She told him about her father, a hard-working and brilliant scientist who used to enthrall her with his nightly bedtime stories. Nicole shared how close she was with her mother, a feisty, independent soul who had always been supportive of her activities and goals, and was still her go-to person when she needed advice. She talked about her older sister, Jessica, a busy and successful architect who lived in Seattle, and her sister's two young daughters, whom Nicole adored.

"I used to spend a lot of time with the girls every week when I lived up there," Nicole said nostalgically. "Ever since they were babies, I've been taking them shopping and sledding and to the beach and the park and the movies. Whenever I came over, they'd always squeal and come running. 'Aunt Nicole! Will you read me a story?' Lenora would cry. Or 'Aunt Nicole, will you build a tent with us?' One time we made a hundred silver paper stars and hung them from their bedroom ceiling. One year, I helped coach Devon's soccer team. It was great fun."

"You must miss them."

"I do. I visit whenever I can. But . . . it's not often enough. I miss Seattle, too. I lived in a great house there with my best friends. They keep asking me to come back. We had a big garden, and they insist I'm the only one who took care of it right." She sighed.

"Have you ever asked yourself why you left Seattle?"

"I told you: it's because I left nursing. Because it was too hard to be around my friends who were always talking about what was going on at the hospital."

He looked at her. "I think, deep down, you were punishing yourself."

"What do you mean?"

"You felt you'd done a terrible thing and didn't deserve to be happy. So you left behind everything that had meaning for you: the city you loved, your work, your friends, your family, your skis, even your piano. And every day that you've been away from them is part of the penance you think you deserve."

Nicole took that in with an uncertain shrug, and said nothing.

Michael asked about the man Nicole had dated, the relationship she said had not worked out.

"We were together for four years while I was working at the hospital," Nicole explained. "It was a mutual parting. He was a good man. For a while we thought we loved each other, but something was missing." *Now that I've met you*, she thought, *I know what was missing. I know what true love is.*

They talked about the early years when Michael homesteaded his property, and how difficult it had been to build his first log cabin on his own and put up a barn. They pulled out the journals he'd kept over past 150 years and spent hours reading sections aloud to each other. Many of the entries were humorous, others were deeply heartfelt, and they brought back dozens of memories that Michael had long since forgotten.

They talked on until the first rays of the morning sun began to light the sky. They talked about everything except the future, a subject Nicole was burning to broach, but she still didn't have the nerve. As dawn broke, she found that she could barely keep her eyes open.

"This whole nocturnal thing is hard on a human," Nicole said, yawning, as they climbed into Michael's bed. "Don't you ever get tired?"

"I am a little sleepy now," he admitted, pulling her into his arms.

Nicole closed her eyes, burying her face in his shoulder. "How are you holding up in other ways?"

"Other ways?"

"You know. With the whole *I shouldn't drink her blood* thing."

"Oh, that. I'm determined it won't happen again," he said firmly. As if to prove his resolve, he lifted her curtain of hair and planted a kiss at the side of her throat, then settled back on his pillow.

"I admire your restraint, but I have to admit . . . I wouldn't mind if you bit me again."

"You wouldn't mind?"

"No."

"Well, I would. Don't tempt me, Nicole. I told you, it's dangerous. Once was enough."

His eyes flashed darkly as he spoke, sending an unexpected shiver of alarm through her.

"Okay," she said, chastened, trying to hide both her disappointment and her fear, "but is it . . . difficult for you when we're lying so close together like this?"

"Like what?" he asked. His hand slid down past her collar bone to stroke her naked breast with infinite slowness, a touch that made her shiver with delight. "Like this?"

"Yes. Like . . . that."

"It is exquisite torment," he whispered huskily. Then he rolled on top of her and brought his mouth to hers.

NICOLE AWAKENED HOURS LATER to a light-filled bedroom. Michael was lying naked beside her, gazing at her from the next pillow with affection, holding a perfect red rose and a small spray of white orchids.

"Hello," he said softly, laying the red rose on the pillow beside her and reaching out to tenderly tuck the delicate orchid blossoms behind her ear.

"Hello back." Her first thought was that she'd never awakened to find him beside her before, and it made her smile. Her second thought was the memory of her eager wantonness under his hands in this very bed, just . . . how many hours before? She stretched and glanced at the bedside clock over his shoulder. It was nearly one o'clock in the afternoon. "That was a good sleep." Picking up the rose, she inhaled its fragrance. "Mmm. What a beautiful rose. And thank you for the orchids." Remembering what he'd told her before about his limited need for rest, she asked, "How long have you been awake?"

"Awhile."

Damn, she thought. *I wish I didn't have to sleep at all. Every minute with you is so special, I hate to miss any of it.* It dawned on her that this was probably their last day, and a melancholy washed over her.

Aloud, she asked tentatively, "Has the highway been cleared yet?"

"No. Still piled high with snow."

"Good." She said it with such enthusiasm that they both laughed.

"Not too eager to get back to work, I see," Michael observed.

"Not so much," Nicole replied. *Not so much about work,* she thought. *I just don't want to leave you.* How *could* she leave him? She loved him with all her heart—she burned to tell him so. "What have you been doing, besides picking flowers?"

"I fed the horses, watered the garden, and worked awhile in my study." As he spoke, with one hand he sensuously grazed the naked curve of her back, causing tremors to cascade through her.

"Considering the outside temperature," she replied, "I hope you didn't do all of those activities naked."

"I assure you, I was fully dressed," he returned softly. "One wouldn't want to shock the horses or frighten the neighbors."

"But you're naked now."

"All the better to watch you sleep."

Nicole laughed, her heart pounding. "That doesn't sound very exciting."

"Oh, but it is, my love." The deep tenor of his voice seemed to penetrate her skin and ripple like a caress through her veins and nerves, as luscious as a warm bath. "It's a rare and wonderful thing to have a beautiful woman in my bed. I admit, I've spent the last two hours very happily just lying here looking at you."

His hand now swept up to tenderly caress the vulnerable flesh of her throat, before he lowered his head to kiss her.

The kiss was long, hard, and rapturous, and sometime during the length of it he whispered against her lips, "I love you,

Nicole. I'm deeply, deeply in love with you. I have imagined you so many thousands of times, but the dream never came close to the reality of you."

"I love you, too, Michael," she whispered, her heart soaring with wonder and joy.

Blood slapped in hot gushes through Nicole's heart. As they made love, their gazes found each other, and the meeting was as sweet and rapturous as their physical union. Nicole felt as if an essential part of herself was being unlocked, as though they were two distinct beings who had melded one with the other, to form another, greater self.

As their passion soared, Nicole saw red flames burning in the blue of Michael's eyes, and gave a little gasp. His face and fangs revealed that other desperate longing he could no longer hide. Her pulse raced in anticipation and alarm, desperately wanting it yet fearing it. Would he bite her again?

Some deep inner strength seemed to take hold of him, taming the impulse. The fangs receded and he brought his mouth to hers in another deep, searing kiss. His lips and tongue felt hot against her own. In an urgent communion they shared sweet liquids and scorching breaths. It was like drinking fire; it was like hurtling through sizzling nectar; it was like being swept away by a shooting star into a blissful oblivion.

THEY DECIDED TO WALK TO THE LAKE.

It was cloudy and overcast as Michael drove down the back side of his hill and parked outside the barn, where his road ended. From there, they were obliged to strap on snowshoes and begin the quarter-mile trek over rugged backcountry terrain which was buried in deep snow.

"I'll go first and make a path," Michael insisted. His snow-shoes sank a good twelve inches into the soft snow with every step, and he took care to tamp it down firmly to make it easier for Nicole to follow. Even walking in his footsteps, he knew, would require a great deal more energy for her than it did for him. As he glanced back, Nicole did seem out of breath, so he kept conversation to a minimum.

It was very cold. The clouds hung low on the mountains around them, completely obscuring the sun, but visibility was good in the protected valley where they walked. The world was a winter wonderland, the pine trees heavily draped in white, the slender, naked branches of the aspens reaching for the sky. Some areas, where the wind had blown hard, were barren, revealing numerous rocky outcroppings and dark expanses of dead under-brush beneath the trees. After a while they came to the frozen stream and walked along its snow-covered banks until it opened up onto the gentle crest above the small frozen lake.

They stopped at the edge of the ridge beside a smooth, giant boulder as big as a henhouse, at the base of some giant pines. Sitting down side by side on a narrow ledge cut into the side of the rock, Michael wrapped an arm around Nicole's shoulders, smiling as he watched her drink in the view. Her cheeks were a very becoming shade of pink in the frosty air, matching her lips, which were curved in a radiant smile.

"It's lovely," Nicole murmured.

"In every season it looks different, but equally beautiful."

"What's it like here in spring?" she asked.

"The spring? I love the spring," he said, resting his cheek against the waving wonder of her red-gold hair. "It's so crisp and definite. Everything is green. The sky and the lake are a brilliant, sparkling blue. The meadows are lush, the wildlife comes out, and you see golden eagles swooping and soaring above. The streams are running, the clouds are white and puffy, and the air is so clean you could cut it with a knife."

"And summer?"

"The same. It's still cold. We're so high up, it never really gets hot. But it's green and more humid. The mosquitoes come out. They're fierce and huge, as big as hummingbirds."

Nicole laughed, a delightful sound that he felt ripple through his body. "And the fall?"

"The fall is like the spring: gorgeous, idyllic. Herds of deer and elk come down from the mountains into the valley. The elk make a sound that's like a bugle with the last note a screech; you can hear it for miles. All those groves of barren aspens that you see—they're covered in tissue-thin, tear-shaped leaves that turn a brilliant golden yellow. They shimmer in the faintest breeze, undulating up and down the hillsides with a rustling sigh. People call it Colorado gold."

"Oh . . . it sounds spectacular."

"It is."

This was the moment, he thought, the perfect moment to bring up the subject he'd been wrestling with over the past twenty-four hours. He hadn't dared to broach it before this, still wasn't sure if it was even possible. Would a woman like Nicole, with so much to offer and her entire life ahead of her, want to spend her life sequestered in these remote Colorado mountains with a being like him? He doubted it. He didn't believe it was right for her. But she seemed to love it here. She'd said she loved him. His own love for her was so powerful, he'd been able to hold his primal instincts in check. Perhaps, he thought, there was a chance, a slight chance, that she'd consider it and that it could work.

He should ask her now.

He was about to speak when he heard a sudden, faint rustling behind them and tensed, the hair rising on the back of his neck. "What was that?"

"What was what?" Nicole asked.

He paused, listening hard, but the sound was gone. "I thought I heard something. Wait here."

Michael shifted off the rocky shelf and padded quietly through the snow, past the giant rock toward a nearby stand of trees. Something was watching them; he sensed it. He had a terrible feeling and guessed what it might be. But where was it hiding?

He heard it again—but now it was behind him. He whirled around to see a tawny flash of movement springing up from beside the boulder. Nicole wasn't even aware of its presence behind her, but to his horror the deadly creature, huge paws extended, was hurtling directly at the back of her neck.

CHAPTER 19

*M*ICHAEL VAULTED TOWARD NICOLE in a flash, colliding with the cougar before it touched her. Nicole's scream and a feral snarl rent the air as Michael wrestled with the writhing beast, its teeth and claws tearing through his garments and his flesh. In seconds, his hands sought and found the animal's neck, and with one sharp, powerful twist he both felt and heard its spine snap, then silence as the creature dropped to the snow at his feet. It lay unmoving, mouth partly open, fangs protruding, all long legs and sharp claws, its ocher fur a stark contrast against the white snow.

Nicole stared mutely at the dead beast, as if too stunned and horrified for words.

Michael embraced her, relieved to see that she hadn't suffered a scratch. "It must have been hiding behind the rock, watching us."

"Is it a mountain lion?"

"A female. They're stealthy. The consummate predator. It was flying straight for your neck. One more second, one bite, and you would have been dead."

"Oh my God. Thank you," she whispered vehemently, hugging him tightly and kissing his cheek. She seemed to be about to say more when she tensed suddenly, as if in response to something over his shoulder. "Michael!" she screamed in terror.

Michael spun. To his astonishment, another mountain lion, bigger than the first, was flinging itself into the air at him, just inches away from contact. A roar of fury ripped from Michael's throat as he deflected the animal's attack with blinding speed. The cougar lithely flipped to its feet in the snow and instantly leaped up again, latching onto Michael's body with grinding claws and sinking its teeth into Michael's shoulder, pulling intently as if to drag him off.

Nicole screamed and shrank back. A burning rage spread through Michael's body as he struggled against the vicious, thrashing beast. Michael felt his eyes blazing to life like hot beacons as he dug his fangs into the cougar's fur-covered flesh. The animal screeched and fought back with ferocious power and agility, the angry stab of its own fangs and nails ripping at Michael's flesh and shredding his clothes.

Blood spurted everywhere. Michael felt light-headed, odd, unable to recognize himself in the welter of fury and emotion that grew like a torrent inside him. There was nothing but him and the beast, two wild animals biting and clawing their way to the death. But he wasn't going to die. He would defend himself to the end.

At last it was over. The huge beast lay in a bloody heap at his feet beside the first. Michael stood over them both, breathing hard, his eyes still burning, vaguely aware that some kind of fabric was hanging half off of him. He felt blood pouring down his arm. He heard screaming—a sound—*Michael!* What did it mean? From the corner of his eye, he glimpsed the source of the sound—a red-haired female in dark clothing with luminescent green eyes. It was looking his way in terror. A human, and clearly the cougars' intended prey.

Michael slowly turned and fixed her with his gaze. His pulse pounded. His mouth watered. His jaw ached.

The cougars were dead, no longer a threat.

She was *his* now, all his, and he would have her.

Michael covered the distance between them in a millisecond, hurling her to the ground as he ripped the scarf from her neck to expose her throat. Again, he heard that inexplicable sound—*Michael!*—but ignored it.

Pinning her with his body, he sank his teeth into the soft white flesh of her neck. She screamed and writhed beneath him, fighting him just as the cougar had but without claws or fangs and with only a tenth of its strength. Weak, weak humans. Such easy prey. His eyes closed. Her blood flowed into his mouth. The ecstasy cascaded through him. Every nerve in his body seemed to be on fire. All senses slept except the exquisite rapture of the taste and smell of her blood. He wanted more; he required it to sate his brutal hunger; he needed it to live. He would not, could not stop.

From somewhere, it seemed to be leagues away, a new sound hovered at the edge of his consciousness. Like a strangled cry.

The creature was still pushing pathetically against his chest. Vaguely, through layers of mind-clouded obscurity, he sensed that there was something he was supposed to do, some concern he was supposed to be aware of. But what? What could be so important that it interfered with his need to *eat*, to consume this delectable substance, the very essence of his survival?

He heard it again: a small moan. What was it? Was something watching him? A growl built up within his chest. This prize was his, his alone, he deserved it, and he wouldn't share it with anyone.

Irritated, he drew his mouth away, licked his lips, and opened his eyes. Beneath him, he saw the pale flesh of his trembling victim. Her throat was pierced and bleeding, her mouth was slightly open, and her green eyes were wet and wide with panic. He frowned, his mind whirling with sudden confusion. Something felt wrong. Very wrong. And then, as if descending from a cloud height, a great horror washed over him as he knew.

Nicole.

NICOLE CRIED OUT, her heart pounding. She'd stood frozen in terror moments ago while Michael fought and killed the second, larger mountain lion. She'd screamed when she saw what the beast had done to him—yet he hadn't seemed to be aware of his injuries.

He'd turned to her with the look of a wild animal himself, his eyes blazing crimson, as if infused with a bucket of blood—a look that had filled her with panic. Then he'd pounced on her, ignoring her pleas to stop, drinking her blood like some angry, feral Thing.

Now his red eyes became blue again as the Michael she knew and loved returned with the swiftness of a lightbulb snapping on. He stared down at her, aghast.

"Oh my God. Nicole. What have I done?"

Tears ran down her cheeks and she couldn't speak.

"I'm so sorry, my darling. Forgive me. I don't know what happened. I didn't mean to . . ."

Nicole scurried out from under him and stood, fighting a wave of dizziness.

Guilt, disappointment, and self-loathing hung in Michael's gaze as he slowly staggered to his feet, grimacing in pain. "I'm sorry," he said again.

Nicole steadied herself and went to dry her eyes, when she realized with horror that her gloves and clothes were covered with blood. *Whose blood?* She stared at Michael. All concern for herself was instantly forgotten as she took in the condition of the man before her.

Michael's bloody coat, shirt, and pants were hanging off of him in tatters, as was much of his exposed flesh. His right arm and shoulder were one enormous, gaping wound that was bleeding profusely. Scratches, punctures, and torn, bleeding flesh were everywhere—on his arms, legs, chest, back, and neck, and his face was deathly pale. His body rained blood onto the snow, so much blood that she didn't see how he could still be standing, much less alive.

"Michael!" Nicole cried, fresh tears welling in her eyes. As she watched in dismay, Michael teetered a bit, then slowly sank again to his knees. She dropped down beside him in the snow, afraid to touch him lest she hurt him. "My God, you're bleeding everywhere."

"I'll make it stop."

He bent his head and began to lick the scratches and bites on his arms, but Nicole could see that it was useless. There were far too many wounds. He might be able to cure the small ones, but the larger ones, especially the shoulder wound, were so severe that she doubted they could be healed by vampire saliva, even if he *could* reach them with his tongue—which in many cases was impossible.

With alarm, she recalled what he'd told her: *even a vampire can bleed to death.* "Lie down," she said urgently, "let me help you."

"No," he ordered. "Go back to the house. You shouldn't . . . be anywhere near me."

"Don't be ridiculous. I'm not leaving you. You're losing blood too fast. Lie down!"

With reluctant obedience, Michael stretched out in the snow, still licking the wounds he could reach, but he was fast losing strength along with his blood. Working quickly, Nicole pushed the shredded flesh of his arm back into place and held it there. He groaned in agony.

"It hurts, I know, I'm sorry," she said compassionately. "I'm going to pack the wound now." She ripped pieces of the tattered lining from his coat and draped them over the wound, exerting pressure to try to stem some of the bleeding.

"You can . . . use—" he began.

"Snow, I know," she said, already ahead of him. Scooping up handfuls of snow, she packed it over and around the entire wounded area to keep it cold and decrease the flow of blood. She then found her scarf and bound his arm and shoulder with it, holding the snow in place.

He lay back, too fatigued now to continue his own healing technique. She wrapped and tied strips of cloth over the worst of his many other lacerations.

"Your shoulder needs stitches," she told him as she worked, "but since we're still snowbound, should I go back and call 911 to send in a Medivac unit?"

"No. No hospitals. Get me back to the barn."

"The barn?"

"It's closer than the house. You'll have to sew me up. Use the medical supplies for my horses."

"Okay. Can you walk?" She tried to help him to his feet, but he got halfway up and then sank to his knees again.

She took his pulse. It was rapid, weak, and thready. *Damn,* she thought, deeply worried. He was never going to make it back to the barn. The rough terrain and snow cover made driving impossible.

With some difficulty, Nicole dragged him to the nearby boulder and propped him against it in a sitting position. "Don't move. I'll go back and get one of the horses," she instructed, wondering even as she said it if she was out of her mind.

"You don't . . . have to do this," he managed weakly, his eyes still haunted by guilt.

"Stop talking. Save your strength."

He grabbed her wrist. "I'm sorry . . . *so sorry* . . . about what I did."

"I know."

"Can you ever forgive me?"

Could she? The memory of his attack made Nicole tremble anew, reminding her that Michael *did* have a monster inside him—a monster who had truly terrified her. It was the part of his makeup he'd warned her about and despised. And yet, it was a part that had saved their lives today. She understood what had happened: it was an instinctive reaction, a mistake deeply regretted. He had come to himself in time and hadn't done her any irreparable harm.

"I already have forgiven you," she said with deep feeling. "That wasn't you—it was the beast you became to fight the cougars. It's over now and I'm all right. Just hang in there. I'll be back as soon as I can."

With an attempt at a smile, he added, "Stay calm. Horses smell fear. I'll be fine." Then he passed out.

He'll be fine, Nicole repeated to herself, running as fast as she could in the awkward snowshoes. *He'll be fine.* It became her mantra as she put one foot in front of the other, using the path they'd trampled on their way down to the lake. She loved him. He'd just saved her life—*again*. He was a good man who deserved to live. She was going to make sure he did.

It seemed to take forever to reach the barn. Nicole arrived gasping for breath and dying of thirst. Under the portico, she ripped off the snowshoes and pulled on the barn door. To her dismay it was half frozen. She had to try several times, yanking with all her might, before the huge door finally slid open.

Nicole raced into the barn. Posse and Pockets were looking at her over their stall doors. Nicole made a beeline for Pockets' stall, then stopped in her tracks. Now that she was here, the reality of what she was attempting to do began to sink in. She'd only ridden a horse once, the afternoon before. *Once.* And that had been with Michael close at hand—*Michael*, who could talk to a horse with his mind. This horse was used to being ridden by a vampire. How would it respond to a greenhorn who didn't speak Horse?

Michael's parting words rang in her mind: *Stay calm. Horses smell fear.*

She didn't have much time; she had to get Michael back here fast so she could stitch him up. Still, she took a moment to steady her breath and try to collect herself, so as not to spook the animal. She quenched her thirst by drinking deeply from the wash hose. She didn't know a thing about saddles. She'd have to ride bareback, the way Michael had taught her. She grabbed Pockets' woven leather bridle from the hook outside her stall and opened the stall door. The horse stepped back as Nicole entered.

"Hi, Pockets," she said quietly, fighting back her fear as she approached. "Michael sent me. He needs your help. Let's go for a little ride."

The horse stared at Nicole with both curiosity and fear, seeming to realize that there was a problem. Pockets' nostrils flared as if she was smelling the air. Then she thrust her head out and snuggled her nose against Nicole's blood-stained gloves and coat. Did the horse know it was Michael's blood?

Pockets let out a low whinny and dropped her head, putting her nose into the bridle as Nicole slipped it over her head. "There's a good girl," Nicole said softly. She quickly removed Pockets' blanket and glanced about the stall, wondering how, without stirrups, she was going to climb on. Spying a bale of straw stacked by the stall's back wall, Nicole took the reins in her hands and tried to lead the horse to it. Pockets resisted, pulling in the opposite direction, straining to head out of the stall.

"I can't fly onto your back like your master," Nicole insisted, annoyed, as she tugged at the reins. "I need a boost. Come here."

Reluctantly, the horse moved in the requested direction. Nicole stepped up onto the bale of straw, but the horse was anxious to go, shuffling her feet restlessly back and forth. It was like trying to climb onto the back of a moving target.

"Stay still," Nicole commanded. Suddenly she remembered what Michael had told her about ground tying—it was like telling a dog to stay. Nicole dropped the reins to the ground. Instantly, Pockets stopped and stood calmly, as if anchored to the spot. *Nice.* Nicole slipped her leg over the horse's back and climbed aboard, picking up the reins again.

"Walk," Nicole said aloud, gently nudging the horse with her legs the way Michael had taught her—but Pockets already knew what she was supposed to do. Immediately, the horse ambled out of the stall and through the open barn door, then instinctively turned in the direction she'd no doubt taken thousands of times before, following the path through the snow that Nicole and Michael had made.

Nicole's heart hammered with anxiety as she fought to stay upright on the horse, holding on with her thighs. It only took three or four minutes to cover the ground back to where Michael was lying immobile against the boulder in the blood-drenched snow, the dead mountain lions a few feet away. As they approached, the horse tensed in fear, her head shooting up and her nostrils flaring. Nicole remembered Michael had said the mountain lion was the horse's most deadly enemy other than man.

"It's okay, girl." Nicole soothingly stroked the side of her head. "Those beasts are dead. They can't hurt you."

The horse's gaze turned toward her master, and her fear seemed to dissipate. She quickened her pace and trotted up to him, lowering her head to nudge him gently with her nose. Nicole slipped off the horse's back and dropped to the ground, letting the reins fall from her hand so that Pockets wouldn't move.

Nicole crouched down at Michael's side. At the horse's gentle prodding, Michael came to and opened his eyes. "I brought Pockets," Nicole said rather unnecessarily, since Michael was already lifting one hand and stroking the horse's face.

"Good . . . girl," he said. Nicole wasn't sure if he meant her or the horse, but it didn't matter; at least he was coherent. He looked into the horse's eyes and they seemed to be silently, briefly communicating. Pockets remained calm as Nicole helped Michael up. Using the boulder for support, they both climbed onto the horse's back. Michael slumped forward over Pockets' neck, Nicole steadying him with one hand as they rode back.

When they reached the barn, Nicole half-carried, half-dragged Michael onto a pile of hay bales, spreading out clean towels beneath him that she found in a trunk. He lay conscious but unmoving. The horse stood by quietly while Nicole covered Michael with a horse blanket to keep him warm. Removing her gloves, she methodically grabbed bottles of Betadine and rubbing alcohol from the medical supply cabinet in the tack room, along with sterile dressings, cotton wool, a roll of adhesive bandaging material, scissors, antibiotic spray, a book of matches, and a large, curved sewing needle.

Returning to Michael's side with the supplies in a bucket, she said, "I can't find any surgical thread."

"Horsehair," Michael said.

"What?"

"Pull a few hairs out of her tail. Old school. Still effective."

It was a method she'd never heard of. Nicole secured the horsehairs and set to work, unwrapping and cleaning off the gaping wound on his arm and shoulder, then examining it. The snow had done the trick: the bleeding had stopped. "This wound is deep. It really should be stitched by a surgeon."

"No need." His eyes met hers and gently twinkled, despite his obvious pain. "I have a nurse."

He had more confidence in her than she had, Nicole thought. "I don't suppose you have any anesthetic?" she asked quietly.

"No. Just . . . do it."

Nicole sterilized the wound and needle, then sat close beside him and began to stitch.

He inhaled sharply and briefly closed his eyes. With great effort, in between quick breaths, he said, "Horsehair won't bear any . . . great amount of tension . . . but you can place the sutures closer together than . . . other suture material . . . without danger of strangulation of the . . . skin margins. This . . . assures quite satisfactory results and . . . only a reef or granny knot is required . . . being smaller than an . . . ordinary surgical tie."

"Thank you, doctor," Nicole said with a little smile, aware that he was talking to help block out the pain—but her smile fled when she saw how weak he was becoming.

As Nicole stitched diligently, she felt Michael's eyes on her, assessing her progress with apparent satisfaction.

"If I'm ever injured again, nurse, remind me to . . . ask for you."

"You might change your mind when you get my bill," she retorted, hoping her worry didn't sound in her voice.

As Nicole finished tying the last knot and was about to reach for a bandage, he said, "Wait. Let me . . ." He struggled to sit up. She understood his intention. With one hand on his back, she helped him lean forward so he could apply his tongue to the skin around the injury. Now that the gaping wound had been sutured, his saliva could help heal the surface gap. What he touched slowly mended, but he could only reach a small part of it.

Nicole offered to let him lick her fingers so she could spread his saliva across the rest of the sutured wound, but Michael shook his head and lay back again, saying, "It has to come straight from my tongue, and it can only penetrate so far. The deeper tissue will take longer to heal."

Nicole bandaged his shoulder, then cleaned and treated his smaller wounds. He lay shivering beneath the blanket now, exhausted. His face looked gray and he was breathing in quick, shallow gasps.

Nicole took his pulse. It was still rapid and weak. His skin was clammy and even colder than usual. The symptoms were unmistakable, she thought with alarm. She'd stopped the bleeding, but it wasn't enough. He'd lost too much blood. She'd never imagined that a vampire could go into circulatory shock, and yet he was.

"Michael, you need a transfusion. You have all that blood at your house. I could get it and—"

"It's not my type. That blood is just to consume."

"You're in shock. Vampire or no, you could die from this. If I was at a hospital, I'd have other resources. There must be something I can do to help you."

"The only thing—" He broke off, shaking his head.

"What? What can I do?"

"Nothing. Forget it."

"What?"

Finally, reluctantly, he said, "The blood I just took from you has probably gotten me this far. If I drink more fresh blood, it will help me to . . . to regain my strength and speed my healing."

"Drink more fresh blood?" she repeated, grasping his meaning. The blood in his refrigerator was far from fresh; it had to be many days or weeks old. To heal, she realized, he would have to drink *her* blood again.

The very idea, which had once become appealing, was now frightening. He'd just drunk her blood like a wild animal in heat. Was it safe to give more? Could she trust him to stop? She knew, if she did this, she might die—but she didn't care. Pulling back the cuff of her jacket, she offered her bared wrist up to his mouth.

"Take it. Take my blood."

"No," he said emphatically. "I'd rather die than hurt you again."

"You won't hurt me."

"I took so much before," he insisted. "I can't—"

"You didn't take that much. I'm fine. My body is replacing it as we speak."

"No," he said again, turning his head away.

"I won't let you die!" Nicole grabbed the scissors and repressed a wince as she incised a sharp line across her wrist. Her blood streamed out, and she held her dripping wrist to his lips. *"Drink,"* she ordered, gazing meaningfully into his eyes.

Michael lost all will to resist. He slowly lapped up the fresh blood she offered. As he slowly gained strength, he grabbed her wrist and pressed it more firmly against his mouth, holding it there while he feasted.

CHAPTER *20*

THE SCENT OF APPLE invaded Nicole's senses. She felt cold and groggy. Opening her eyes, she found herself lying on a bale of straw. The last thing she recalled was Michael drinking her blood.

Since she was still alive, it meant he'd had the self-control to stop from taking too much. Nicole heaved a relieved and satisfied smile. Michael was sitting beside her, gently stroking her head and holding a slice of apple to her mouth. Love lit her heart at the sight of him.

"Eat, Sleeping Beauty," he murmured.

"No, please, not another apple," Nicole complained wearily.

He scooped his arm under her and gently lifted her to a sitting position. "You need to get your blood sugar up. Eat it."

With a sigh, Nicole accepted the apple and bit into it. The cut on her wrist, she noticed, was healed.

251

"How do you feel? Are you dizzy?" he asked.

"A little. *You* look a lot better," she observed with relief as she chewed. Color had returned to Michael's face and his energy level seemed to be back to normal. Through the tattered remnants of his clothes, she could see that most of his smaller wounds and scratches had healed.

"The restorative powers of human blood." He smiled at her with gratitude. "Thank you for everything you did. That took a lot of guts."

She retrieved another apple slice from his hand and ate it. "I was happy to save the life of the man who had just saved mine."

He frowned, a haunted look returning to his eyes. "Well. You certainly proved something today."

"What did I prove?"

"That you're no longer afraid of blood—giving it or working around it. I was bleeding like a stuck pig and you never hesitated. You saw what needed to be done and you did it."

Nicole took that in with a silent, surprised nod.

"I'm proud of you. You should be proud of yourself."

"Thank you." Nicole started to stand, but her knees felt wobbly and she sat down again.

"We'd better get back. You need to get some liquids in you."

Nicole took another long drink from the wash hose, then Michael offered her his arm and they returned to the truck. It was still overcast and the sun hung low in the sky. They drove back to the house in silence as Nicole finished off the rest of the apple, her head beginning to feel less woozy.

Just as the truck crested the rise of the hill, a sound rent the air: the distant roar of another truck engine.

Nicole's breath caught in her throat and her heart lurched in dismay. On the main highway far below, a massive snowplow was slowly cutting its way forward through the deep snow, clearing one side of the road.

NEITHER OF THEM SPOKE. Michael parked in the garage and they went inside. A heavy stillness filled the air.

"I'll go and get changed," Michael said quietly before darting up the stairs.

Methodically, Nicole threw her bloody clothes into the washing machine, then went up and put on clean clothes. Wandering into the kitchen, she found a can of soda in the fridge and popped it open. The cool, sweet beverage felt good against her parched tongue, but she barely tasted it. Deep inside she felt only welling sadness.

She took the can with her to the front windows where she stopped and looked out, drinking in the beauty of the snow-draped landscape, which glistened beneath a hazy late afternoon sky. The highway below was half-cleared of snow now, a stripe of black against a field of white. Soon, it would be open in both directions. Tomorrow, she could go home.

Tomorrow.

Michael joined her at the window, dressed in a clean pair of jeans and a black T-shirt. They stood in silence for few minutes, gazing at the view. His expression was unreadable.

Nicole was the first to speak. "I've been thinking about something you said last night."

"Oh?"

"You said I should go back to nursing. You were right. I thought maybe I could get a job up here at the hospital in Steamboat Springs."

"Steamboat Springs?" He stared at her. "That's a ski town. How many pediatric oncology cases do you think they get there?"

"There are other nursing specialties—"

"But that's *your* specialty. You have skills that the world needs. You have to work in a city hospital with a pediatric oncology center, and you know it."

"But you live *here*. If I worked up here . . ." She saw him frown and rushed on uncertainly. "I wouldn't have to live with you. I could get my own place—"

"Forget it, Nicole. If you were anywhere nearby, I'd want us to live together, to *be* together—as man and wife. I've fantasized that maybe, somehow, we could do it, but now I know that's impossible."

"Why is it impossible? Because I'll grow older every day, and you won't age?"

"Of course not! I'd love you at any age."

"Then why? Because of what happened today?"

"*Yes*, because of what happened today! I almost killed you!"

Nicole twisted her hands, glancing away briefly. She *was* frightened by that part of him; very frightened. She couldn't deny it. But her love was stronger than her fear. "Michael: you saved my life from those cougars. You *had* to become a beast to fight them—otherwise we both would have died."

"I almost killed you, Nicole!" he repeated. Shame and guilt were etched in his face as he strode to the sofa, where he stood with clenched fists. "I lost myself. I became a wild animal. I wasn't even aware of who you were. I drank your blood and I had no intention of stopping."

"But you *did* stop. It proves that the man inside you is stronger than the beast. And when I let you drink from me again, you had enough self-control to only take what you needed."

"We might not be so lucky the next time. Which is why there can never *be* a next time. I could never risk that happening again—and neither should you."

His despairing tone cut through Nicole's anguished hope like a blade. "You told me not to spend the rest of my life worrying that I might make a mistake and hurt someone. The same goes for you. I'm willing to take the risk."

"Why? Why would you take that risk?"

"Because I love you! Because I can't imagine my life without you!"

"I love you, too." Michael's eyes glowed with such deep affection it made her heart ache. "I love you with all my heart. And I'd give anything if we could be together. But we can't." He turned away. "The anxiety I'd have to endure every day, worrying about you, about what I might do *to you*—I couldn't live with that."

Nicole hadn't considered it from his point of view before, the stress that he must be under. She didn't want that for him. "Oh," she said quietly. "All right. I understand." Did she even dare to speak her next thought aloud? She had barely acknowledged it to herself. Crossing to where he stood, she said, "There is . . . another option."

He whirled to face her again, his eyes and tone darkening dangerously. "Don't. Even. Say it."

"I have to say it!" In a choking voice, she went on, "When I let you drink my blood in the barn just now, there was a moment when I thought: so what if I die? He'll save me. He'll bring me back. He'll make me a vampire."

"I told you *I will never do that.*"

"But if it's what I want?" she persisted.

"You don't know what you're asking!" he cried angrily.

"I'm asking for a chance to be with you, to share the life you have here. And if that's the only way it can happen—"

"Do you really want to exchange your human life for an existence like mine? To spend a lonely eternity hiding from people and the sun?"

"We wouldn't be lonely if we were together."

"If I made you a vampire, it wouldn't guarantee that we'd be together."

"Why not?"

"Because," he said bitterly, "in all probability, you wouldn't want me anymore."

"Of course I'd want you! I—"

"Nicole. Have you forgotten what I went through as a newborn vampire? It's not just a physical change. It's emotional, psychological, and it's all-encompassing. In those early years, I cared nothing for the people who'd once been important to me. My parents, my siblings, my fiancée whom I once loved—I didn't give a damn about anyone but myself. I lived a life of utter decadence, selfishness, and lawlessness. It didn't matter how many people I murdered or how much I drank, I was never satisfied. And it went on that way for *half a century.*"

Nicole's knees buckled and she sank onto the sofa, dashing away tears. "And you think it would be that way for me?"

"I know it would. I saw it with all my kind."

"But you learned to rise above it, to fix yourself," she said desperately. "You passed for a human and lived among people for decades."

"Yes, but after killing how many hundreds, thousands of others first? Even now, no one is truly safe around me. Do you really want that for yourself?"

Tears spilled down her cheeks. "No."

"I'd give up this accursed excuse for immortality for the chance to be human for just one more day," he said brokenly. "To be able to eat food, to feel the sunlight on my face, to enjoy the company of other people and not be tormented by the thirst for blood." Tears studded his eyes as he sat down beside her, taking her hands in his. "Nicole, life is meant to be lived, and you deserve to live yours to the fullest. To marry, to have the children you've always wanted. I could never give you that."

"I don't want those things anymore. I just want you."

"You do want them, my darling." He tenderly stroked her cheeks and wiped away her tears.

Nicole sobbed quietly, knowing deep down that he was right. "But I love you. No one has ever understood me as well you do," she whispered. "I've never been looked at so closely in all my life—and no one has ever made me look so closely at myself."

"I feel the same," he said in return, a tear running down his cheek. "I never imagined it could be like this to love someone. But you're young—so young. You'll meet another man someday. A good man who will understand and love and treasure you every bit as much as I do. A man who can take you out to dinner and share a meal and a glass of wine with you. A man who can take you on a real tropical vacation, not some facsimile on a mountaintop. A man who can make love to you without fear of hurting you. You'll fall in love and raise a family together. You'll be happy. You'll see."

She shook her head. "How can I leave you here all alone?"

"I've been alone for centuries, my darling. I've survived. My heart will break to see you go, but you must."

"No. I can't do it. What we've had is too rare, too wonderful."

"But it was never meant to last. It's been four stolen days." With deep sadness, Michael kissed her hand and added softly, "The road is open, my love. We both know that it's time for you to go home."

NICOLE COULDN'T BEAR TO CLOSE HER EYES that night. "I don't want to sleep away even a moment of this precious time with you," she said, her heart aching.

She wanted to stay another day at least, but Michael insisted that would only make it harder.

"Every day you're here is just another day that you're in danger," he said, unable to hide his regret.

They spent the night reading aloud to each other from the books in his study. They played piano far into the night— sad, pensive nocturnes that matched their mood. They strolled through his garden conservatory, talking, then lay down on a soft carpet of moss in a bower of orchids and made love slowly, desperately, aware every instant of the risk they were taking but unable to stop themselves, knowing it was the last time.

The next morning, the car rental company arrived and towed away her damaged vehicle. Nicole reserved a flight home that left Denver late that afternoon.

"I'll drive you to the airport," Michael insisted.

She packed her suitcase through tear-glazed eyes. Michael loaded her bags into his Range Rover. They were silent for much of the three-hour ride to the Denver airport. Nicole was too choked up to speak.

As they drove, Nicole tried to imagine what her life would be like now. What would she do when she got home? First, hug her beloved cat. Then call her mother, her sister, and her nieces. And then? *Then*, she promised herself, she would quit her job and move back to Seattle—the city she loved and missed. She'd banished herself long enough from all the things that had once mattered to her. She'd move back in with her friends. She'd play piano again, play with her nieces again, and return to the nursing job that had once so fulfilled her.

Nicole thought of the years ahead and her heart ached. Was this truly the last time she'd ever see Michael's beloved face? *No*, she told herself. Somehow, some way, someday she'd see him again—even if just for a week or a day or an hour. The promise of that meeting would help her go on. *Life is meant to be lived*, he'd said. She knew he was right. She knew what true love was now, and that memory would sustain her. In the meantime, she could read and reread the books of Patrick Spencer with intimate knowledge of the head and heart of the man who wrote them. Through his words on the page, she'd be with him again every day, if only in spirit.

When they arrived at the airport, Michael parked the car and stayed with Nicole while she checked in for her flight, which was leaving shortly. He rolled her carry-on suitcase toward the line at the security control point, where they both stopped to face each other.

It was time to say good-bye. The tears Nicole had been holding at bay welled up and spilled down her cheeks. Answering tears glistened in his blue eyes.

"You've changed me, you know," he said, tenderly running his fingers through her hair as if trying to memorize its weight and color.

"How?" she whispered.

"I was used to being alone. I was good at it, resigned to it. But I wasn't happy. I was closed off, bitter, and angry. I don't feel angry anymore. I feel . . . alive. Just knowing that this kind of love is possible—that you're out there somewhere, living your life—that we once had four brilliant days—that will make me smile."

"You've changed me, too," she said with great emotion. "I see my life more clearly now. I understand what I want and where I need to be. I'm so grateful to you for that. But I'll never forget you. Not one day will pass that I won't think of you."

"Every day, I'll remember what we had, and wish that you were here beside me."

"Thank you . . . for everything. For saving my life— twice—on that snowy road. For taking me in. For—" Her voice broke and she couldn't continue.

He pulled her into his arms and held her tight. "I love you, Nicole."

"I love you, Michael. I always will."

He kissed her fiercely. "Have a good life. Be well. Be happy."

Nicole's throat was so full she couldn't reply. She sobbed as he turned and walked away, melted into the crowd, and disappeared through the doors toward the parking garage.

Blinded by tears, Nicole moved into the security line. *How does anyone live through such sadness?* she wondered, the finality of their separation so profoundly painful that she thought her heart would break in two.

Her suitcase, as she lifted it up onto the moving belt, was heavier than Nicole remembered. When it appeared on the X-ray monitor, she glimpsed a small, rectangular shape inside which the TSA agent studied intently, then let pass by. What was it?

At her gate, the plane was already boarding. Determined to find out what was in her suitcase, Nicole quickly knelt down, lay her case on the floor, unzipped it, and tearfully searched inside. Buried among her clothes, she found what felt like a small wooden box. She brought it out and gasped in surprise.

It was a music box. *The music box.* The one with the exquisite red rose and music motif.

MICHAEL TURNED ONTO THE HIGHWAY, staring through the windshield with tear-glazed eyes. His CD played, the lyrics and melody of his favorite song so beautiful that he thought his aching heart might burst.

What was he going to do now? How could he go on, day after day, year after year, with only the memory of her to console him?

As he drove, he pictured her in his mind. How could he keep that image fresh and alive as the decades, the centuries unfolded?

An idea began to form. An idea for a love story that featured a captivating, green-eyed, red-headed heroine—the kind of woman he'd only been able to conjure in his imagination before, but now could see and hear quite clearly in his head. Yes. Yes. Work had always been a solace to him, a distraction from pain and loneliness. He welcomed that distraction now. In writing about her, he would have the joy of bringing her to life, hearing her voice, and being with her again every day and every night—forever. It was not the same, it could never be the same, but it was all he had, and he would devote himself to it.

He knew what he would call the book. He'd call it *Nocturne.*

THROUGH MISTY EYES, Nicole ran her hands lovingly over the smooth varnished surface of the music box, then lifted the lid and listened to its beautiful tune.

It was such a precious gift, and knowing that Michael had made it with his own hands made it doubly precious. Had he written her a note? There was none inside the music box. She looked through her things again, thinking a note might have fallen into her suitcase, and discovered a parcel she didn't recognize. It was the size and shape of a book, neatly wrapped in brown paper. Had Michael given her one of his novels? she wondered, her heart skipping a beat.

As the last boarding call was announced, Nicole zipped her suitcase, raced up to the ticket agent, and hurtled down the jetway, boarding the plane with the parcel in hand. After stowing her luggage above, she dropped into her seat by the window and unwrapped the gift.

Her breath caught. It was indeed a book—a very, very old book—of Scottish songs and poems. The type and spelling were very old-fashioned, the leather spine was soft from frequent readings, and its pages were brown and tattered with age.

Inside the front cover was an inscription in Michael's handwriting. As she read it, her heart seized and her eyes filled with fresh tears.

My darling Nicole,
My red, red rose,
This is one of my most treasured books. I know you'll appreciate it as much as I have. I hope when you listen to the music box, it will make you smile.
Have a good life, my bonnie lass. Look forward, not back. Be happy. Have no regrets. Fall in love again—do it for me. And know that I will love you until the end of time.
Michael

A page of the book had been marked by a scrap of paper. As the plane pulled away from the gate, tears streamed down Nicole's cheeks as she turned to the designated page and read:

O My Luve's Like a Red, Red Rose
by Robert Burns (1759–1796)

O, my Luve's like a red, red rose,
That's newly sprung in June.
O, my Luve's like the melodie,
That's sweetly play'd in tune.

As fair art thou, my bonnie lass,
So deep in luve am I,
And I will luve thee still, my dear,
Till a' the seas gang dry.

Till a' the seas gang dry, my dear,
And the rocks melt wi' the sun!
And I will luve thee still, my dear,
While the sands o' life shall run.

ACKNOWLEDGMENTS

I AM DEEPLY INDEBTED to the following people for their help during the creation of this book:

Mary Ann Elder, devoted horsewoman, for her enthusiasm, generosity, and patience in providing so many invaluable details on every subject from the care and training of horses to blizzards, barns, Colorado winters, road clearing, wild animals, medical emergencies, and sports. I'm especially grateful for her verbal inspiration in helping to design the layout of Michael's property, her descriptions of Colorado in all seasons, and her suggestion regarding an unexpected use of horsehair. Mary Ann has the soul of a poet, and I will be forever grateful to her.

My cousin Adam Rosenberg, DVM, for his time and knowledge on a wide range of topics including Colorado wildlife, blood banks, backup generators, communications systems, driving conditions, and for researching and pinpointing the exact spot in the Colorado mountains where it was feasible to be snowed in for four days. Most particularly, I'm grateful for his suggestion that Michael keep horses, a brilliant notion that helped to define his character and shape this story in so many ways.

My cousin Jessica Rosenberg, RN, PNP, CNS, for giving me such wonderful insight into her particular specialty in the medical profession, for sharing her expertise and personal experiences, and for helping me to craft the crisis at the heart of Nicole's character. I can never thank her enough.

My friend Michelle Shuffett, MD, for her invaluable input with regard to all the injuries and treatments in the book, and her careful review of all pages with medical content. Thank you!

My friend Cynthia Bosworth, for the Audrey Catburn story that made me laugh, and the phrase about the face of a ladybug and a caterpillar.

My brother, Mel Astrahan, PhD, computer guru, and horseman extraordinaire, for so generously coming to my rescue when my computer died, sharing his passion for bitless horseback riding and the Indian Hackamore, all the memories with Posse and Pockets, and for teaching me how to ride bareback.

My sister-in-law, Cheri Astrahan, for the war stories from her sojourn in the world of medical insurance claims.

My agent, Tamar Rydzinski, for her tireless support and encouragement, and for insisting—*immediately*, when I gave her no more than a paragraph synopsis—that *this* was the book I was supposed to write.

ACKNOWLEDGMENTS

My publishers, Georgina Levitt and Roger Cooper, for seeking me out and for trusting me to write the book that was in my heart; Francine LaSala for reminding me that sometimes less is more; Chrisona Schmidt for her light yet precise copy-edit; Annie Lenth for her diligent work getting the text and page layout just right; and, of course, the rest of the wonderful Vanguard team; thank you so much for the beautiful cover, which really knocked my socks off!

My son, Ryan, for inspiring me to write from two points of view, and for his usual thought-provoking feedback, delivered in such a timely manner, while incurring much loss of sleep.

My husband, Bill, for his loving attention and devotion when I needed a sounding board, for being so understanding and supportive of the vampiric hours and habits I was obliged to keep during the writing process, for helping me find the music, and for suggesting his favorite song—a song that was so perfect, it moved me to tears.

AUTHOR'S NOTE

I FELL IN LOVE WITH Nicole and Michael while writing this novel. They became so real to me that I feel as if they truly do exist, and this story really happened. I wouldn't be the least bit surprised if, while driving around that particular bend of Highway 40 high in the Colorado mountains, I was to actually see Michael's beautiful house perched up there, nestled between the pines.

I hope you found this book exciting and romantic. It came to be because the wonderful team at Vanguard Press, who'd read my novel *Dracula, My Love*—which features a dashing, highly accomplished, and charismatic Dracula—asked me to write a romantic vampire novel for them. I couldn't resist the offer.

It was the first time I'd agreed to write a book without knowing what it was going to be about. But almost immediately, inspiration struck. There is something very compelling to me in the idea of a "good" vampire—a tortured being who cares deeply about humanity, and struggles daily to overcome his primal instinct to kill. What if, I thought, a woman was stranded for days with a reclusive, gorgeous, fascinating, mysterious man, who turned out to be just such a vampire? What if they fell deeply in love, and when she discovered his terrifying secret she had nowhere to run? I was excited about that idea, and so were my agent and publisher.

For some reason, I just knew the story had to take place on a mountaintop in Colorado. I delved into my research. The challenge was to create an entire novel that has only two characters and takes place in a single location, and yet keeps the sexual tension, twists, turns, and surprises coming. Before I knew it, the story and characters began to appear fully formed in my head. The tale poured out of me, as if I was downloading it from the universe—or as if it was a true story and I was simply recording it.

The most satisfying part of any story, for me, is the character's arc. No matter the genre, I think the main characters must go through some kind of learning curve. I like to begin with a haunting, deeply felt inner wound that has in some way prevented the character from moving forward in his or her life. Over the course of the story, they grow and change, and come out on the other side transformed and ready to tackle life's challenges with new insight and perspective. I believe that Nicole and Michael did that for each other; that the four magical days they spent together have changed them forever.

I loved every minute of the time I spent with Michael and Nicole. I got so deeply inside their heads and hearts that I feel as though I've lived their lives . . . that I personally experienced their traumas and heartaches, and the joy of their life-changing encounter. I was so possessed that I rarely left the house while writing this book, and my eating and sleeping habits became as erratic as any vampire's. When it was finished, I cried. To me, Michael and Nicole are each other's perfect other half. I so wanted them to end up together—even though there seem to be very good reasons why they can't or shouldn't be.

But I'll tell you a secret: in my mind, Nicole and Michael's story is far from over. I fully believe that they'll see each other again, and not just for a week, or a day, or an hour.

Because I believe in the power of true love.

True love always finds a way.

NOCTURNE
by Bestselling Author Syrie James

AUTHOR QUESTIONS AND ANSWERS

1. **Question:** One of the surprising elements of the book is Michael's amazing relationship with his horses, even though he is a predator. Though Michael is confident that he can restrain his true nature around the horses, why can't he have that same willpower around Nicole?

Answer: Michael acknowledges that his horses might instinctively see him as a predator, which is why he's had to work so hard to learn to communicate with them. During the years when Michael forced himself to feed exclusively on animals, he would have taken blood from any other creature in the forest before he would have touched one of his horses, because they were his friends. It is this emotional connection, founded on Michael's innate sense of decency, that helps to keep his primal instincts in check, both with regard to horses and human beings—but as we've seen, that control could falter in a heartbeat if he's enraged by a dangerous wild animal. Michael's problem in Nicole's case is further complicated in that it's not just about his thirst for blood; the intense passion of lovemaking can also cause him to lose control.

2. **Question:** You must have had a lot of fun including real historical personages, such as the Scottish poet, Robert Burns, and Charles Dickens as friends of Michael in his past life. How did you

choose which characters in his long and storied past you wanted to interweave into the story?

Answer: That *was* fun! I didn't really plan which historical characters to include in the story—they chose me. I wanted Michael to have a signed novel in his library. It had to be a famous British writer from the Regency or early Victorian era, but it couldn't be Jane Austen or one of the Brontës, whose books were published anonymously during their lifetime. I didn't know it was going to be Dickens until Nicole pulled the book off the shelf, and then it was fun to invent how and when Michael knew him in a way that was historically accurate.

As for Robert Burns—I asked my husband to please help me find a wonderful, romantic song to serve as the theme for the novel that could also be played on a music box. Bill played the CD *My Luve is Like a Red, Red Rose*, and it was so perfect I immediately started crying. When I learned more about Robert Burns, I decided that Michael *had* to know him, and I added a jaunt to Scotland to Michael's backstory.

3. **Question:** Music plays a major role in *Nocturne*. In fact, a major turning point in the novel is when Nicole and Michael really connect as they discuss Chopin's Nocturne and then play a duet together. How and why do you use music in your writing? And do you think music can be used to highlight or emphasize important themes in the novel?

Answer: Music plays a big role in this novel, and one of the great pleasures of writing it was finding the right pieces of music to include, both to showcase the theme and the characters' emotional state. At different points in the story, Michael and Nicole each sit down at the piano and play pieces that are difficult and dramatic, emphasizing the frustration they feel at the time. Their shared love of music and the piano is one of the many things that draws them to each other. The title of the book is both a tribute to music and a description of the story itself, since a nocturne is, by definition, a short, lyrical piece of music of a dreamy or pensive character especially for the piano that is appropriate to the night or evening. And the centerpiece, *My Luve is Like a Red, Red Rose*, represents the theme of the story: that Michael's love for Nichole is everlasting, and like Michael himself, it will last till all the seas go dry and while the sands of life shall run.

4.   **Question:** How much research into the medical profession and into details about blood transfusion did you need to do to write *Nocturne*? And Nicole's passion for pediatric oncology is fascinating. Why did you decide to make both characters healers at different points in their lives?

    Answer: I interviewed a pediatric oncology nurse who specialized in blood transfusions, and both she and several doctors reviewed those chapters for medical accuracy. I loved the idea that Nicole worked with blood, which is so vital to a vampire's survival, and serves as such a core element of the story. Because Nicole and Michael spend such a brief but intense time together—for the story to work, they had to fall in love almost immediately—I wanted them to have a great deal in common. Their mutual passion for healing the sick is just one of the many things that brings them together.

5.   **Question:** Ironically, it is the devastating attack at the climax of the book that actually finally heals Nicole and gets her over her deep, emotional fear of blood. Why did you choose to set this cathartic moment in Nicole's life during one of the most terrifying times in her life?

    Answer: When a person suffers from a deep, emotional wound, it often takes extraordinary circumstances to draw them out of their shell and cause them to face their fears—which they must do if they are to learn and grow and move forward in life.

Because Nicole's fear of blood was the very antithesis of Michael's basis for survival, it set up an interesting disparity between them. I wanted her to deal with and overcome her fear in a way that was exciting and dramatic, and served to remind her of her own special skills, while at the same time allowing her to save Michael's life, just as he had already saved hers so many times.

6. **Question:** Is there significance to your use of the apple Michael hands Nicole after the attack to help her get her strength back?

Answer: Interestingly, the forbidden fruit mentioned in the Book of Genesis is not identified, although popular Christian tradition holds that it was an apple. Magical, golden apples are featured in both Greek mythology (as growing on the Tree of Life) and Norse mythology (they keep one young forever), and they appear frequently in fairy tales such as the poisoned apple in Snow White. I had all this in mind when Michael hands Nicole that slice of apple. It's a symbol of *all that he is:* the forbidden fruit, a combination of poison and youth elixir, whose very bite could kill her yet make her immortal. At the same time, the apple is a source of life: the nourishment she needs to recover and survive.

7. **Question:** In the novel Michael says the worst kind of pain is hurting one you love most. When Michael loses himself in the cougar blood frenzy, he calls Nicole, the person he loves most, "the creature." How do you use this lack of identity to reinforce danger and obsession?

Answer: I was very particular about which parts of the book were told from Michael's versus Nicole's point of view, and that scene—the cougar attack—simply had to come from Michael. I felt it was important for the reader to get inside Michael's head to understand the transformation he goes through when the beast within him takes over. Only by seeing him truly become a wild animal with no connection whatsoever to Nicole can we truly appreciate the kind of danger he poses, and understand his decision at the end.

8. **Question:** Your description of Michael's indoor garden paradise is fantastic. Do you have experience gardening yourself? What is it about this greenhouse that fulfills such a special need for Michael?

Answer: I have a beautiful garden, a koi pond like Michael's, and a fondness for plumeria trees and rose bushes. Although I don't have time these days to maintain the garden myself, I've enjoyed many wonderful hours in the past planting and pruning, and I love strolling through my yard and watching the butterflies flit from flower to flower. Michael's greenhouse fills two very special needs for him: the need to be surrounded by nature, which is difficult for a being that must avoid direct sunlight; and the need to nurture things and make them grow, which serves as a daily reminder that he is rising above the monster inside him—because he can create life, rather than destroy it.

9. **Question:** Michael is an author in this novel and draws inspiration from his past lives. What inspired you to write this novel?

Answer: In *Dracula, My Love*, I thoroughly enjoyed exploring a new, more sympathetic version of Dracula—a man who was a good person in his human life, and has spent an eternity struggling against the evil inside himself, on a determined quest to improve his mind and talents. A union between a vampire and a human is fascinating and compelling, yet so problematic—and as I wrote, I fell completely under its spell. When I finished the novel, I was eager to write about another such vampire, and another such relationship—but this time, I wanted to invent my own characters from scratch.

I've noticed that, when reading some novels, I sometimes skim the subplot and jump ahead to the parts that interest me the most: the parts that focus on the main, romantic characters. I wondered: was it possible to write a book that focused *entirely* on the hero and heroine, and didn't include a single other character? The challenge inspired me, and this novel was born.

10. **Question:** Though Nicole sees a gentle and kind man in front of her, Michael admits he has killed many times before, and not just because he was hungry. Why does Michael expose this side of his character to Nicole when he could keep the past a secret?

Answer: From the very beginning of the story, Michael's intent and struggle is to somehow keep Nicole safe. Fearing every moment that his true nature might assert itself, he feels it is his duty to tell her the truth: that he is a monster and she's better off keeping her distance from him—even though it costs him dearly to admit it, because by that point he's deeply in love with her.

11. **Question:** Michael tells Nicole: "Even legend is founded in a kernel of truth." Do you believe that is true for the most part? Do you believe there is a kernel of truth to people's superstitions and beliefs in vampires?

Answer: The universe is a fascinating place, full of wonders that mankind has yet to understand, discover, and explore. Many of the advances that modern scientists have made and which we take completely for granted today were once considered impossible—the stuff of superstition—and would have gotten our ancestors burned as witches. It is certainly possible that many things *we* see as mere superstitions could be true, or founded on a kernel of truth. I believe that anything is possible.

NOCTURNE
by Bestselling Author Syrie James

READING GROUP GUIDE

1. In *Nocturne*, the two main characters are actually the only two characters in the novel. Why do you think the author chose not to include any other characters in the story? Have you ever read a novel like this before?

2. Why do you think Nicole and Michael argue so much at the beginning of the novel? Have you ever felt attracted to someone and yet felt the need to disguise it with a cold or uncaring attitude? If you did, why did you make this decision?

3. Discuss the many things that Michael and Nicole have in common as well as their differences. What draws them together? How do they complement each other? Do you think that Michael and Nicole are the love of each other's life?

4. Do you believe in true love? Why or why not?

5. What do you think is it about being injured and snowbound with a dangerous person that piques people's imaginations? A decade ago, people were compelled and terrified by the blockbuster novel and movie *Misery*. What do you think is it about the fear of being cared for by a monster (human or inhuman) that fascinates us?

6. Both Michael and Nicole are accomplished pianists. Why do you think the author chose to make music such an important

part of the novel? And what do you think it is about the nocturne in particular (a short, lyrical piece of music of a dreamy or pensive character especially for the piano) that is so important to the characters' love story?

7. Could you be attracted to someone like Michael, even if you knew how many times he had killed in his life and how dangerous he was to everyone around him? Did you like Michael and find him sympathetic? Why or why not? Have you ever been attracted to a person that your friends or family have thought was bad for you? How did you handle that situation?

8. Nicole and Michael fall in love very quickly. Have you ever had a romance like this where you fell in love so quickly and intensely? Was it short-lived or did it turn into an enduring relationship?

9. Discuss the clues that mount up in the first half of the book before Nicole realizes that Michael is a vampire. How would you feel if you had been in Nicole's shoes, and that frightening myth had suddenly become reality? Would you have been terrified?

10. Discuss the scenes that explore Michael's backstory. How do all the parts of his history contribute to the man he is today? Were you surprised to learn he had been a doctor years ago, and that he continued to work as a doctor for many decades after he became a vampire? What does that say about him?

11. If you had an eternity before you, how would you spend it?

12. Describe all the aspects of the property that Michael has built for himself in the Colorado mountains. Why does he call it his "sanctuary"? Did you find it appealing? Why or why not? Do you think you could live in isolation the way Michael does, when the surroundings are so spectacular? Or are you too social?

13. What was your reaction to Michael's indoor conservatory? What is it about gardening that Michael and Nicole each find so fulfilling? Do you have experience gardening yourself? If so, in what ways does gardening fulfill a special need for you?

14. Forbidden love is one of the most enduring themes in great literature. What other great love stories have you read? Compare and contrast them with *Nocturne*.

15. Have you ever experienced the kind of loneliness Michael has? How did you deal with it? Has there ever been a time in your life you wished you could just pick up and move away from everyone you know?

16. Discuss Nicole's emotional growth throughout the novel. How would you describe the crisis at the heart of Nicole's character? Did you find her to be a sympathetic character?

17. Nicole and Michael make a heartbreaking decision at the end of the book. Do you really believe this is the end for them? How do you think they could make this relationship last if they were to get back together? The more creative answers, the better!

18. The two lovers only spend four magical days together and yet both of them are utterly transformed by their time together. In what ways do they each grow and change? Have you ever had a transformative experience? What was it? Discuss what you learned.

19. If you were Nicole, do you think you could have gotten on that plane and left the love of your life behind you? Why or why not?